Praise for Annabel Pitcher

On MY SISTER LIVES ON THE MANTELPIECE:

It's funny. It's truthful. It lives off the page. It has a warmth you can bask in; an honesty you can cut with a knife…This is one of those stories which has elements that will stay with me for good. Clear your shelf for the awards, Annabel Pitcher.

Philip Ardagh, THE GUARDIAN

This is a warm-hearted, funny tale…Painfully honest and beautifully written, you'll devour it. COSMOPOLITAN

This appealing story explores tolerance and intolerance, and ways of grieving and loving.

Nicolette Jones, SUNDAY TIMES

On KETCHUP CLOUDS:

Powerful and utterly original…

Natasha Harding, THE SUN

Pitcher's tale of troubled family life is deftly done…A moving and ultimately highly compassionate tale. To be human is to err, after all.

Martin Chilton, THE TELEGRAPH

Silence is Goldfish is Annabel Pitcher's third novel. Her debut, *My Sister Lives on the Mantelpiece*, won the Branford Boase and a Betty Trask Award in 2012 and her second novel, *Ketchup Clouds*, won the 2014 Waterstones Children's Prize. Annabel's work has been shortlisted for many prestigious awards including the Dylan Thomas Prize, the Galaxy British Book Award, the Red House Children's Book Award and the Carnegie Medal.

Annabel graduated from Oxford University with a degree in English Literature and an ambition to be a children's author. She lives in Yorkshire with her husband and two young sons.

@APitcherAuthor
www.annabelpitcher.com

SILENCE IS GOLDFISH

SILENCE IS GOLDFISH

ANNABEL PITCHER

Indigo

First published in Great Britain in 2015 by Indigo
This paperback edition published in 2016 by Hodder and Stoughton

1 3 5 7 9 10 8 6 4 2

Text © Annabel Pitcher, 2015

The moral right of the author has been asserted.

A CIP catalogue record for this book
is available from the British Library.

ISBN 978 1 78062 002 2

Typeset by Input Data Services Ltd, Bridgwater, Somerset

Printed in Great Britain by Clays Ltd, St Ives plc

The paper and board used in this book are from
well-managed forests and other responsible sources.

MIX
Paper from
responsible sources
FSC® C104740

Indigo
An imprint of
Hachette Children's Group
Part of Hodder and Stoughton
Carmelite House
50 Victoria Embankment
London EC4Y 0DZ

An Hachette UK Company

www.hachette.co.uk
www.hachettechildrens.co.uk

For Isaac, in the hope he will always
know where he belongs

PART ONE

CHAPTER 1

There must be a list on the Internet of what to buy when you're running away, but my phone is typically dead, like I swear it just passes out whenever things get stressful. It's unconscious in my pocket so I can't look up a list of essential items for life on the road, but a children's torch in the shape of a goldfish seems a very sensible choice. It looks friendly enough with its little orange face and definitely I could use a mate right about now, so into the basket it goes where it sits in the corner, gazing at me with shiny black eyes as I pick up tampons, tissues, two chocolate bars and a magazine.

It's a two hour train journey from Manchester to London, so I'll need something to read as well as something to hide behind because knowing my luck Jack will alert the police when he realises I'm gone. By the time I pull into Euston station, there will be pictures of me plastered over the loos with the caption *Find My Tessie-T* in extra large bold letters. Let's face it, Jack isn't the type to downplay a drama, and a child going missing must be the worst thing that could happen to any parent. This realisation makes me want to drop the basket and run back home, so I remind myself that my so-called dad is now my number one enemy after what I saw on his computer. My heart still aches though when I think about the expression on his face as he stares at my empty bed with its *Star Wars* duvet, which I bought last year, pretending it was some snigger-worthy ironic statement when actually I just wanted to sleep with Luke Skywalker, and who can really blame me when you think about how he handles his lightsaber.

Mum will shout, 'Jack, come here!' with her voice more strained than it should be at seven o'clock in the morning when she always bursts into my room with a cup of tea, like a cuckoo in a Grandfather clock that, yes, is reliable, but also quite irritating. I'm not even kidding, I haven't drunk that tea for three years. It just seems too hard to lift my head off the pillow at that ungodly hour, but I am grateful and Mum knows it, squeezing my foot when I croak, 'Thank you.' That is love, making endless tea for someone who never drinks it, just in case this is the one morning they might actually want a sip, and I want to throw the tea back in Mum's face but also savour it, and I can't do either of these things because I will never see her again. In about an hour's time she will realise I'm gone, gazing in horror at my empty bed where Jedi will jump up to give me a lick, whimpering when he sees I'm not there.

And I whimper too, walking up and down aisles on feet

that throb in silver Dr Martens because this is the most amount of exercise my legs have done for give-or-take four years. Once upon a time it was the best thing in the world to sprint with the wind whistling through the gap in my front teeth. I would stretch out my arms and fly like a fat butterfly and oh God I remember my dazzling colours, but then they faded and now I plod. I've been plodding since ten past two this morning when I crept out of my house, needing to feel solid ground beneath my feet, to know the Earth was still there though my world had just crumbled. I wandered familiar streets feeling lost in the darkness, too scared of the stuff inside my head to be afraid of anything outside it. And now I am here with a plan that involves a goldfish, who looks shocked because this is not at all what he thought was going to happen when he woke up this morning next to the bottles of de-icer in the Texaco Garage that is the only home he's ever known.

My eyeballs swell like rain clouds. There's going to be a downpour and no one wants to see that now, do they, so I pretend to be someone else, someone in their thirties with their life sorted and a train to catch for an important meeting in the centre of London, rather than a fifteen-year-old with dyed black hair, bad roots, and no dad. I say *no dad*, but he could be over there, working behind the till, though that man doesn't look the type to have fathered large offspring. No offence to myself, but I do have big bones with a fair bit of beef and that man is lean chicken with a hen-like face. He stares straight through me as I put my basket on the counter then pecks at the till with a scrawny hand, typing in the price of the goldfish because it doesn't have a barcode.

'Sorry,' I say, as if it's my fault. The man doesn't acknowledge my apology, which is bad manners or what have you, but I don't really mind because it is better for everyone if I don't exist.

I know what planet I am, thank you very much, and I am sick of trying to bump myself up the solar system when my true position is obvious, just ask my old dinner lady, who spotted it a mile off. At primary school when people tried to find friends, I tried to find space that my imagination could fill with whatever it wanted, nearly always butterflies because to me they were perfection, like real life fairies with prettier wings. At playtime I turned myself into them, not just one butterfly but hundreds of them, my arms a kaleidoscope of colours as I danced across the wet grass while my class played tag, chasing each other round a few metres of tarmac. I didn't understand it, like *wasn't it too crowded* I asked them all the time in my head.

'Don't you worry, cherub,' the dinner lady said when she caught me watching the other children in confusion. 'You're Pluto. Happiest away from the heat of the action.' She smiled a wrinkly smile. 'Nothing wrong with that.'

I believed her until the start of high school, when there was a welcome disco for Year Seven with a DJ who wasn't

[6]

even somebody's dad but an actual teenage boy with a tattoo of a Chinese symbol on his bicep.

'Kung Pao Chicken,' I replied when two wide-eyed girls asked me what I thought it meant, 'with egg fried rice.' They frowned and danced off so I escaped the noise of the hall for the room where the teachers were selling sweets, and oh goodness the chocolate bars were in such a mess that I had no choice but to stack them in neat piles for Mrs Miller, and then I disappeared outside to sit on a wall beneath a tree.

At home, Jack asked me if I'd had a good time, sounding as if he already knew the answer to that one, but I defied the odds and nodded, thinking of the way moonlight had shone through the branches to make silver patterns on my skin.

'You did?' His voice perked up, his face too. 'Really? That's great, Tessie-T. Really great. New school and everything. New start. What did you do?'

'I sat under a tree,' I told him and his face fell.

'With a friend? Tell me you were with a friend, Tess. We've talked about this.'

I examined my toes through my tights. Before the disco, Mum had painted my nails bright pink even though no one would see.

'Tess?' she said, half-hidden by a pile of marking in the armchair. 'Dad's talking to you. Did you go outside with a friend?'

"Course she did,' Jack replied. 'She remembers our discussion, don't you, Tessie-T? About the importance of fitting in? That's what you're doing, isn't it? Fitting in?'

There was only one right answer, that much was obvious. They didn't want a Pluto. They wanted a Mercury or a Venus at least. I nodded, my head going straight up and down then jolting forward as Jack slapped me on the shoulder blade where my left butterfly wing used to be.

'Atta girl!' he said, and if his voice had perked up before, it positively soared now, high high high above the fear I would always struggle to fit in. 'Tell us about her. Or is it a him?' he said, giving me a wink as he pulled me onto the sofa. It creaked like always and we had to adjust the cushions like always and we both did this exaggerated groan when Mum squeezed in on the other side. She poked us with a red pen before saying, 'Go on, Tess. Give us a name.'

'Anna,' I said, not even caring it was a fib. They were glancing at each other over my head with these *eyes* that were full of a thing I didn't recognise, and then it dawned on me that it was pride. I was surrounded by it, warm and full of hope, this golden cocoon promising to transform me into something more desirable than even a butterfly. When I went to bed, I knelt in front of Jedi and made a solemn vow. I'd try to be an ideal daughter if he'd try to be an ideal pet, and he hung his fluffy white head because he knew that meant no more fighting with Bobbin, his nemesis, who belongs to Andrew next door.

I raised my hand and he lifted his paw.

'May the force be with us.'

It sort of was for a few years. Jedi didn't bite Bobbin for ages, and I made this big effort to fit in, trying to be louder and livelier and more fun than I felt inside, wearing my personality like a clown hat to make everyone laugh. Jack in particular.

Well, not anymore. Not after the words I read on his computer. I'm off the hook, which means Jedi is too, so can someone please tell my dog that the deal is OFF. A leopard can't change its spots and a dog can't change its temperament and a planet can't change its position in the universe. I'm Pluto, which is why I take the receipt in the petrol station without saying anything to the man who's not saying anything to me, but that takes some effort let me tell you after four years of being the one to fill the awkward silence.

I wait for the red light to halt the non-existent traffic on this not-so-busy road that actually doesn't require me to stand on the pavement, hanging around until some machine tells me it's time to cross. That sort of behaviour belongs to a girl trying desperately to do the right thing, and I am trying desperately to do the wrong thing, so I step out onto the road without looking both ways, ignoring the Green Cross Code because I am that much of a rebel.

'Use your bloody eyes!' a van driver yells, slamming on the brake. Of course I check him to see if he's the one, but he's too loud to be my dad, shouting *blah blah this* and *blah blah that* because I made him screech to a stop, ruining his brand new bloody tyres that cost a bloody fortune, don't I know. 'Look where you're bloody going next time, love!'

My real dad would never be this rude, I just know it. Even if he was angry, he would hold up his hand to apologise. I would hold up my hand to apologise, and he would hold up his hand even higher to take more of the blame, but I would hold up my hand highest of all to show that it was actually my fault. And with our fingers almost scraping the sky we would smile identical smiles then he would gasp, 'It's you!'

'Yes!' I would reply, and then we would embrace, right here in the middle of the road, with everyone clapping and cheering like a film with a happy ending that will never happen in real life, Tess, so don't go getting any strange ideas.

I make it to the pavement doing a semi-waddle, which is my version of a run these days, and when did that happen, when did this stripy dress that is supposed to be A-line but looks more O-line on my body get so damn tight is what I am asking myself. I'm supposed to care that I'm getting fatter according to Jack, but I am fine with my size, in fact sometimes when I pose in front of the mirror with my boobs in my hands, I think there are a lot of men out there who would pay good money to see my body, and not just the ones with a fat fetish, so there.

I strut along the pavement, belly-first, like *bow down and worship at the great altar of Tess* is my suddenly awesome vibe as I look out for a taxi to whisk me away on an adventure. I've got a load of change in my coat pocket and the prospect of getting in a cab feels sort of magical, like wow I can just fling out a hand to stop a black chariot and pay a few gold coins to go anywhere I want within reason and a nine-pound budget. And the place I want to be is Manchester Piccadilly train station because the place I ultimately want to end up is Finsbury Tower, One-hundred-and-three to One-hundred-and-five Bunhill Row in London, and I chant these words again and again in my head so it's a surprise to hear my mouth tell the driver my home address when I finally flag one down.

'That up by Chorlton Grammar School?' he asks as we do a u-turn. There's still time to change my mind. I am ready to go and the goldfish is too, but I mutter, 'That's it, yeah. The first right after the school. It's one of the middle terraces about halfway down the road.'

We set off in the opposite direction to the station, and in no time at all we are turning onto my street. Something more should be happening, something big enough to account for the mad beat beat beat of my heart, but no, we're decelerating, coming to a stop outside my front door. Everything about my house is the same. The same silver number is displayed above the same silver letterbox. The same curtains are hanging in the same lounge window. And this evening no doubt I will be the same girl sitting on the

[11]

same sofa, watching TV in my tiger-print onesie when a mouse one would be far more appropriate.

'Six pounds fifty, when you're ready.'

I hand over some cash but don't get out, pretending for a few more seconds that I really might do something big and brave for once in my decidedly small and timid life.

'This is the one?'

'Yeah,' I reply, but I make no move to open the door. The driver almost-but-not-quite turns to look at me.

'You are okay, aren't you?'

It's nice of him to ask, but his voice is heavy with obligation and his eyes are tired, like *here's just another messed up teenage girl wandering the streets after a disastrous evening* is the precise look on his face as he half-surveys my own. Maybe if he'd twist a bit further, or cut the ignition, or take his hands off the steering wheel rather than gripping it so tightly, maybe then I'd tell him what I saw last night.

Instead, I pull myself together. 'I'm fine.'

The sky is crying, relieved or disappointed by my return, it's hard to tell. I stand in the rain, staring up at the house, taking in the fact Mum and Jack's bedroom curtains are still closed so they will never know I ran away for four hours and thirteen minutes. The cab disappears as I unlock the front door. I tiptoe into the house, wondering why it still feels like home.

CHAPTER 2

The kitchen smells of burned spaghetti, proof that last night happened, there's absolutely no denying it. Listening out for Mum and Jack, I avoid the creaky floorboards, creeping to the sink to get a glass of water. The cold tap is awkward, but I turn it on the perfect amount to get a good flow without any splash.

The house is quiet. Not silent exactly, but the noise of it is so familiar it barely registers.

I listen harder, transforming the creaks and groans and pops into something strange then force myself to look. The door to Jack's study is open so I can see it from here, just a bog-standard laptop, but somewhere hidden away in the deepest, darkest part of that computer is a file called DCNETWORK BLOG containing six hundred and seventeen secret words.

And Jack typed them yesterday.

Jack typed them, and that's a hard fact sitting in my brain giving me acid indigestion of the mind, particularly behind my right temple, which is throbbing.

Jack typed them, probably doing his usual sigh as he bedded in for a few hours with a cup of coffee on the *Master of the House* coaster, which he bought in the foyer of the theatre with the glittering chandeliers because even the ceiling was wearing its best jewellery to see *Les Misérables*. And wow that was such a good night, but then again, maybe not for Jack. Maybe it was this huge great big effort for him to climb to his feet during the standing ovation where we both grinned at each other, clapping until our hands stung. I elbowed him in an eloquent way, like that jab of my bone on his arm said, *This is the best moment of my life*. He elbowed me back to say, *Mine too*, but now I am wondering if actually he was trying to knock me off the balcony because, no doubt about it, he would be happier if I didn't exist.

Jack's slippers with the trodden-down backs are still under the desk where I kicked them off when I discovered the truth. Jack's slippers. Dad's slippers. Dad's old familiar slippers I used to put on whenever my feet got cold because dads and daughters can share foot-sweat no problem. I will never wear them again and suddenly that seems the saddest thing of all, like my toes start to grieve, throbbing in my boots as I turn away from the study, unable to believe he wrote that blog.

When Tess finally emerged after two hours of pushing, all I felt was revulsion, and I could no more easily pretend to love the peculiar creature in my delighted wife's arms than hide the

*resentment that burned inside. It wasn't my daughter. It was
her daughter – hers and some sperm donor's I had never met,
but what could I do? She was here and she was my wife's and I
loved my wife even if I didn't love the ugly red thing gnawing
at her –*

'Oh no! Oh help!' Mum had shrieked as the smoke
alarm had gone off and Jack had burst out of the study
as I'd run in from the lounge. Mum was flapping her
hands at the sticks of spaghetti jutting out of the pan that
had caught fire in the flames of the gas hob. 'What's the
rule?'

'Watch yourself, Helen!'

'What's the rule?'

'What are you talking about?'

'The rule about fires!' Mum exclaimed as the smoke alarm
yelled *THERE IS AN EMERGENCY THERE IS
AN EMERGENCY THERE IS AN EMERGENCY.*
'You're not allowed to throw water on certain types of fire.
Some of them need an extinguisher. What is it? I can't
remember. Quick! Do we need an extinguisher?'

'What? We don't have an extinguisher.' Jack went over
to the awkward tap, turning it on the perfect amount to get
a good flow without any splash. He filled a jug of water.

'Don't just throw that on it. It might cause an explosion. Is
it gas fires? Is it gas that needs carbon dioxide or something?
Does that sound right? We need to check! I think it is gas
fires.'

'You've turned off the bloody gas, Helen. It's not a gas fire. It's just a fire. Fires need water,' Jack said, but he was hesitating now, staring at the hob. 'The gas is off, isn't it?'

'The fire's getting bigger!' So were Mum's arm flaps. They were ridiculous and I smirked as I watched the spectacle, ignoring the alarm urging me to *LEAVE NOW*.

'I can see that,' Jack replied. I don't know how. Mum was practically star-jumping in front of the pan as the alarm got louder, screaming *YOU ARE IN DANGER*, not that I paid any attention to it. 'I can see that, but I don't—'

'Quick, Jack!'

'Don't tell me to be quick. You're the one slowing—'

'Just pour!'

'No, I can't now. We should check.'

'We haven't got time to check.'

'Just check, will you?'

And that's what I decided to do, slipping into Jack's study, normally off-limits, but this was an emergency. Besides, my parents were too busy arguing to notice, all this hot-faced bickering that steamed up the windows. I put on Jack's slippers that he'd left under his desk then sat in his bum print, bashing a few buttons to wake up his laptop.

'Come on,' I said, wiggling the mouse when nothing happened, almost knocking over the framed poem on his desk – *The Road Not Taken* by Robert Frost. I stared at the words without seeing them because there was a glorious picture inside my head, and it was of me saving the day, finding out the information in the nick of time.

'POUR!' I imagined shouting, a split second before the pan exploded. 'POUR, DAD! TRUST ME!'

I wanted to impress my dad, that's why I was drumming my fingers on his notepad, urging his computer to wake the bloody hell up before I missed my chance. I wiggled the mouse again, but the screen stayed black for what felt like ages. I will always remember it, the blissful darkness of not knowing before the harsh glare of reality hit me between the eyes, and the alarm *BEEPED* and *BEEPED* and *BEEPED* because there was an emergency, after all – it just had nothing to do with burned spaghetti.

CHAPTER 3

Mum doesn't look at me as she places my favourite pig mug on my Sudoku book, and she doesn't look at me as she moves my curtains to one side to groan at the rain, and she doesn't look at me as she takes my lunchbox out of my school bag to wash it out so she can fill it with salad now Jack has banned bread of all types, not just the white stuff. She doesn't look at me because for the past one thousand mornings when she's delivered my tea, I have been dead to the world, my face buried in my pillow.

This morning is different though.

I am lying on my back with a rigid spine, gripping the duvet with tight fists as I stare up at her. When she finally notices, she jumps out of her skin because there are the whites of my eyes, I can feel them glowing in the darkness.

'Wonders will never cease. Are you actually awake?' She is all smiles and long brown hair as she leans over me, checking my pulse with jokey fingers nowhere near the right place in my neck. 'Well, well, well. Your body must be in shock after such an unprecedented event. Here, let me see.' She grabs my wrist feeling the pulse there too, pretending to time it *tick tock* on a nonexistent watch. 'Yes. Yes. A little fast. Just what I thought. Are you feeling okay?' she asks in mock concern, and here it is, the perfect opportunity to scream *NO* at the top of my voice.

I wait for it to happen, but the word doesn't even nearly come.

Mum puts her hand on my forehead.

'Slightly raised temperature but that's hardly surprising. All that effort it must have taken to peel apart your eyelids at this time in the morning. You must be exhausted. Do you want to lie down? Wait. You're already lying down. Thank goodness! Don't want you overstraining yourself.' She grins at her own joke then lifts my tea by the rim of the cup, offering me the handle. 'Can you manage this for once? Go on. Make my day.'

She cheers as I take the cup and I smile, like I actually do this massive grin, and what the Holy Crap is that about I ask myself in disbelief. I'm supposed to be causing a scene, not playing along ever so nicely, but I let Mum plump up my *Star Wars* pillows then take a sip of tea that tastes really good after my failed attempt to run away. I grip the mug tightly, relieved I am not in the station drinking weak tea from an unfamiliar polystyrene cup, waiting to board a train that will take me away from everything I've ever known.

But then Jack appears around my bedroom door. Tea

goes down the wrong way and I start to cough. I can't stand to look at him, but I can't take my eyes off him either, so I gaze at him without wanting to, resenting the pull he has over my eyeballs. His red hair is wet from the shower and his pink cheeks are freshly shaved and he looks clean, too clean for someone who writes dark confessions about his so-called daughter to post on the Internet.

The betrayal hits me again and it takes effort not to double-up and hide under my duvet like I did last night before I ran away. Typing *DCNETWORK* into my phone, I found that it stands for *Donor Conception Network*. Holding my breath, I visited their website all about sperm and egg donation where it outlined the procedure and talked about how it felt to conceive a child through assisted fertilisation. Loads of people had written about their experiences, but not one of them had said anything about disgust. Jack obviously spotted a gap and decided to fill it with his story, willing to tell the world his secret, but not me his own flesh and blood – well, not exactly I have to keep reminding myself because the fact he isn't my real dad still has not sunk in.

'Look at this!' Mum says, meaning me. 'It's a miracle.'

'Now there's something you don't see every day.'

Jack steps into my room, drying his face, but the mask of Perfect Dad does not rub off in the towel. He uses it to grin at me as if he is just so goddamn delighted to find me wide awake in the room he painted when I was ten. I got to choose the colour from a shiny brochure, and of course the only logical choice was the mystical Midnight Blue. I couldn't wait for Jack to start, jumping up and down when he covered my furniture with sheets to make a den that I sat in even though I was too old to pretend my desk was a cave and I was a troll.

'Don't you want to be a princess?' Jack asked as I scratched my warts then belched, rubbing my belly with a hairy hand.

'I eat princesses for breakfast.'

Jack shook his head then shooed me outside. I climbed up on the shed roof in the backyard. Craning my neck to peer through my bedroom window, I saw Jack bend down to prepare the paint that I just knew was the exact colour of magic. When he caught me spying, he waggled a finger and I laughed, leaping off the shed because I didn't want to spoil the surprise, not really.

It was a shock when he said *voilà* and I burst through my door to my new blue room that wasn't blue at all but pale yellow.

'It's First Dawn,' he said as my chest constricted. 'Not Midnight Blue. I thought it was prettier. Much nicer for a girl. Look how it catches the light, Tessie-T. That blue would have been too dark. This one makes your room look so much bigger, don't you think?'

I nodded even though the walls were caving in, squeezing out oxygen, they must have been, because I couldn't breathe.

Tears teetered on my eyelids, globules of disappointment that I had to hide no matter what because Jack was waiting for me to be delighted. Somehow I managed it, I don't exactly know how, keeping my eyes open until they stung and saying the words he wanted to hear.

'Thanks Dad, I love it.'

'Your old man knows best, eh?'

I have never hated my yellow walls more than I do at this moment as Jack clutches the towel to his chest and pretends to have a heart attack.

It's brilliant how he does it, I have to admit it. Mum is in stitches and normally I would be too, maybe even joining in with a companionable cardiac arrest of my own. It takes a lot of willpower, but I make rocks out of my eyes and keep my expression stony as Jack staggers to my desk, clawing at his heart. I watch impassively as he holds out a dying hand to grip the coat I wore to run away last night. It's damp, it must be, and Jack is surely about to notice – but no. It's just a prop, and he collapses on my chair and dies with his face pressed against my hood, not even wondering why it's wet.

I jolt up suddenly, screwing my anger into a black ball, toying with it so dangerous and powerful in my hands. It's a grenade that could blow up this ordinary day, shattering the image of my perfect family into a thousand little pieces. All I have to do is let it explode.

Mum sees me sitting up in bed. She pretends to gasp then nudges Jack and he gasps too. They look at me with eyes precisely the same shade of blue – information I've known my whole life that now takes on brand new meaning. Here it is, proof that someone else was involved in my conception because I might not always pay attention in Biology, but I am pretty certain that two blue-eyed parents cannot produce a brown-eyed child.

'I—'

'She's talking,' Jack says. 'She's awake and she's talking.'

'I—'

'Woah, be careful!' Mum laughs.

Jack strolls over to my bed. 'Don't strain yourself on our account, Tessie-T.' He touches my shoulder with fingers that typed those six hundred and seventeen words. There is contact between us, and the strange thing is it doesn't feel strange because he has been my dad for fifteen years and Jack for only twelve hours. 'Just relax, Tessie-T. Lie back, lie back. Why change the habit of a lifetime, eh?'

He pushes me down onto my *Star Wars* pillows, and I disappear into the familiar universe of them like nothing at all has changed.

CHAPTER 4

I go through the motions, pretending everything's okay, which is what I need to do until I can work out what I want to do. I eat the porridge Jack makes every morning as he checks my homework, moving a thin finger across my maths book, not finding any errors even though it only took me twenty minutes because I am that good at trigonometry. He hands it back with a smile that normally I would return then reminds me to pack my flute for a lesson I might not attend if I decide to run away. *It's still a possibility* I tell the goldfish inside my head, even though the plan seems ridiculous in the cold light of day. I picture him, impatiently darting about beneath my bed, chanting the address of the Human Fertilisation and Embryology Authority where information about sperm donors is stored. *Finsbury Tower, One-hundred-and-three to One-hundred-and-five Bunhill Row in—*

'Tess?'

I come round to see Jack finish the last of his porridge then lean back in his chair.

'What do you think, then?'

'Yes?'

Nine times out of ten *yes* is the right answer. Sure enough, Jack nods then takes our bowls to stack in the dishwasher, strictly his domain. He takes great pleasure in it, putting the plates and the cups in the right order so we can fill the dishwasher completely, twisting his head this way and that, trying to work out where everything should go.

Today it's a plastic jug that's proving tricky. Jedi races in, scampering across the kitchen floor so he can thrust his nose in the cutlery. Jack hates it, but I love it, his pink tongue licking the butter knife with no regard for the rules.

'Out of there, boy. Come on. You know the score. Yes, that's what I thought, Tessie-T. Ask her about it. There's not a lot of point learning the flute if you don't do grades, is there? Suzie's just done one. Do you fancy having a go? We don't want to hide your light under a bushel, do we? We want to give you chance to shine. Really show what you can do, you know? Stand out.'

'I thought I was supposed to be trying to fit in,' I say, surprising myself, but not as much as Jack. He dumps the jug then straightens up.

'Who wants to fit in? Who wants to be ordinary?' he asks, sounding genuinely shocked. It's exhausting, trying to keep up with him, and it's a relief I don't have to do it anymore. 'Do you want to blend into the background, Tess? Is that what you're telling me?'

I mumble the appropriate response, but it's harder than usual. There's a scream of protest in my chest where there used to be silence and my eyes are ablaze. This is new, this heat, burning into Jack's back as he shakes his head then disappears upstairs.

I get changed in my room, grabbing an old school skirt because my trousers are in the wash, holding it up against my legs to see if it will still fit. Probably not is my guess, given that it was a squeeze six months ago, but with a few pulls and pushes I just about manage to get myself into the green fabric. Shoving my feet into the black Dr Martens I wear for school, I gaze down at my bottom half, telling myself that curves are beautiful until I love the way my bum juts out of the emerald material like some sort of epic green mountain. I am big and I am strong and I am powerful – a girl of Everest proportions who won't easily be conquered. I brush my hair vigorously then give my teeth an extra-fierce scrub, looking in the bathroom mirror at my face so full of fire.

Something's coming. I don't know what or when, but it's going to be huge.

'You ready, Tess?' Jack calls from the hall. 'I'll give you a lift. It looks like it might rain.'

I get my flute and my bag then pick up my salad from the kitchen before slipping on my coat, still wet from an adventure that already seems a million years ago.

'Miserable, isn't it?' Andrew says as he emerges from

the house next to ours. 'But, look at you, Mr Turner. This working lark becoming something of a habit, is it?' He locks his door with a quick turn of a key.

'Not really,' Jack replies, locking ours with more of a fumble.

'Life not beaten you into submission then, mate?'

'Not at all, mate.'

Andrew's proper laugh jars with Jack's false one. 'Glad to hear it. So you've not yet given up on the great acting dream?'

''Fraid not. Still flying the glorious flag, mate.' Jack points at his suit. 'This is nothing serious, just a temp job over in Ashton. A bit of pocket money in the run up to Christmas while I wait for my agent to find me a new role.' All of a sudden it seems pathetic, a forty-five year old man answering phones for a Volvo car dealership, scornful of anyone *on the treadmill* or *in the rat race*, turning up his nose at people with theirs *pressed to the grindstone* as he waits for auditions that never seem to come. 'Anyway, best be off. Have a good one, eh?'

We walk to our car parked in a space on the other side of the road. 'You spoil her!' Andrew shouts. 'School's only two minutes away. I never give my Suzie a lift.'

'Yeah, well.' Jack points at the sky. 'It's threatening.'

'The fresh air does them good! Toughens them up. Bit of exercise before school and all that.'

They both glance at me, the same thought pinging into

their minds as the button of my skirt almost pings off onto the pavement. The look on Jack's face makes me feel big, bigger than this car and bigger than this street, bigger even than a country, pretty much the size of Africa if famine had been eradicated.

'So, what've you been auditioning for recently?' Andrew asks, ambling over to us. 'Will we see you in that detective thing again? *Morse*, was it?'

'*Lewis*,' Jack says, zapping the car.

'*Lewis*. That's right. They're going to write you back in it, are they?'

'Nah, I don't think so. But whatever. It's good to get some variety on the old CV. I'd turn it down even if I was offered it again,' Jack lies.

'What will it be instead?' Andrew asks, not taking the hint as Jack climbs into the car and starts the engine. 'Adverts or something? Will we see you dressed up as the Honey Monster?'

'Don't think they have that anymore, do they? Adverts aren't my thing, really, to tell you the truth. Soulless. I'm concentrating more on theatre work at present. I am in this local pantomime. Helping them out, you know? Starts this weekend, actually. Tomorrow at seven, and then three Saturdays after that. You should check it out, if you get chance. Didsbury Players. Got myself roped in as Captain Hook, didn't I? Tess is in it too. You're loving it, aren't you? I mean, it's an amateur dramatic thing but it's quite impressive, isn't it? High quality?'

'Mmm.'

Jack looks at me funny because this is not at all how I usually respond.

'Half dead this morning,' he says to Andrew in a voice full of exasperation at the lethargy of teenagers. 'You know what it's like.'

'Suzie's a morning person, actually. We struck gold there.'

'Yeah, you did,' Jack says in a way that makes me feel distinctly bronze. 'Anyway, there might be one or two tickets left if you're interested.'

'Sounds good. I'll definitely try to make it,' he says, even though he won't.

'Brilliant,' Jack replies, meaning the total opposite. 'See you later, mate.'

'Yeah, mate. See you later. And you, Tess. Enjoy the lift with your chauffeur – I mean your dad.'

CHAPTER 5

We wave at Andrew but it's not him I'm looking at. I can't take my eyes off our hands. Mine's broad with short fingers and Jack's is narrow with long fingers and they make contrasting patterns as they fly through the air like birds definitely not from the same species. There's a fresh shaving cut on Jack's chin the complete opposite of my chin that's too large according to these girls at school. *Man Skull* they call me on account of my heavy jaw and big nose, bigger than Jack's I am suddenly realising because nothing about us is similar. He's thin to my fat, small to my tall, and ginger to my natural blonde.

Panic flutters in my chest. We're moving now so I can't leap out of the car, but I lean away from Jack as far as possible then stare out of the window with eyes that don't blink. He isn't my dad. I'm sitting next to a stranger. An imposter. The flutter becomes a swoop that makes the whole world lurch. I grip the seat and try to focus. There's a pavement.

People. Puddles. I see all of it and none of it. Jack tuts and I jump.

'That's one thing Andrew and I do agree upon. This weather's miserable.' I open my mouth to reply, but no – I am not going to make small talk with the enemy, let's be clear about that. I bite my tongue, sitting on my hands until they start to tingle. 'He won't come tomorrow, mark my words. Men like Andrew hate the arts. More fool them, right Tessie-T? You did ask Anna if she wanted a ticket, didn't you? Gran's too old to cope with it, but I mentioned it to Uncle Paul and Aunt Susan so that's a couple more if they can make it. You okay, Tess? You're quiet.'

The rest of me tingles too. Skin. Bones. Blood. 'I'm fine.'

Jack slows down as we approach school. He peers into the car park then drives straight past the entrance because Holy Crap he's going to do it again, even though I've told him countless times it's absolutely not allowed.

'That's ridiculous,' he said when I held up the letter for him to read as he stirred a pan of some mysterious sauce because he'd swung by the organic shop after work to grab a selection of ingredients, totally at random. 'Wang us the salt, Helen. This sauce needs a bit of bite to complement the sweetness of the plums. *Strictly no cars allowed in the bus park at any time.* Mrs Austin is a fantastic Head, but has she seen the car park? It's always gridlocked. What does she expect me to do?'

'Obey the rules,' I replied, too quietly for Jack to hear,

not that it would have made any difference to him. It's not just recipes that are for other people, it's rules as well.

He turns left then stops slap bang in the middle of the bus park because there's nowhere to pull in. Anger floods my face, washing over my body in a red hot tsunami.

'So, this isn't bad, eh, Tessie-T?' he says, oblivious to the wave of fury moving in his direction. It's going to knock him off his feet any second now, I swear to God. I wait for it to happen, but there's not even the quietest splash. 'Door to door service.'

He looks around for somewhere to drop me off. There's still nowhere to pull in and no way of reversing out because there's a bus behind us now, blocking the exit, so we stay where we are for a minute that feels way longer than sixty seconds.

When I was small, being in the car with Jack was up there with going to bed. I loved hiding under my duvet after school. It was a cave. A cocoon. And the car was the same.

'Our own little world on wheels,' Jack used to say, grinning at me in the rear view mirror as I sat with my legs dangling off the booster seat. He'd put on music and sing show tunes, even the female parts, to make me laugh. I'd give anything to hear that falsetto voice now.

At last there is a puff of exhaust fumes as a bus splutters into action. Jack sneaks into the space, ignoring the *honk honk* from the bus behind us. I go for the door the instant he pulls the handbrake.

'Zip up your coat, Tess.' Normally I would obey this sort of order no problem, but today I hesitate. 'Come on. Look at that. It's really starting to come down. You don't want to sit in a damp uniform all day, do you? You'll get a cold. We've got the pantomime to think about. Opening night tomorrow. You and your old man, eh? You don't want to come down with flu and miss it,' he informs me as I picture myself sneezing and smiling about it.

I never wanted to be involved in the first place. Jack heard about the audition from his friend, Derek, who'd been hired as the director, telling me about it as he plonked himself on the coffee table directly in my line of vision. I was watching *Embarrassing Bodies* and this just so happened to be the good bit where they showed the scrotum they'd mentioned at the start of the show. As Jack banged on, I slowly peered over his shoulder, trying not to be too obvious about it, hating myself a little bit for how much I wanted to see this testicle apparently the size of an orange.

'The audition's this Saturday,' Jack said, but I wasn't listening. The thing on the TV was more the size of a melon, I'm not even kidding. 'Derek's asked me if I want to be involved, and I said yes. Bit of a favour to help him out. It's only an amateur thing. No money involved, obviously, not even for a professional. But it will be fun. I haven't been in anything, theatre-wise, since I played Hamlet. Last year of stage school, that was. Back in the eighties. I had long hair.'

'I loved your long hair!' Mum said. 'Long flowing locks

and Shakespeare? My idea of heaven, but then I did have dyed red hair and a flower-stud in my nose.' She started to laugh and Jack did too. 'All those lines, darling. I don't know how you did it. Remember Yorick the mascot?'

'*A fellow of infinite jest and Sellotape.*' I loved the look they gave each other, my mum and dad, still together after all this time. 'He was terrifying, but he was perfect. Where did you find him again?'

'Some market stall in Oldham where I had that awful teaching placement. God, those kids were tough. I was walking home after school. The play was on just before Halloween, do you remember? I couldn't believe my luck. A plastic skull on a market stall! He was a little battered and broken, but we patched him up, didn't we?'

'And he worked. That show got brilliant reviews.'

'You got brilliant reviews, you mean.'

'I'll have to try and find him,' Jack said. 'He must be in the attic somewhere.'

'It will be good to see you on stage again, darling.'

'Yeah, I am looking forward to it, actually. Especially if it's a little quiet on the work front. I bet you fancy it too, eh, Tess? *Peter Pan?* You and your old man? Treading the boards?'

He expected me to say *yes* so I put on my happy face and nodded. That's how it worked. Jack suggested something and I agreed to it because I had a vow to honour, a vow I'd made when I was eleven years old with music from a school disco ringing in my ears. I'd made a promise to a fluffy white dog to be a better kind of girl, a more perfect kind of daughter for my perfect dad, so I chiselled away at myself, trying to become a chip off the old block, but no matter how much I shaped myself, I never quite got it right.

And now I know why.

'I won't say it again, Tess. And don't look at me like that, please. You're the one who chose to wear a skirt in this weather. It's ridiculous. It's not exactly skirt-weather, is it, and besides, it's—' he stops dead and clears his throat '—it's a bit too short for my liking.'

I look at my skirt. It almost comes down to my knees.

'Did you pick up your salad?' he asks, proof, not that I need it, that it's the tightness of my skirt, not the length of it he's thinking about. 'I don't want you going hungry, that's all.'

Usually I'd be appeased by this lie, but today I see it for what it is – manipulation, pure and simple, because he *does* want me going hungry, that's the whole point of giving me salad rather than sandwiches.

He smiles. 'I put some pineapple in it.' Pause. 'It's just that, well, kids can be mean, can't they? They can say things. That skirt. I don't want you standing out, that's all. Becoming too much of a target.' I snort loudly. 'What?'

The rain doubles in force. It's spectacular, the noise it makes on the roof of the car and the amount of water on the windows. We both fall silent and watch it for a while, letting the awkwardness fade between us, and then I zip up my coat before Jack can tell me again so that it's absolutely my decision to do it.

'Remind me what subjects you've got on today. Geography first, is it?'

'Yeah.' I don't want to talk but my mouth isn't obeying my brain.

'You enjoying it?'

'Yeah,' I say again, even though I'm not.

'Good. That's good.'

There's nothing good about it, and I long to be in London rather than stuck outside school. In twenty minutes' time, I am going to open my exercise book and write down the date as if this is just an ordinary Friday morning rather than the very first day of the rest of my life. I need a new timescale because there's a *before* and *after* now, and if the Christians were allowed to invent a new calendar after the birth of a baby in a stable, so am I after the rebirth of myself, Tess Turner, a Pluto in the solar system of life, who no longer needs to impress Jack or answer his questions I have to keep telling myself because it's going to take some getting used to.

'Still on volcanoes?'

'No. We're starting a new topic today.'

'Precipitation by any chance?' He elbows me in the ribs. 'Don't need to study precipitation when we have a first class example like this. Put up your hood, Tess. What is it then?

Footpath erosion? Tourism?' The rain's not going anywhere so I open the door without looking at him. 'Glaciation?'

I set off, biting my lip to keep from answering.

'Tessie-T?' He sounds baffled because I am leaving without saying goodbye. 'Sweetheart?'

I spin round. 'Oxbow lakes, okay?'

'Ah, my favourite! Enjoy, Tessie-T. Have fun with Anna – though not too much fun, mind. I know what you girls are like. You're at school to work, remember? Ask her if she wants tickets for tomorrow. And ask your flute teacher about those grades, okay? Right. You got everything? You sure? Good. See you tonight then,' he says, and I nod resignedly because in all likelihood he will.

CHAPTER 6

A large man with blond hair and brown eyes is who I am searching for, so I check every male teacher in the corridor. If I've lost my old dad then I need to find a new one is the main feeling in my heart, pumping with adrenalin. Mr Stevens from Design Technology is too thin, and Mr Crosland, my English teacher, is too red, with his red hair and red face and red ink always covering his red hands, especially after marking one of my essays.

Numbers are more my thing. Life is confusing and the only place where two plus two ever equals four is in a Maths lesson. Even when things look complicated, actually they're pretty straightforward. My teacher, Mr Holdsworth, creates chaos on the whiteboard with *Xs* and *Ys* and none of it makes sense until he makes it make sense, and the chaos becomes simple and the mess transforms into a neat answer that he circles twice in green marker pen.

He's wending his way through the crowd with a coffee in the yellow mug not the blue mug this morning. He's dark not blond, thin not fat, but that's okay because I'd rather be his wife than his daughter if there's a vacancy going in his family. As we pass in the corridor, I twist the dry ends of my hair round the fourth finger of my left hand then swipe my card to get through the security gate in the library.

It is an understatement, the fact I am pleased to see her, my one friend, the only person on planet Earth who I can now trust: Isabel. She's been my happy secret for two years and I intend to keep it that way. Jack would never understand her appeal, but she is the most interesting person I know, and the bravest too, because who else would sit in a packed library at an empty four-seater table, completely at ease with their solitude, is what I am pointing out to myself as overwhelming evidence of my friend's brilliance.

She's leaning on the bulky case of her cello, mousey head resting on upturned palm as she reads with squinty eyes, totally engrossed in *The Lord of the Rings*. I hurry over and touch her arm. She startles then grins.

'Greetings, Gandalf the Grey. Or should that be Gandalf the White?'

I have seen the films so I stoop over my imaginary staff and say with great wisdom, 'I have returned.'

'Nice skirt, Gandalf. Seriously. You look *wizard*.' She waggles her eyebrows as I sit down, glad to take the weight off my achy legs. I glance at the clock behind Miss Dyson's desk. Isabel's going back to her book so I grab it and chuck it to one side because there isn't a lot of time. 'Hey! I'm on a really good bit!'

'Listen. I need to talk to you. I did something crazy last night and—'

'Gandalf's back!' She pats the book with all this affection as if it's a living, breathing thing. 'He's back. The balrog is defeated. His old grey robes have been cast off. He's back and he's white and, oh, it's just so marvellous! I'm going to write a balrog into my story tonight.' She gestures at the notepad she carries everywhere but never lets me read. 'It's going to be epic. I've got it all planned out. Rather than Gandalf, the mysterious but beautiful elf, Isawynka, will defeat it. Me.' She beams. 'I am going to—' she swishes an imaginary sword – 'and then' – she spears an imaginary beast – 'to save the day.'

'Good. Good, I'm glad.' I raise my arms in mock celebration. 'Go Isawanka.'

'*Isawynka.*'

'Whatever. Woo, elf.' I lean in close, lowering my voice to practically a whisper. 'I need to tell you something.'

Isabel's eyes narrow to slivers of pale blue. 'Is this about Mr Holdsworth because I swear, Tess, you're getting obsessed, and it's a waste of time because, unfortunately for you, Mr Holdsworth doesn't strike me as a paedophile with a penchant for teenage girls.'

'A what?'

'A penchant. A proclivity. An inclination for underage females.'

'No. It's not about Mr Holdsworth. Though I have just seen him in the corridor.' Isabel pretends to yawn, but it is good-natured. Despite everything I smile, grateful for the normality of our conversation. 'He was looking particularly fine.'

'Yellow or blue?'

'Yellow.'

'Curious.' She means it too.

'That's what I thought. It was blue last Friday.'

'He's obviously trying to keep you on your toes.'

'Do you really think so?'

'No, Tess. I don't. Luckily for you, I don't think Mr Holdsworth is aware that you keep a tally of his cup choice in two carefully drawn columns in the back of your homework diary.'

'Three carefully drawn columns. There was the Morning of the Random Red Mug, remember?'

'How can I forget?' She smirks. 'It was momentous. So, what's up? What do you have to tell me?'

I look at her raised eyebrows and then at her cello and then at the bookshelves, trying to think how to say it out loud, the unspeakable truth that Jack is not and never wanted to be my dad. The stark reality of the situation hits me harder than it did on the streets at three o'clock in the morning when I was tiptoeing through the moonlight that made everything silver and surreal, only half-there so only half-true.

When Tess finally emerged after two hours of pushing, all I felt was revulsion, and I could no more easily pretend to love the peculiar creature in my delighted wife's arms than hide the resentment that burned inside. It wasn't my daughter. It was her daughter – hers and some sperm donor's I had never met, but what could I do? She was here and she was my wife's and—

'Tess?' Isabel says, sounding shocked. 'Are you crying?'

'No.'

'You are!'

'I'm okay. Honestly,' I say dishonestly because I don't want to cry, not here, not at school and besides Jack's not worth it I tell myself angrily. 'I'm fine.'

'You don't look fine. What is it?' She clutches my hand over the top of the cello case, our arms making a wonky bridge that I long to cross, but it is impossible. I sit, not so much lost for words, as full of words that can't be spoken. 'Tess, come on. You can tell me,' she says, but I don't know how to explain the past few hours of my life, and how I ran away from Jack last night, only to return this morning to eat porridge with him.

It's ridiculous.

I'm ridiculous.

I'm relieved to hear the bell. There's something reassuring about the prospect of my life being divided into predictable fifty-minute portions for the next seven hours at least. I make to leave but Isabel doesn't move, grasping my fingers as I try to pull away.

'We'll be late for registration,' I tell her.

'I don't care.'

'You do. What about your punctuality stamps?'

No one else in Year Eleven cares about the time-keeping scheme, but Isabel's been turning up for registration bang on time every morning since September because the reward for getting a term's worth of stamps is a fifty pound book voucher.

She steels herself. 'It doesn't matter.'

'You're a liar.'

'Yes, I am,' she squeaks, standing up suddenly. She shoves her things into her bag but packs her notepad carefully, hiding it in a discreet side pocket. 'I want that book voucher. I'm sorry. I have to get it. There's an illustrated *Complete Works of Tolkien* in Waterstones.' She gives me a quick one-armed hug that turns into a long hug because I don't let go. 'Talk properly at lunch?'

'Absolutely,' I say, but I don't believe the words. There is a cold, slithery sensation in my stomach – the truth burying down, worming its way into my guts. 'You run.' I pump a fist. 'Go get that stamp.'

CHAPTER 7

Mr Gledhill's hair is precisely the right shade of blond. It catches the light of the projector, flickering on an image of the Blitz. He points a ruler at a burning building, asking us to imagine in great detail the shocking annihilation of everything we hold dear.

'Picture the devastation,' he says so I do, thinking of a porridge bowl cracking in half as family photographs rattle on the walls then smash to the ground. 'How would you survive?' I am not sure of the answer to that one yet. 'How did England defend herself? Anyone? Lola? Ahmed? Tess, how about you?' He comes a little closer, surveying me with a pair of blue eyes so I cross him off my list that stretches to the ends of the Earth containing every single white man on the planet.

The world is too big and I am too small, just one girl searching for a stranger in a population of billions. I feel it, swirling around me, vast as the ocean, a sea of faces I don't recognise. My lungs tighten. I'm drowning, struggling to breathe, trying to hold onto something, anything, solid. But there's nothing. My whole life has been a lie, every birthday and Christmas and Father's Day and average Tuesday and bog-standard Sunday, eating roast dinners round the kitchen table, nearly always chicken because I don't like beef.

'How can you not like roast beef?' Jack said, just a week ago. 'I don't know anyone who's not a vegetarian that doesn't like roast beef. A nice pink joint of meat?' He laughed as I winced, and I glowed with pleasure because amusing my dad is pretty much my favourite pastime.

Except he isn't my dad. And Mum isn't the woman I thought she was. And I'm not Tess Turner because half of me, fifty percent of my genes, belong to some other man.

I have to find him. Somewhere beneath my bed, the goldfish lifts up his little orange head as I chant the address of the HFEA, picturing Finsbury Tower on Bunhill Row where I'm going to march through the door maybe even this weekend, demanding to see my file.

'You should have written to us,' the man on reception will no doubt say at first. 'You need to complete a form applying for information about your donor and then we can check the records to see what we've got.'

'I know that from the website,' I'll reply. 'But I only turned fifteen in August. I can't apply for information until my sixteenth birthday, but I thought if I turned up here and explained my situation then you might be able to help.'

'If you're not sixteen, I can't help you, dear. I'm sorry. You have to be sixteen to access the basic details about your donor – what he looked like, hair colour, height, that kind of thing – and eighteen to get any identifying information, if we have it.'

'Like a contact address?' I'll ask, breathlessly.

'Like a contact address. But you have to be eighteen for that. Fifteen-year-olds get nothing, I am afraid. Though you can ask your parents to apply on your behalf?' I'll shake my head firmly because this just isn't an option. 'Then I really can't help you, dear. I'm sorry.' Conservation over, he'll turn his attention to a Sudoku puzzle, no doubt looking baffled by it, gnawing the end of a pen.

I'll lean over the desk to point at the top of the grid. 'The three goes there,' I'll say, doing it upside down, working it out in a flash. 'And the five goes there. And the nine is at the bottom.'

'I'll take you up to the files,' he'll say, sounding awestruck. 'Anyone that good at Sudoku is clearly mature enough to—'

'Tess?' Mr Gledhill calls, snapping his fingers, and has my mouth been hanging half-open is my major concern as I shake off the daydream and glance at Anna, who sure enough is turning her head in my direction very, very slowly. 'You've been quiet today. You can make an educated guess, at least.' He perches on top of a filing cabinet. 'We're all listening, Tess. We're all ears.' I look him straight in the eye, but it's Jack I am seeing as I shrug. 'Well, that's disappointing.'

Every head swivels back to the front, apart from one. It sits, still as anything on a long pale neck, cool to the touch I imagine with a very slow pulse. It's a beautiful neck, there's no denying it, and I can't help admiring its elegance, stretching out of a shirt whiter than any in the class. My treacherous mind conjures an image of Jack, smiling in delight after the pantomime.

'So this is the famous Anna,' he'd say, and I would shrug like it was no big deal to be friends with the most popular girl in school. 'I'm so pleased Tess got you a ticket.'

In the real world, Anna takes in my tight skirt then blows out her cheeks. When the bell rings, she stands up, one foot hitting the floor then the other, her hands shaking either side of her legs to mimic the wobble of my thighs. I try to lose her in the corridor, but she follows me to Dining Room Three where I am due to meet Isabel in our usual spot by the lunch menu. I can't face her comments, not today of all days, so I swoop my hair forward, hiding behind the black curtain.

I can still hear her though.

'Man Skull's wearing a skirt,' Anna says to her friends, just a statement of fact in a perfectly ordinary tone that blends into the background so no teacher would ever pick up on it. I sneak a look through the gap in my hair to see seven pairs of sleek ballet pumps. The laces of my boots aren't even done up in a bow, and it bothers me all of a sudden, like I actually have to fight the urge to bend down and turn the ugly knots into something prettier. 'I didn't know they made them in man sizes. How does she fit her fat legs inside it?'

'Must have been an effort,' Tara replies. 'Imagine her trying to do up the zip.'

She acts it out, huffing and puffing, and the girls giggle, a light tinkle of laughter, this sprinkle of broken glass that cuts me to the core. I count to ten, trying not to cry, determined not to give them the satisfaction, but it's harder than normal and I feel angry, so angry, at Jack for making me this vulnerable.

'I hate you,' I whisper at the girls and at Jack and at myself most of all for standing here and taking it. Anna moves closer, hovering by my shoulder full of words she's ready to drop like bombs in my very own Blitz, but I am no England putting up a fight. I am a country with no clear boundaries, letting my enemy trample wherever she chooses.

'She's so fat she turns my stomach,' Anna says. Jack nods along as he types the words, making them bold on a screen that flashes in front of my eyes. 'Really ugly. Especially in that skirt,' she murmurs, her mouth almost touching my ear. 'Who does she think she is?'

I couldn't reply even if I wanted to. Thanks to Jack's blog, I have absolutely no idea anymore.

CHAPTER 8

'Sorry. Sorry. It took ages. They put pickle on it so I had to get another one.' Isabel holds up a baguette wrapped in a napkin. 'It was the same dinner lady who screwed it up last week as well. How hard is it? No pickle. *No pickle.* I said it twice like that but she still got it wrong. Hey, are you okay? Was she giving you bother again?' she asks as Anna disappears into the dining room. 'She was, wasn't she?' Her eyes glint dangerously as she takes in my forlorn expression. 'Of all the cold-blooded savagery! Two Shakespearean terms for you there, Tess. Two of my favourites out of all the great bard invented. *Cold-blooded savagery.* Describes her perfectly, don't you think?'

We head outside into a day drying up, just a few puddles left.

'She's creepy. *Evil.* I swear, if she was cast as one of Macbeth's witches, she wouldn't even have to act. I don't see why everyone thinks she's so pretty. It's just make-up and false eyelashes, isn't it? There's nothing natural about it. We're the real beauties.' I smile at this, catching sight of our reflection in the drama studio window – one fat girl with bad roots and one thin girl with limp hair. 'Ha. We are, Tess. Honestly. We're gorgeous.'

'Yeah, total hot stuff,' I manage. 'Absolute babes.'

'You say it, sister. Say it loud and proud,' she hollers in the voice of an American cheerleader, dropping my arm and starting to wiggle.

'Isabel! Stop it! Someone will see!'

'So? Shake your booty, shake your booty, shake your booty!' she chants, holding the baguette like a pole in a dodgy nightclub. 'Dance with me, Tess.'

'Oh my God. Stop it right now!' I grab her shoulder, so horrified I can't help laughing.

She shimmies. 'Dance with me, beautiful. Shake your booty and shake your beauty. Shake your booty and shake your beauty. Ooh, word play,' she says in a sensual voice, rotating her hips round and round in a circle. 'Nothing more arousing than a good pun.'

'Was it a pun?'

She bends over the baguette then bats her mousey eyelashes. 'It can be a pun if you want it to be a pun.' That makes me shout with laughter, and I celebrate the surprising burst of happiness by drawing back the curtains of my hair and letting sunlight bathe my face. 'Better? Good. Let's eat. I'm starving.'

We make ourselves comfortable on our usual bench by

the Science block, covering it with our coats because it's still wet. Isabel takes one look at my salad then offers me half her sandwich, the better half too with more of the filling by my reckoning. The baguette is gloriously white and strictly forbidden and tastes better for being banned because it is ham and cheese seasoned with rebellion and just a pinch of *Screw you, Jack.*

'So, are you going to tell me what's going on? Oh that's perfect,' she says, talking with her mouth full in some sort of sandwich heaven that is a spiritual experience, judging by her half-closed eyes. 'It's the onion that does it, Tess. It's the bloody onion.' She swallows. 'So, do you want to talk? I can sit here and eat this beautiful, beautiful creation and you can just go for it, if you like. Spill your heart out.' She takes another big bite. 'I'm an excellent listener.'

I know she is, and I want to tell her, but it would be easier to go back to the Big Bang and explain the history of the universe than talk about everything that has happened since Jack's computer flickered into life.

'There's no pressure either way, Tess,' she goes on, cheeks bulging. 'Honestly. You don't have to tell me if you don't want to. I'm here whenever you're ready to talk.' We fall silent for a while – probably not even ten seconds actually, before she blurts out, 'Like now, for instance. Now would be a good time to talk, don't you think? We have privacy. We have half an hour before afternoon registration. We have chocolate.' She rummages in her coat pocket and pulls

[51]

out a packet of Maltesers. '*The lighter way to enjoy chocolate,* so naturally I bought twice as much.' She produces a second bag that she chucks towards me. I open it and stuff three little balls into my right cheek, letting them melt there for a while. 'The time is right, my friend. The time is so right. If ever there was a good opportunity to come out then this is it. If ever there was . . .'

'I'm sorry, what?'

'. . . an ideal situation in which to inform a dearly loved friend that you are gay and gorgeous and some other positive adjective beginning with the letter g then this is surely—'

'I am not going to tell you I'm gay, Isabel.'

'Aw, really?'

'What about Mr Holdsworth? Have you forgotten about him?'

'Could be a cover up. Or you could be bisexual.'

I stare at her in disbelief. 'You are joking, right? You don't actually think that I'm—'

'No. No.' She glances at my boots. 'Maybe a little bit sometimes.'

'Er, hello, do you want a side order of cliché with that stereotype? I thought you were supposed to be open-minded,' I say, pretending to be disappointed, hitting her where it hurts. The colour rises in her cheeks, gloriously pink, and I hide a smile because this is part of the game.

'Stop trying to get a rise out of me.'

'I'm not doing anything,' I reply innocently, in awe of

myself and dazzled in general by the human spirit, how one minute it can be crushed and the next putting up a valiant fight. I cheer myself on and the roar sounds good, blocking out Jack's words for the first time in hours. 'I was simply stating the facts. You're not open-minded, but that's cool.' I add a shrug for good measure, just one casual shoulder up and down that turns her face from pink to red. 'It doesn't bother me either way.'

'And your opinion doesn't bother me because I know I am open-minded.'

'Well, I think we've just established that you're not, but like I say, it's okay. It's cool. No worries.'

'But I am open-minded, Tess,' she says getting annoyed now, these little flecks of spit appearing in the corners of her mouth. 'I am the most open-minded person that I know.'

'Prove it.'

'Okay. I want you to be gay. How's that? I'd *love* you to be gay. I'd wear a gay pride T-shirt on your behalf and dance around with a tambourine in the gay pride parade, chanting your name as I jangled my bells – which isn't a euphemism, by the way.'

'You'd wear a gay pride T-shirt for me?' I ask, all touched to the bottom of my heart that I clutch with my hand. She nods enthusiastically. 'That's nice. That's really nice.' She pops a Malteser into her mouth as if the problem has been solved. I let her relax, lulling her into a false sense of security, before saying really slowly, 'I'm just wondering one thing, though.'

'What's that?'

'I'm wondering why you'd wear a gay pride T-shirt for me but not a *non*-gay pride T-shirt. That's not very politically correct.'

'Shut up, Tess. I don't mind you being straight as you very well know.'

'Woah. Woah woah woah,' I say, holding out my hands. '*You don't mind me being straight.* Is that what you just said? Oh,' I shake my head, 'it's worse than I thought.'

She hits me. 'Stop it!'

'Let's get this straight.' I take a deep breath, gathering all my pretend thoughts into a frown. 'You, tremendously open-minded you, would only celebrate my sexuality if I was a *lesbian*. Is that what you're telling me?'

'No! That's not what I am telling you. That's not what I'm telling you at all.'

'That's what you just said though.'

'I didn't. I didn't say—'

'You don't *mind* me being straight but you'd *love* me to be gay. Your words, Isabel.' I wave a finger in front of her face and she swats it like a fly. 'Your words. Your prejudice, heterophobic words.'

'Argh! Tess! I'd celebrate your sexuality whatever it was, okay?' she shouts at the top of her voice, and we both start laughing because I've riled her up good and proper.

It's hysterical, the way she's climbing to her feet, unable to resist the urge to defend herself, even now. 'Do you want to know the truth? Here's the truth. The truth is—'

'You can't stop saying *truth*?'

'The truth is—'

'You have an addiction to the word *truth*?'

She snorts, making us both laugh even harder. 'The truth is I'd wear a T-shirt for you whatever your sexuality, okay? I mean it, Tess. Man. Woman. Boy. Girl. Dog . . .'

'Eww,' I grimace.

'No. Not *eww* to me. Not *eww* at all. If you fell in love with a dog, I'd wear a *My Friend Loves Bestiality And I Am Proud Of It* T-shirt because that's how accepting and tolerant I am. So there.'

The idea of that T-shirt makes me collapse in a good way. I hunch over my legs, laughing until my sides hurt, loving the achy feeling of joy in my lungs.

'You can pay me later,' Isabel says when we're still fizzing but the bubbles have died down, pretty much like lemonade five minutes after being poured. It feels good, sort of sparkly. We grin at each other, and isn't it amazing, the fact that my mood affects her mood, and her mood affects my mood because we are symbiotic creatures, let's be clear about that. 'For the therapy. It'll be fifty quid for the laughter and one hundred English pounds for the baguette pole dance. A bargain.'

She falls serious, sucking her last Malteser as I look down

at my boots, preparing myself for what I know is coming next.

'What was it though, Tess? What did you want to tell me this morning? Come on. You would've spilled the beans in the library if I hadn't gone on about Gandalf like some sort of *Lord of the Rings* freak.'

'You are a *Lord of the Rings* freak. Didn't you used to have an imaginary friend called Frodo?'

Isabel sighs. 'At least tell me you're all right. If you say you're okay, I won't badger you, I promise.' She holds up three fingers on each hand like a Boy Scout then puts them behind her ears. 'Elves' honour.'

'Is that a thing?'

'It is now. And answer the question. Are you okay?'

'I'm okay,' I lie because I want it to be true, and I don't want to destroy this mini moment of peace, here in the sunshine, with the pain in my chest more manageable than it was this morning.

'You're not upset?'

'I'm not upset.'

'And the crazy thing you did last night, whatever it was, you're not going to do it again?' This time I pause, thinking about the goldfish waiting impatiently for our trip to London. 'Tess?'

'I'm not going to do it again.'

'Elves' honour?'

'Don't make me do—'

'Elves' honour?' she says again, looking at me with too much white round her eyes. 'Isawynka won't believe you unless you do it.'

'Are you ever going to let me read the stuff in your notepad?' She stares me down. 'Fine. Fine. Elves' honour – *Isawanka*.' I copy the action by my ears for a split second only before changing the subject without meeting her gaze.

CHAPTER 9

After school, Isabel and I head towards Chorlton Park, not exactly the most exciting place to hang out, but there's a kids' play area where we can sit and talk and go on the swings, saying *wooo* with just enough irony to disguise that we're loving it. Friday afternoons are my favourite. Isabel doesn't have cello or clarinet or orchestra practice and for once I don't have to be home on the dot of four.

'It can wait until Saturday morning, can't it?' Mum said when Jack was breathing down my neck to get my homework done one Friday evening. 'What difference does it make?'

'She'll feel better if she gets it out of the way.'

'Have you asked her that?' Mum laughed as I half-sprawled on the sofa. 'She seems happy enough to me.'

'Sit up, Tess.' I shuffled round at once. 'And take off those ridiculous boots, will you? They're filthy. How many times do I have to tell you?'

I speed up, marching along the pavement, not even trying to avoid the mud. Home is behind me, the park up ahead, and I am rushing towards it like Jedi, straining on his leash, his nose sniffing madly like maybe freedom has a smell. I breathe it in. The sky's a purple line above a long, straight road. There are rows of identical red houses and a tram full of people, gliding smoothly on a solid track. *Clack clack* it says, in a repetitive, reassuring rhythm. *Clack clack.*

It disappears around a corner as two planes fly majestically overhead. My dad is out there somewhere and I will find him is the sudden conviction in my heart as I scan passers-by for a man with blond hair and brown eyes and a body big enough to have created mine.

'Why are you staring at the Jehovah's Witness?' Isabel asks as we approach the park.

He's standing on the other side of the road in front of a clothes shop, preaching through a megaphone and giving out leaflets with an over-energetic thrust of his hand that people are swerving to avoid. He's the right size and has the right hair colour and is the right sort of age, Praise the Lord, to have produced an abundant sperm sample sixteen years ago. Heart in my mouth, I watch him almost take out a pensioner with a pamphlet before apologising profusely, running his fingers through his hair the way I do when I am nervous.

'Tess? What the—?' Isabel cries because I'm darting across the road.

'The Bible is the key to your salvation!'

Pretending to be interested in the Eternal Kingdom of

Heaven, I move closer to inspect the man's eyes. There they are, lighting up as I approach of my own accord and take a leaflet like a miracle teenager sent from Jehovah or what have you, but his eyes glint green not brown so he isn't the one.

All of the feeling trickles out of me until I'm more of a dummy than the mannequin in the shop window. The man's loving it, this captive teenage audience, no idea at all that I'm not listening to him describe my ticket to salvation because I am too busy thinking about a ticket to London. I have to go. I need information to narrow down my search.

'What was that about?' Isabel asks when I return. She snatches the leaflet and starts to read. *'The good news of the Kingdom will be preached in all the inhabited Earth.* Matthew's Gospel, chapter twenty-four, verse fourteen, apparently. *My friend is a complete mentalist.* The Gospel of Isabel, chapter one, verse one. *She's totally and utterly lost her mind.* Verse two. *I have no idea what's going on but she's going to confide in me, her only friend in the world, right this very second.'* She pokes me as we walk into the park. 'That was verse three. You can't argue with verse three. You have to tell me. The Bible says so.'

We make our way to the play area.

'I thought you weren't supposed to be badgering me.'

'I'm an irrepressible badger. You should know that by now.'

I perch on a swing as a man appears, holding the hand

of a little girl with auburn pigtails. She sprints towards the seesaw and her dad follows just as quickly. He scoops her up and she shrieks in delight as he puts her on one end then hurries round the other side to sit down himself. They're giddy with excitement. Giddy on each other. It hurts, but in some faraway part of me. My body's dispersing, my head wafting away . . . away . . . away as my limbs drift apart. I am not Tess Turner. I am not anyone. I float in bits beneath a sky the exact colour of a bruise.

'Tess?'

It doesn't even sound like my name.

'I'm sorry.' I really am too. Isabel's my best friend, my only friend, and she deserves an explanation. 'I know I'm being weird. It's just that—'

'What?' Isabel interrupts, pointing at her ear even though she heard me just fine. 'What did you say?'

'I'm being weird, but I—'

'What was that?'

I grind my teeth. 'I'm being weird.'

'Oh, you think?' She starts to laugh. 'Tess, you have never acted more freakishly in your life and that is saying something, trust me.'

I bite the bullet one more time. 'The thing is—'

She yawns loudly. 'You know what? I'm not that interested anymore.' I look at her in dismay. 'I mean, why would I care what's going on, hmm? Hmm? *Hmm*?'

'Be serious, will you?'

'Fine. I'm ready, Tess,' she chants in a monotone. 'I'm serious enough to hear whatever it is you have to say.' My eyes fill with frustrated tears. 'All right, all right. That was the last one, I promise.' I glance at her warily but she's quiet now. Listening. I'm just about to speak when her phone starts to ring.

'Sorry, sorry!' She pulls it out of her coat pocket. 'Give me a sec. *Hiya Dad.*' Her voice is casual, unconcerned, because absolutely without question, *Dad* is what he is. She smiles at something he says and it's warm and easy, oh so full of trust. '*With Tess. In the park. No. No young men, Dad.*' She rolls her eyes for my benefit. '*Apart from the rapist. There is him, but no one else.*'

The seesaw's creaking, the little girl giggling as her dad bounces her up and down. In the distance, a man and a boy my age are walking a dog into the woods. The bruise darkens, the treetops turn black, and I ache with longing to swap places with the boy or the little girl or Isabel telling her dad that she'll see him at home.

She hangs up with this strange expression, sort of nervous but pleased.

'He's got tickets. For tomorrow night. The pantomime. I asked him if he would buy them this morning. You don't mind, do you?' Jack's disapproving face wafts before me. I blink to get rid of it. 'I know you said not to bother,' she says quickly, 'but I want to be there. You, dressed as a Lost Boy, Tess? I wouldn't miss that for the world. Tell me you're okay with it . . . It'll be fine, honestly. I'll give you the biggest cheer.'

I don't want to hurt her so I smile. 'All right.'

'And afterwards I'll introduce myself to your parents and you can finally meet my dad,' she says, happily. 'You'll love him, Tess. I've told him all about you.'

CHAPTER 10

Maybe I'm overreacting.

Maybe Jack will love Isabel and Isabel will love Jack and they'll tease me about how worried I've been. She'll laugh at his bad jokes and he'll laugh at her bad jokes and I'll laugh at my own stupidity for ever keeping them apart.

'I've got a good one. *What did the drunken hobbit say when he bumped into the wizard? Saruman, I didn't see you there!*'

'She's so great!' Jack will tell me after giving Isabel a high-five. 'Much better than that Anna girl.'

'I can't believe you pretended she was your special friend, Tess! How long has that lie being going on, then?'

'Since the Year Seven disco.'

'Hilarious!' Isabel will shout, slapping her thigh.

'She even showed me photos of Anna. On the Internet, you know? She often talked about how pretty she was.'

'Stop it. Oh, stop it. It's too funny!' Isabel will laugh, wiping away silver tears of mirth.

'I know,' Jack will reply. 'And she also said they sat next

to each other in lessons and went for lunch every day in the canteen and talked endlessly about boys and blusher because she's far more interested in that sort of stuff than balrogs and bestiality.'

Isabel's smile will fade. 'But she loves talking about balrogs and bestiality.'

'She doesn't,' Jack will say and Isabel's tears will start to rust. 'Why do you think she invented a friendship with another girl? She's bored of you, Isabel. Bored and ashamed.' His expression will harden. 'And I can see why.'

'It's not true!' I'll cry as Isabel's tears corrode her lovely face. 'Our friendship is the best thing in the world! The very best thing!'

I have to protect it, and this is just one more reason to make sure I disappear to London. I'll go tomorrow, before the pantomime begins – *and that's a promise* I tell the goldfish as I nip into *Tesco* to buy some Eccles cakes for Gran. On Fridays I always drop off a packet with a pint of full fat milk on my way home from school.

I hurry down her drive and let myself in. 'It's just me, Gran!'

It's getting dark now and there's a lamp shining in the hall that smells dusty and old, like time is crumbling second by second to form a powdery coat over the ornaments on the side table. I check the coast is clear then wipe the dust with my sleeve because this right here is what Mum and Jack would call a sign that Gran is no longer coping. They started saying it a couple of months ago, snooping on her, checking her fridge for mouldy food and the kitchen for grime. I can't stand it, Jack wiping his thin finger over the surfaces the same way he drags it across my homework.

Well, they won't find any mess in the kitchen after my visits. I clean it with the secret spray I bought from the supermarket, hiding it at the back of the cupboard under the sink where definitely Gran's too old to stoop down and discover it. When I walk into the kitchen to drop off the cakes and turn on the kettle, I wipe up a dollop of yoghurt and put the empty carton in the bin before popping my head round the lounge door.

'Hello, dear.' Gran lifts a wrinkly hand then returns it to her round belly. The gesture is so familiar and comforting I well up, giving thanks that Gran is on Mum's side of the family. I'm no less her granddaughter than I was yesterday afternoon and it's a relief to see her, this woman whose blood throbs in my veins.

'I've put the kettle on,' I shout so Gran can hear me, the only time I don't mind raising my voice.

'You are good, dear. I'll make us some tea, shall I?' She's wearing a fluffy pink cardigan and the warmth of her voice makes me feel as if I'm snuggled up in it too. 'And don't you dare offer to help. I can still make a pot of tea, you know.'

I look away out of respect. I wouldn't want an audience if I struggled to get out of my chair and Gran is no different. She's human, isn't she, a thing Mum and Jack seem to forget when they talk about her cleaning habits as if Gran is out of earshot rather than sitting right in front of them.

She grips the wooden arms then heaves herself to standing. It's an effort and she staggers, unsteady on her feet, round-shouldered and shuffling as she leaves the room. It will take her a while to make the tea so I have a quick tidy round, nothing too obvious so Gran won't notice. She's proud, no doubt about it, like if her body still worked, she'd have a spine like a metre stick and a lofty sort of head with eyes that stared straight forward.

On the mantelpiece, there are twenty porcelain animals that need dusting. It's hard without polish but I do my best with my shirt sleeve. As always, I'm drawn to the lion without really knowing why.

'You've always liked that one,' Gran says, reappearing with a tray that shakes in her wobbly hands. I don't take it off her though. If Gran says not to help then Gran means not to help, let's be clear about that. 'Do you remember? You always chose to play with it when you were small. Making it purr. Giving it a saucer of milk. That sort of thing.' I smile at Gran, amazed I have no recollection of it. '*But lions aren't tame,* Jack used to say. *They're dangerous, Tess. They roar.* But you wouldn't listen. You saw a cat. Jack saw the King of the Jungle. But that's folk for you. It wouldn't do for us all to be identical, would it?'

I've always known we were different, but I didn't think other people had noticed it too. It's frightening how little we're alike, how little I know about my true identity.

'Are you okay, dear?'

I want a dad. A proper one. I want to look at him and know who I am, to be able to make sense of the awkward parts of me by seeing how they've come together in a man who's got it sorted. I want to watch how he works things out with a brain just like my brain, and how he copes with our peculiar brand of shyness, and how he lives with the DNA I share, a tangle of codes that confuses the hell out of me, giving me a thousand contradictory impulses every minute of every day.

Like now, for instance. I want to ask Gran about Jack and never hear his name again. I want to scream in Jack's face and also disappear for good so I never have to face up to the truth. I want to parade Isabel on stage in front of an audience of millions and also hide her away to protect her from Jack. I want to impress him and defy him and hate him even though I love him in a muddle that hurts my brain.

'I'm fine.'

I don't know what else to say.

And I don't know what else to do except sit with Gran and eat an Eccles cake.

CHAPTER 11

'You're here early,' Jane says when Jack and I walk into the theatre that's not a theatre at all but a Methodist church in Didsbury.

Everything I need to get to London is hidden in my bag beneath my costume and my make-up kit. I'll put on my Lost Boy outfit so as not to rouse suspicion, but slip out before I go on stage, changing back into my normal clothes at the train station where definitely I will be buying a ticket in precisely two hours and twenty minutes.

Jane stares at us through the dead centre of a square pair of glasses. 'I haven't even set up Front of House yet.' She grabs a stack of pink tickets and a pile of programmes then perches behind a table.

'That's Front of House sorted, then,' Jack jokes and actually it's pretty funny so I laugh without meaning to. It rings out over the church, this blessed holy noise, and for the tiniest instant it's just like old times. It's been happening all day, these moments where everything seems normal and I almost forget.

'The dressing room isn't ready. I haven't even had chance to turn on the electric heater.'

'In that case, I'm leaving,' Jack says and I snort again. 'Take no notice of us, Jane. We're pulling your leg.'

She sniffs. 'Are you staying or not?'

'If you don't mind. Sorry to be a pain. I'm the same on set, I'm afraid. They got to know my ways on *Lewis*. They used to let me arrive a couple of hours early when I had a big scene,' Jack says, and the moment passes, just like that. He never had a big scene, and I wait for a hint of embarrassment at the lie, but it doesn't come.

Jane's intrigued without wanting to be. 'Did you meet him, then?'

Jack scratches his cheek then gives his fingernails a brief once-over. 'Who?'

'What's his name? Kevin . . . Wheately, is it?'

'Oh, Kevin Whately. Oh yes. I know Kev.'

'Really?' Jane replies, dropping any pretence of disinterest now. She leans forward, her large chest squishing against the table to make a ledge of bosom.

'Yes. He's a great guy. A really great guy. Great actor too, of course. On the screen.'

'Is it very different then, being on stage to being on television?'

'Chalk and cheese, Jane.'

[70]

'Really?'

'Oh, absolutely.'

She beams at him with all her teeth. 'Fascinating.'

'So, how're the sales going? Picked up yet?' For some reason Jack glances at me.

'A little,' Jane says in a way that makes me think they haven't at all. 'Thirty-two.'

'That's not bad,' Jack replies, sounding like he thinks it is. 'Thirty-two's an audience.'

'Thirty-two's plenty and we could still sell more. Bob, the lighting guy, said a couple of his sisters might come along with their kids, so that's another five or six if they make it.'

'And my agent might turn up.'

This is news to me. I imagine Jack finishing the blog and switching to his email in the study where clearly he gets up to all sorts of secret business.

Jane looks impressed. 'Your agent, hey? Very glamorous.'

'Invited him up from London. Dropped him a line a couple of days ago. Thought it would be good to remind him I can do theatre work as well as TV because it's, well, not exactly difficult. It's been a good year if anything.'

It's unnerving, how easily Jack lies to everyone about everything and me most of all, every day of my life, which is five thousand five hundred and seventy-one I worked out this morning. If I lined up the false words that have emerged from his lips, I reckon they'd stretch at least twice round the Earth. That's how it feels, like my world is surrounded by lies and made up of fibs and built on mistruths. I need facts – facts that can't be denied, written down in black and white in an official file with an index where I can look up the secrets of myself and find the answers.

'Still, it can't be the easiest way to make a living,' Jane says.

'It's the road less travelled, certainly. You know the Robert Frost poem? *The Road Not Taken?*'

'No, I'm not familiar with it.'

'It's about the importance of doing things differently, getting off the beaten track. This man stands in the woods at a fork in the road. One path is clear, downtrodden by hundreds of pairs of feet, and the other is overgrown. Untried. Untested.' He makes a grand, sweeping gesture down at himself. 'That's the route I've chosen, obviously. It isn't easy, but I thrive on it. The unpredictability. The unexpected twists and turns. The chance to be great, to do something great, to challenge myself and prove what I can do in front of an audience, you know? Silence the doubters, that sort of thing?'

'I can't imagine you have many of those,' Jane says in this voice that's half a flirt.

Jack gives her more than half a smile. 'It will be nice for my agent to witness this. Home-grown drama. Grass roots stuff.'

He looks around, taking it all in like he's trying to imagine it through his agent's eyes. I take it in too: the programmes printed off someone's computer; the pretty decent homemade set; the foyer of the church, repainted especially for tonight. I don't know what's worse, how bad this whole thing is or how good everyone's tried to make it.

'I'll keep a ticket to one side,' Jane says, but Jack doesn't respond right away. He's lost in some thought or other that creases his brow.

'That's good of you,' he says, straightening it out. 'Thanks.'

'And are you looking forward to it, Tess?'

'She can't wait,' Jack replies before I've even had chance to consider the question. Irritation tingles my skin. 'She's really excited, aren't you? Aren't you, Tess? *Don't mumble.* No one will hear her in the audience if she speaks like that, will they? She is excited. Always going on about it at home, aren't you?'

The irritation's burning now. I swallow hard, resenting Jack, hating him, but forcing out the word he wants to hear. 'Yes.'

'She's loved it, being in a play with her old man. It's been a treat for both of us. Just nervous, that's all. Opening night of the first play she's ever been in. Debut performance. It's a major deal.'

'Yes, it is,' Jane agrees. 'Well, good luck both of you. Enjoy your big moment, Tess.'

'Oh, I will,' I say more loudly. Clutching my bag, I follow

Jack into the dressing room to wait for that big moment to
come.

'I need Nana the dog as well. Has anyone seen him?' Derek
asks. 'Where is he?'

Daniel shuffles out of the toilet, cue the laughter, because
a man in a dog costume is automatically hilarious and this is
just one of the rules of the mainstream universe that I don't
have access to being Pluto, thousands of miles away, floating
out here on the very edge of things. It's just not funny, Jack
woofing his approval as Daniel wags his tail and spins in
a circle, but everyone's rolling around. These are Jack's
people, all right, and I am not going to join them. I stand
alone and it feels good, like I'm remaining true to myself at
long last. I am a storm cloud and I am thunder and I am big
and black and angry, lurking on the horizon.

'That's enough now, gents,' Derek says, red-faced due to
the power of the electric heater and the stress of opening
night. 'It's time.'

The overture rings out over the dressing room, just one
man on a piano playing for me and the goldfish and the start
of our adventure. Trying not to think about Isabel waiting
in the audience, I move to the seat nearest the fire exit,
propped open to let in some fresh air. The smell of freedom
wafts in on an icy draught that gives me goose-bumps, this
prickly sense of anticipation that something huge is about

to happen. I can almost see it, my destiny crystallising in the frozen air.

Jack propels his arms in a circle then double-cricks his neck to the left and right, a movement I've seen him do a thousand times before, but I pay close attention to it, memorising the look of his body as he bends over a skinny man's paunch to touch his toes. He pulls his chest to his knees and holds it as he counts to five. His lips move as mine do too, counting down these last seconds together before he stands up with flushed cheeks, gives Yorick a pat, then walks out of the room without looking back. He doesn't sense my eyes boring into his red waistcoat, urging him to turn round because it is not so easy after all to be separated from the only dad I've ever known.

I edge towards the door. It looms bigger and bigger, the sliver of night getting wider and wider as I approach with a pulse that seems unusually conspicuous. I am very aware that I am alive, with a heart and a stomach and a tongue swimming with double the usual amount of saliva. I pause, summoning up courage, then dash outside.

Other people follow.

I curse. This wasn't part of the plan. The plan was to slip through a crack in the door and disappear without being seen, not throw it wide open to let out five Lost Boys, three pirates, and one Indian desperate to escape the stuffiness of the dressing room. They huddle on the steps, this motley crew tinged with moonlight, watching me watch them as I peer over my shoulder to see if I can sneak off without being seen.

I take one step, then another, then stop with a grimace reflected back at me in a jeep window and the windscreen of a BMW. There are three of us, all looking as frustrated as the other as the chance of escape vanishes before our eyes. If I disappear they will alert Jack, who will hunt me down, and can you even imagine it, him in a pirate costume chasing me as a Lost Boy in a weird case of life imitating art.

'Let's Talk,' he'll say, but no thanks, Jack, I don't want to Talk about what I saw on your computer, not now or ever for that matter. Talking will make it real and I am not ready for that yet. With his voice full of shame, Jack will have no choice but to deny he meant those six hundred and seventeen words, vowing with his hand on his heart that he really does love me, his non-daughter. I can't stand the thought of this lie being told right to my face. I am too proud to hear his fibs, and too scared of the prospect that he might not tell them at all if he's braver than I imagine and willing to stand by that blog.

I wish I'd never seen it. I wish it so hard I actually say the words out loud, my legs trembling in the car park that's too full of cars, this claustrophobic mass of metal surrounding me, blocking any chance of escape.

'Where are you off to?'

I leap out of my skin because I didn't hear any footsteps, or even sense that someone was standing by my elbow, which they are with their fingers on it, shaking my arm gently to get my attention. I turn to see Mr Darling.

'Derek's looking for you. The others are back inside.' He means the Lost Boys, and sure enough there's no one on the steps now apart from Daniel, dog-helmet on his knees, staring up at the moon, part-man, part-beast. 'You're not doing a runner, are you?'

'No.' Mr Darling is not convinced, studying my bag with shrewd eyes that look as if they belong beneath a pair of glasses. 'Do you wear contact lenses?' I ask because it seems important to know.

'What?'

'I was just wondering,' I say a little embarrassed, acting not like myself at all. I feel odd, sort of strung out and reckless, throbbing with adrenalin in the cold night air. 'Your eyes are wise enough to pull off glasses. The type a professor would wear in a university. It's a compliment,' I reassure him and he looks pleased.

He studies me again, contemplating my bag and my boots ready to march down to London. 'It's okay to be nervous. It's all part of it. It's not a very pleasant feeling, but it won't kill you. You're tougher than you think.'

I'm not, but it's a nice thing to say.

'Thanks.' He smiles a truly lovely smile, and isn't it a pity that his hair is brown not blond and his eyes are hazel because he would make a wonderful dad. 'Do you have children?'

'Three of them.'

'They're lucky,' I reply, a lump forming in my throat.

'I'm not sure they would always agree with you. Come on. Let's go back inside.'

I look at the road beyond the trees that leads to Manchester Piccadilly station. I think of the train waiting to go to London, and Finsbury Tower on Bunhill Row that could contain the answers I'm searching for. *I'm sorry*, I tell the goldfish because I am a disappointment, no doubt about it, the only runaway never to run away and the only rebel never to rebel and the only storm cloud never to let out a roar of thunder. But Mr Darling is putting his arm around me, and right now that wins.

CHAPTER 12

My only line in the play is coming up – *Honest, Mr Hook, I have no idea where Peter is and that's the truth* – fourteen words, easy enough to remember but difficult to get out of my mouth when I am this uncomfortable being on stage.

'Don't just say it in a monotone though, Tess. Use your voice. Intonation is important. You need to put some emphasis on the key words.' That's what Jack said earlier today when he made me practise in the lounge. 'Emphasise *no* not *idea* and *that's* rather than *truth*,' he told me, or maybe it was the other way round.

Honest, Mr Hook, I have no *idea where Peter is and* that's *the truth* I try out in my brain, but that doesn't sound right. I switch it, but that sounds wrong too. I repeat the line over and over, getting more and more desperate, until the words lose their meaning altogether.

I do a bit of acting, tending the fire made out of foil and spray-painted toilet rolls. The lights are dimmed, just one on Wendy, illuminating her pale skin as she starts a monologue about missing her mother. Jack paces up and down in the wings, mouthing his lines, acting offstage so he can start with a bang onstage in about ninety seconds is my alarming estimation that sets off a bell in my chest where my heart used to be. I lubricate my throat, trying to clear some phlegm with a cough that comes out louder than anticipated. Wendy glares at me, waxing lyrical about her mother's dainty hands with a face that looks as if she'd rather chop them off.

'Everyone needs a mother, and I miss mine. Oh, how I miss mine.' The audience claps. I use it to disguise one more cough, a proper cough this time with all my lungs behind it, but the phlegm will not be dislodged.

Jack marches onto the stage. There's a chorus of boos, Isabel louder than anyone in the very front row. Her dad tells her to calm down, but she boos again and he laughs then joins in. They're identical. Carbon copies. Cut from the same cloth, definitely the same colour, all gold I imagine, just like the wrappers of the Werther's Original sweets they've been sharing tonight. I've been watching them work their way through the entire bag, family-size most probably, and isn't that just perfect for their perfect relationship I think with a painful pang of jealousy that makes me feel ashamed.

Jack bursts into the Wendy House, searching for Peter.

'He's not here!' Wendy cries, the fifth line before mine, which, oh God, I suddenly can't remember at all. I rack my brains as Captain Hook ransacks the Wendy House, upending chairs and emptying shelves. I take cover beneath a low table, usually a squeeze, but tonight I bolt underneath it like a girl half my size.

'He is!'

'He isn't, you fool!' shouts Tinkerbell.

'Someone must know where he is . . . *You*,' Captain Hook says, grabbing my foot. I am supposed to make it easy for him to drag me out, but I cling onto the table leg. Snarling with rage, he clutches my bare calf and tugs hard, too hard for me to resist, so I scuttle back, giving in to Jack as always.

I face him, expecting to crumble, but something incredible happens, and I don't.

'Where's Peter?'

The line comes back to me easily, and that's a shock to find it waiting patiently behind my lips. Captain Hook grabs me by the scruff of my neck and gives me a shake, demanding my response. I cough again and this time it works. I swallow, giving thanks to God for mucus that behaves itself in the nick of time.

My throat is now gloriously clear, no blockages at all, and the line's on the tip of my tongue so I can say it no problem, and yet I just – *don't*.

'Where's Peter? Where's Peter I say?'

I stare at Captain Hook, seeing past the fake eyebrows to Jack underneath. Something shifts in his expression and he sees me too. Jack's hand tightens round my neck, the hook pressing into my flesh with a lot more than pretend frustration behind it. Time slows down, the seconds throbbing in the space between us as Jack demands that I speak and I stare into his black pupils and keep my mouth closed.

'Where's Peter?' The voice of the pirate has disappeared to be replaced by good old Dad in a towering rage. 'Where's Peter? Did you hear me? I asked you where Peter was.'

I heard him all right, but just for once let me stand here and do what I want for a change, which is to categorically *not* say the words Jack wants to hear. He gives me a shake, trying to stir me into action, and the audience laughs, wanting this awkwardness to be part of the play. It dies quickly and they shift about, merging into one body twitching uneasily on one big seat, fidgeting as I gaze at Jack and still do not reply.

You're not my dad, I tell him with eyes that don't blink and lips that don't move, my pulse a strange high-pitched hum, buzzing in my ears and my veins so I vibrate with all this power I've never felt before. Spit flies from Jack's mouth as he repeats the line one more time. It takes an age for it to fall, these tiny droplets glowing in the spotlight. They hover in mid-air and I hover there too, somewhere between before and after as Jack's shoulders rise but do not fall. He's holding his breath, waiting to see what I'm going to do next, and in this instant so magnificent and unexpected, I take back control.

Fear flits across Jack's face like a moth with frantic wings.

He mouths the words at me, all fourteen of them – *Honest, Mr Hook, I have no idea where Peter is and that's the truth* – reminding me of what I have to do, but I haven't forgotten. I know precisely what's expected of me, just like I always have.

But I am Pluto and I am cold and I am dark, so I take a step back, moving out of Jack's reach with a silence that speaks volumes.

Just listen to my noiseless thunder roar.

CHAPTER 13

'Jack, come on now. Stage fright can't be helped,' Mr Darling says, no doubt thinking of my attempted escape at the start of the play. 'You covered it up out there. There were only a few seconds or so when the audience might have noticed something. Not enough to worry about when the rest of the show was such a success. Here. Have a Pringle.'

He holds out a red tube, and how do you get to be like this, just a decent human being I wonder, deciding that when I'm an adult I'll model myself on his good manners. But right now I am too angry to be anything other than difficult.

'Was that it then, Tess? *Stage fright?*' I turn my back, feeling the world spin on its axis so Antarctica freezes Jack out, cold and unyielding. 'Tess? I'm talking to you.'

He's quieter now but more audible over the cast holding its breath, waiting to see how I'm going to respond.

I walk to my bag.

That's it.

Put one foot in front of the other, nothing complicated, but everyone seems surprised and in some cases impressed, definitely Daniel with his long, low whistle.

'Pathetic,' Jack mutters, but I don't feel pathetic or look it either – in fact, I am quite certain that I have never in my life appeared more powerful.

I dawdle in the dressing room, giving Isabel plenty of time to disappear because Jack's in no fit state to meet my friend. I go to the loo for ten minutes then spend ages getting changed. I lace up my silver Dr Martens, loving the feel of them on my feet, these boots the colour of the stars. I leap into the sky then jump from one star to the next, all the way across the galaxy to my rightful position at the very edge of the solar system.

It's quiet out here, just how I like it.

The dressing room is deserted now. Catching sight of myself in the mirror, I break into a grin because I've done something, haven't I, something big and brave for once in my decidedly small and timid life. I'm radiant. Beaming. And I can't let Jack see. Nipping the edges of my smile together, I draw it back into my mouth before stepping out into the night that's my night, let's be clear about that. I'm at one with the darkness. The black cloak envelops my skin as I draw curtains on the world with my hair.

It smells like it might rain. It smells of November and bonfire night, which is over, and rebellion, which is not.

Change is in the air.

[85]

I can't resist carrying on my silence in the car park where we meet up with Mum but not the agent because he didn't turn up, after all.

'He could have been in the audience, though,' Jack says as he opens the boot and throws in his stuff. 'He could have been in the audience, and she still messed up the damn scene.'

I dive onto the back seat because Isabel's waiting for me, standing outside the church, twisting her head this way and that. I hate seeing her worry, so I turn on my phone to send her a message, spying through the window as I wait for it to wake up. Her dad points at his watch. She checks one more time – out into the car park and back inside the church – then nods because it's time to go. Her dad puts up a brolly and holds it above her head even though it isn't raining.

'But he wasn't there,' Mum says as I shove my phone back into my pocket without writing a word, 'so no harm done, right?'

'I don't know about that. Everyone else witnessed the debacle. Can you imagine if he had been in the audience? Or my dad, for that matter, if he'd said yes to those tickets? It would have been even more humiliating than it already was.'

'It wasn't that bad, Jack. Not from the audience's perspective. It just looked like a thirty second blip.'

'Thirty seconds is a long time, trust me. Thirty seconds

is endless when you're in the middle of a performance and the person you're relying on lets you down. And why's that? What was it, Tess? Stage fright? A bad mood? Mind went blank? Come on. Fill us in.' He glares at me in the rear view mirror. 'Will you stop ignoring me? It's rude. At least have the courtesy to speak.'

I don't, not on the way home or when we get out of the car or when we walk into the lounge where Jedi bounds up to me, licking me to death, giving me a hero's welcome with an extra-fast tail, thumping on the carpet. Jack drops his bag, tossing Yorick on top. Jedi barks with delight then runs off with it clamped between his jaws.

'You may as well have it, boy. Fat lot of good it did me.'

Mum ushers me into the kitchen, pushing me into a chair before crouching down with her hands on my knees.

'Talk to me, Tess. What's going on? Are you ill or something?' she asks in this voice of hope, obviously praying for the flu because that has a predictable prognosis, just a week in bed with my old hot water bottle. I haven't seen it for years, the heart-shaped one, worn and comforting with a rubbery smell I used to breathe in as Mum stroked my hair whenever I was ill. 'We've got a bottle of Lucozade in the fridge. Do you want some?'

She surveys me for signs of fever, her long brown hair brushing my thighs as she fingers the beads around her neck, working them like a rosary. For a second I want nothing more than to answer her prayers, to tell her that I am fine, just a bit off colour and not to worry because I will be right as rain in the morning. But she lied too, every day of my life and on all those Father's Days in particular, encouraging me to make cards for The World's Best Dad.

'What's going on, Tess?'

I sit in the middle of my silence, protecting myself from the truth I might be able to forget if I never have to hear myself say it out loud.

'Are you crying?' I'm not really sure because, oh look at that, my face has gone numb. I can't feel my cheeks, let alone any tears trickling down them. 'Make her some tea, Jack, for goodness' sake!' He dithers. 'And get her some tissues.'

'Where from?'

'A piece of kitchen roll or something.'

'There isn't any.'

'Toilet roll then,' Mum snaps, gripping my hand in hers. The dryness of it is so familiar, and also the hardness of her wedding ring that won't break no matter what I tell her about Jack or how incompetent he is when it comes to finding tissues. They're totally in love and happily married and maybe even in it together, for all I know.

'Horrible creature?' Jack might have asked, looking up at Mum as she hovered over his desk in her apron, leaning over his shoulder to peer at the screen. 'Disgusting creature?'

'How about peculiar? Gives a sense of strangeness but also conveys how ugly she was as a newborn.'

Jack probably grinned. 'Perfect.'

'And change sucking to gnawing. *I didn't love the ugly red thing* gnawing *at her breast.* That's how it felt, like she was eating me alive. It was – *oh! The spaghetti!*'

I mean, really, how else could Mum have set fire to some pasta? I am no chef, but even I know to bend spaghetti into a pan of water just as soon as it's pliable, so Mum must have been distracted by something to make such an obvious mistake.

'You *are* crying,' she says because this time there's no mistaking it. Great waves of grief crash through the chasm that has formed at my core. I cry for my childhood that was a lie and for my future that's uncertain and for myself, split in two and torn apart and no longer whole, made up of bits I don't understand anymore. 'Come here, Tess. Come on. Oh don't cry, my poor darling.' With a pained expression she opens her arms, but I don't lean into the hug. 'Will you get me some bloody toilet roll, Jack?'

He leaves, trudging up the stairs, not exactly rushing, still too irritated to sympathise fully. Well, good. I don't want his pity, or Mum's either for that matter. I try to breathe calmly but it comes out in broken pants, my chest convulsing as my shoulders shudder.

'Easy now. Easy does it,' Mum says, clutching my hand once more. I snatch it back because I have boundaries now, boundaries I will defend to the death, so can someone please let the world know that the great country of Tess now has very strict borders. 'You're okay,' she tells me, not sounding certain. 'You're okay, Tess. You are. Just breathe.'

Jack traipses back into the kitchen, dropping the toilet roll into my lap.

'What's wrong with her?' he asks, referring to me in the third person, like I'm one step removed from him now, but this distance suits me just fine. 'Did she tell you?'

'No.'

'She's sulking, Helen. That's all it is. Because I shouted at her in the dressing room. She's in a strop. Am I right or am I right, Tess? Come on, moody,' he says in a lighter tone. 'Enough is enough, now. You're quite capable of answering a simple question.'

'Let's not force it,' Mum says, trying to smile with lips that curl up against her teeth to reveal a pale gum, no blood in it at all. 'She's upset, for whatever reason, so let's leave it for the time being. I'll make her a cup of tea. In the pig mug.' She stands up abruptly and takes it out of the cupboard, presenting it to the room at large. My watery sadness evaporates in a searing flash of anger as Mum makes an *oink oink* noise and Jack smiles at her effort to improve the mood. 'A nice cup of tea in the pig mug. Yes.'

'Good idea. Tea solves everything,' Jack says, so I climb to my feet and walk out of the kitchen.

I flop onto my bed with my phone, planning to get in touch with Isabel. It's muted, so I haven't heard it *beep, beep, beep* in my pocket – and *beep* some more by the look of it because there are thirteen messages from my friend. The first are light-hearted, chatty, but they get more concerned and less patient as time goes on. They're full of questions, queries upon queries about what happened on stage and where did I go at the end of the night and why am I still acting so strangely?

I open a message and stare at the blank space ready to be filled with words that still don't come. Even silent on a screen they're too much for me tonight, so I just type *Long story. I'm sorry. I'll tell you on Monday.* Then I close my eyes.

An open door. A sliver of night. A reflection in the windscreen of a BMW. A fake fire. A packet of Werther's Originals. A perfect dad. And a brolly. And no rain.

The jealousy's back, wilder and more savage than ever, sticking in its claws. Isabel has a loving dad, and a mum who she can trust, and a home where she belongs. I charge to my window, shoving it open with a trembling hand and learning out to gulp in the night. My lungs scream and my heart goes crazy and my vision blurs so the stars become lines and the buildings smudge into one before it all goes black as I sink to the floor.

I almost shout for my parents. Even now I crave them,

like it would be the best thing in the world for them to help me to my feet and tuck me in bed, saying, *Don't worry, Tess. Everything will be okay*. Pride stops me from opening my mouth, but I do open my eyes to find I am sitting next to my bag. The goldfish is staring up at me, but his expression isn't reproachful after our failed adventure. It's understanding and patient and kind so I reach forward, picking him up ever so gently to study him properly for the first time. His mouth is fixed open, but there are no words.

That's okay, Mr Goldfish. I don't have any of those either.

I've never turned him on before, but now seems the right time.

Now seems the perfect time, so I click the switch by his fin. A powerful beam shines out of his mouth onto my mouth, bathing my motionless lips in a warm golden glow.

PART TWO

CHAPTER 14

'Thanks for letting me know,' Mrs Austin says the following Tuesday, standing up to show us out of her office. It's posher than I was expecting, with a shiny desk, a rotating leather chair and a red rug sprawled across a polished wooden floor. 'I'll send out an email straight away to inform Tess's teachers of the situation. You said she's been to the Doctors?'

'I took her yesterday, not that it was much use,' Mum replies.

'Doctor took one look at her throat, saw it wasn't infected, and referred her to a speech therapist,' Jack says. 'We should get a letter in two weeks or so inviting us to a preliminary appointment. Not exactly an express service, is it?'

He tries to smile but it's a huge great big effort, I can tell that a mile off. It's thrilling and also alarming to see his usual buoyant self deflate before my eyes. He glances at me so I pretend to stare into space when really I am picturing myself spinning round and round on Mrs Austin's chair, my hair blowing back in dizzy triumph.

Jack stands up and Mum does too, and they both wait for me to move.

It's remarkable, the power of doing absolutely nothing. I slip my hand into my pocket and fiddle with Mr Goldfish's switch. Jack pokes my shoulder.

'Come on, Tess. I'm sure Mrs Austin has better things to do.'

I cross my feet, nothing very interesting, but no one can take their eyes off my boots. That's remarkable too, how every movement I make is fascinating now I no longer speak. I flex my ankles and, sure enough, everyone watches the specks of dried mud fall off my soles onto the rug. Mrs Austin purses her lips. Jack's expression darkens. Mum goes pink. And I just sit, humming a tune inside my head where no one but Mr Goldfish can hear it.

'Mrs Austin's very busy, Tess,' Mum says, gripping her handbag, the Mulberry one she rarely uses. The tune disappears to be replaced by Mum's words last Christmas.

'Oh my goodness, Jack! I love it!' she said when she opened the present, beautifully wrapped with a big gold bow. 'But it must have cost a fortune. Can we afford it?'

'Totally worth it, for that reaction,' Jack replied, kissing the hand clutching the bag. 'I want my wife to have the best.'

'I'll save it for best.' Mum tried the bag on her shoulder, looking the opposite of glamorous in her purple dressing gown. 'Goodness. Check me out. I love it. I really love it. Thank you, darling. I'll look after it. It will only come out for special occasions. Weddings. Royal ones, at that.'

The bag doesn't belong in Mrs Austin's office.

'Well done, Tess,' Mum says when I climb to my feet, giving my arm a supportive squeeze that just makes me feel worse. 'We'll let Mrs Austin get on. I'm sure she has a lot to do.'

'Just the three reports to write and the two meetings to attend before break,' Mrs Austin replies, opening the door to reveal Isabel in the waiting area. 'Shouldn't you be in lessons, Isabel?'

'I'm here for Tess.'

I love how she says that. I really love it, but then I freeze.

'Isabel?' Jack sounds confused. He frowns, taking in her limp hair and gawky posture.

'I'm her friend.'

'Are you?'

'I'm Isabel,' she says, as if that explains it. 'Are you okay, Tess? What's wrong?'

'She isn't speaking,' Mum replies. 'We're not sure why.'

'What, not at all?'

'Unless you know differently, of course?' Jack says, sharply.

'Me?' Isabel asks.

'I'm just thinking. She didn't call you or anything? Over the weekend? Given that you're *friends*.' He looks at me when he says that.

'No,' Isabel replies because it's true. We haven't spoken

actual words, but we have communicated via text, which is a secret as I am sure she understands. 'But . . .'

Jack's staring at me so I can't shake my head to tell her to keep quiet.

'But what?'

'We're waiting, Isabel,' Mrs Austin says. 'If you know something, you should tell Tess's parents.'

Isabel stares at me before glancing at the window like she's desperate to escape through the glass.

'But what?' Jack says again. 'Did she call you? Or send you a message?'

My heart skips a beat as Isabel nods.

'She did?' Mum gasps with her mouth and also her eyes that turn into big white *Os*. 'What did she say?'

'She didn't say anything. It was a text.'

'What did it say?' Jack asks.

'Just that . . . Just that it was a long story,' Isabel says miserably, talking to a feathery plant on the windowsill.

'A long story? What was a long story? Our argument in the dressing room, is that what she meant? For crying out loud, that was something and nothing so if she's caused all this worry because of a few cross—'

'Let her speak, Jack.'

'She just said it was a long story,' Isabel repeats, still addressing the plant, lucky for her because the heat of my gaze would set her eyeballs on fire. They were private words. My private words, written in the darkness, contained on a phone screen in a rigid box, never to be let out in the open. But now Isabel has done just that, speaking them out loud, ruining the illusion of my perfect silence.

'Is that all?' Mrs Austin asks.

Isabel hesitates then hangs her traitorous head. 'She said she'd tell me on Monday. The long story. I don't know what it was though.'

'*She'd tell you on Monday*. So she was planning to speak?' Jack clarifies, taking a step towards Isabel then turning to look at me, literally coming between us. 'You got that feeling? That she could speak and she was going to speak to you on Monday?'

'Yes. I suppose,' Isabel almost whispers, trying to catch my eye that won't be caught by her, not now, no way. I gaze past her out of the window at the sky the exact colour of water. 'I'm sorry, Tess.' I barely hear her, doing what she can't and breaking through the glass.

I plunge into the sky with Mr Goldfish, swimming about in a fish tank of our own creation that blocks out the world and all of its words. Mr Goldfish opens and closes his noiseless lips as I open and close my noiseless lips, and the sun is the ray of light shining from both our mouths because it's true what they say, silence really is golden.

'And you're sure she hasn't spoken to you out loud since Saturday?' Mum asks, keeping her voice gentle. 'This is important, Isabel. Tess's silence – it's serious. You understand that, I'm sure. We need to help Tess, all of us. And we can do that by being honest.'

'We haven't spoken. I promise you. Apart from that one message, she hasn't even replied to my texts. I tried calling too, but her phone has been switched off.'

'What about the others?' Jack asks.

'What others?' It's Isabel's turn to look confused. I just about resist the urge to yell at Jack to stop, clenching my jaw because I know what's coming next.

'Anna and that lot.'

Isabel is so shocked she bursts out laughing. 'They're not our friends!'

'Since when?' Jack asks, not hearing my silent scream to shut the hell up. 'When did you fall out? Was there an argument?'

'No! There was no argument because there was no friendship!' She's still giggling, looking at me to share the joke.

'That's not what Tess told me,' Jack says, and the laughter stops. 'She's always talking about Anna. All the time. Never mentions you though.'

'Oh. Right. Okay.' It's me trying to catch Isabel's eye now, but she's staring over my shoulder. 'I've got to get to class.'

She zips up her coat even though we're inside, unnecessarily adjusting her bag straps as if she's waiting for me to say something. But I don't. She doesn't, either. I turn on Mr Goldfish, needing the power stored deep in his batteries to give me strength.

Isabel runs out of straps and zips and stands there with nothing else to do to delay what has to happen next, glancing at me with this expression that pretty much breaks my heart. It's sad but resolute and I'm sad but resolute, and is this even happening is the question I'm screaming into the darkness of my mind as she turns her back on me and disappears down the corridor.

'It's happening,' comes a voice. A strange voice. I look at Mum and Jack and Mrs Austin, but their mouths are closed.

CHAPTER 15

I dash into a toilet cubicle and try to be sane. Torches can't speak, like I know this for certain, but I can't resist looking in my pocket, prising apart the material.

'Hi!' says Mr Goldfish, waving a bright orange fin. 'Nice to meet you.'

I scrunch up my pocket then reopen it almost immediately. Mr Goldfish is gazing up at me, a golden ray of light shining from his mouth – his *plastic* mouth that, let's be clear, is completely incapable of forming words.

'Really? And yet I appear to be talking to you. How funny.'

'This is the opposite of funny,' I reply, but crazy as it is, mad as it seems, it's a relief to be saying something to another person, even if it is in my head to a torch who can't hear a—

'Oh, I can hear you, loud and clear,' he chuckles, which is too much for me. I thrust my shaking hand into my pocket and flick the switch.

'Hello?' I try, but there's no reply. 'Hello? Hello?' Still nothing. I get him out. I get *it* out. I stare at the torch, who stares right back, or seems to, with these knowing little eyes. Exhaling slowly, I try to pull myself together. *Torches cannot speak.*

The toilet door makes a nice noise when I open it, a rational sort of *click* that brings me back to my senses. Obviously, I imagined it.

There's only ten minutes left of first period so I don't rush to go to my lesson, meandering down the corridor that's empty apart from one person.

One magnificent person in the distance holding a mug of indistinct colour. Mr Holdsworth.

My feet make music, a shy *shuffle shuffle* as I walk towards him. I lift my eyes to peep through my curtain of hair, keen to find out if it's going to be a yellow or blue morning, looking forward to filling in my table with its neat, sensible columns, putting a clear mark beneath the colour—

PINK.

Wonderfully, shockingly *pink.*

'Why aren't you in a lesson, Tess?'

I almost keel over at the sight of this brand new cup in Mr Holdsworth's familiar, very sexy fingers. I love how long and clever they are, how easily they flick a pen over the whiteboard, the answer to the universe's most complicated problems right at his fingertips.

Find the value of D in M + D = T if J for Jack is no longer relevant

If anyone can solve the biggest puzzle of my life, it's him. I've seen him do it a thousand times, using his massive brain to work out the most difficult algebraic equations that don't seem to have a solution at first glance, or tenth glance, or one hundredth glance for that matter. Mine's a tricky one, but he'd be able to do it no problem, circling the answer in a perfect ring that would restore my world to some sort of order.

I want to ask for help, but words are banned. They appear in my mouth then fade to nothing on my cold, still tongue.

'Hurry along, Tess. The bell's about to go. Get to your next class.'

I wander to the Languages' block, checking my emails on my phone. I filled in the contact form on the HFEA website on Sunday, but there's still no reply. Probably because of my age. I was going to hide it until I realised they need to know when I was conceived if they're going to track down my dad. I'll keep searching even if they don't agree to help. I'll start in Manchester, and then move to Liverpool . . . Birmingham . . . London . . . and every city in every country until I find him.

It's more than blond hair and brown eyes I'm looking for now. I've found those loads of times, but the men have never been quite right. The *Tesco* delivery guy was too loud. The doctor who referred me to the speech therapist was too small. The transvestite I saw on Sunday when I went shopping for Gran's birthday present had a weak chin. I was excited at first, following the red stilettos all the way down Deansgate to the perfume counter in *Selfridges*. A pair of dark eyes surveyed me warily, no doubt expecting me to make fun of the butterfly-patterned dress clinging in all the wrong places. But I smiled because she looked beautiful, sort of fragile but brave outside her cocoon.

Isabel has moved places to sit with Patrick Smith.

Let me say that again one more time in my head because actually I am not even sure if I believe it.

Isabel's sitting with Patrick Smith.

She gets out her Maths textbook. I wait to see if she looks at it, but no, not even a cursory glance at our names scrawled in the blue triangle on the front cover. I wrote *TESS* on the vertical line and she wrote *ISABEL* on the horizontal one, and the *S* at the end of my name became the one in the middle of hers, and we turned it into an infinity symbol because we just knew we were going to be inextricably linked for all eternity.

Well, isn't that a joke I think to myself as Isabel guffaws at something Patrick says. She throws back her head and flashes her mirth in my direction. My rage reignites, the smouldering ashes sparking into life as I look at her with new eyes, this girl of fickle friendships.

'I hate Patrick,' she said, just before the summer holidays. 'That sounds awful, Tess, but I do. He doesn't even try in orchestra. He sags over his violin as if it's impossible to keep his back straight and play properly. And he picks his nose. It's shameless. Rooting around really deep to get the ones at the back. I *know*,' she said when I started to look sick. 'It's unbelievable. And that's not the worst of it. He doesn't even wipe his fingers. Before he plays, I mean. He smears the bogies over the strings. It's the most revolting thing I've ever seen.'

'Don't watch him, then.'

'Says the girl who's obsessed with *Embarrassing Bodies*,' Isabel replied. I raised a reasonable eyebrow to acknowledge this very fair point. 'Mrs *hashtag-disgusting-hashtag-can't-take-my-eyes-off-it*. Who wrote that on Twitter just last week? Not me, Tess Turner. You.'

'I know. I am a hashtag-hypocrite.'

'Yes, you are. You know what it's like when something's so gross you just have to watch it? I can't stop staring at his grubby little fingers.'

Four months later and she's letting him borrow her ruler.

Mr Holdsworth enters the room. 'Settle down, folks. Let's make a start.'

I pick up my own ruler and draw an untidy margin then write down the wrong date by mistake. I still haven't got used to it, my new unfamiliar life where my dad's not my dad and my friend's not my friend, choosing to sit next to a boy she finds repulsive rather than share a desk with me.

There's a knock.

'Latecomers,' Mr Holdsworth says. He opens the door to reveal Tara and Anna. Tara's flustered and even Anna has two pink spots on her pale cheeks.

'Sorry. Sorry. We had to—'

'You'll stay behind at lunch.'

They don't argue because you don't argue with Mr Holdsworth. He holds out his hand. Automatically they get out their homework diaries. I smile without meaning to and Anna notices, giving me a look that makes me nervous.

'Your parents will no doubt be fascinated to hear of your tardiness,' he says, scribbling notes in their diaries. 'You know the rules, girls. Every minute you're late for me is quadrupled and taken from you at lunch. So, how late were you?'

'Five minutes, Sir.'

'So how long will you be staying?'

'Twenty minutes.'

'Precisely. And what is the square root of five? Get it right, and I'll take it off the time.'

'Twenty-five?' Tara blurts out.

'That's the square of five. Try again.' Tara's eyes roll back in her head as she tries to figure it out.

'It must be two something,' Anna guesses, sounding not really bothered about the answer. 'Below two point five. Two point three?'

'Not a bad effort, without a calculator. I'll give you that.

So, what's that . . . You now owe me . . . seventeen minutes and . . .' He goes quiet for a few seconds, muttering under his breath as he works it out in his head, and it's impressive how he comes up with the answer almost as fast as I do on my calculator. 'Seventeen minutes and forty-five point eight four seconds.' The same number shines up at me. 'I'll let you off the point eight four, girls. I am in a good mood today.'

'Is that because you're leaving, Sir?' James asks from the back of the room.

I almost drop my calculator.

Mr Holdsworth nods. 'I'm afraid so.'

I do drop my calculator.

'You're leaving us?' Mazra asks. 'When?'

'Today's my last day.' There's an audible gasp that I accidentally join in. 'But don't look so worried, folks. It isn't for long.' Mr Holdsworth returns to his desk and takes a swig of coffee. Isabel's head twists slightly in my direction because she's clocked it too, I'm sure of it, the incredible colour of his new pink mug. I can feel the effort it takes for her to resist turning round to catch my eye, and I will her to give in to the impulse. I miss her already, and it's only been two and a half hours. 'I'll be back next term. It's a back operation, not a job move.'

'What's wrong with it, Sir?' Patrick asks.

'You really want to know? It's decidedly dull. Very well, then. It's a lumbar decompression. I get a lot of nerve trouble in my lower back. I need it sorting out. I know the timing's not ideal, but that's the NHS for you. I had a date in August, but that was cancelled. There's nothing I can do about it.'

'Who will we have instead?' Isabel asks. 'Are we having a supply teacher?'

'You are. He's in today, actually. Just having a meeting with the Head of Maths but he should be along – oh, look. Here he is. Mr Richardson is his name.'

A face peers through the glass in the door.

It's a large face with blond hair and brown eyes and a very strong chin. Mr Holdsworth turns the handle, letting in our new teacher, then stands with his arm outstretched like he's found it, after all, the mysterious value of D, the solution to the biggest puzzle of my life.

CHAPTER 16

'Hello.' It's a quiet voice. The right sort of voice. And he waves a hand that looks just like mine. He's dressed head-to-foot in black, the buttons of his shirt straining over his stomach. 'I'm looking forward to working with you until Christmas.'

'I'm sure they will make you welcome,' Mr Holdsworth replies. 'Right, folks. Page fifty-two of your textbooks. Cubic graphs. We're going to plot one first. I don't suppose you could hand out some graph paper, Mr Richardson? You'll find it in the drawer by Tess. Thanks, Sir. Most kind. Tess.' He points me out. 'Just over there.'

Mr Richardson sets off, wending his way through the maze of tables and chairs with all this determination to find me, quite possibly his long-lost daughter. As he gets nearer, my cheeks get hotter and isn't that amazing, how we appear to be two axes on the same graph with our variables directly proportional to each other. He stops by my desk as I reach boiling point.

I look up, shyly.

We are carbon copies, no doubt about it.

'The graph paper?' Mr Richardson says in his quiet, quiet voice because I'm sitting in the way of the drawer.

I want to plot our axes and show him the line that links us together because we are definitely related, I am absolutely sure of it. I pass him the paper, but don't let go right away, and he doesn't tug it out of my hand either. We hold the paper and we hold the paper and we hold the paper, and then he gives me a shy smile that hides in a dimple.

I don't have one of those.

I let go in disappointment. As he leaves me behind, I dig my finger into my flesh. No matter how hard I press, the hole doesn't stay in my cheek. Mr Richardson disappears to the other side of the classroom, and the further away he walks, the more my temperature cools until I shiver with the cold stark realisation that he probably isn't my real dad at all.

It's lunchtime before I know it. Isabel stands up as I do too, and there's this pulse between us, this beat, as we both try to decide where to go for lunch after two years of sitting together on the bench outside the Science block.

We move at the same time, but I'm taking a step towards Isabel and she's walking towards the door.

'Lunch in the canteen, Patrick?' she says, loudly. 'I fancy a change.'

I need a friend. As soon as I'm home, I take Mr Goldfish out of my pocket. It's mental or what have you, but I need someone to talk to, even if it is in my head with a torch who—

'Can hear every word you say,' Mr Goldfish tells me as soon as I flick the switch. The light shines out of his mouth onto my mouth, forging a silent connection between us, actually very warm and comforting. 'And less of the torch, if you don't mind.'

'What are you, then?' I ask, after a pause. If some people pray to an invisible being in the sky and Isabel talks to a hobbit, maybe it isn't all that strange to speak to Mr Goldfish. I gaze into the light, feeling silly but determined to continue because it's nice to talk after so long, even if it is with—

'God?' Mr Goldfish asks, hopefully. 'Or *a* god, at least. I suppose you could just call me Lord, or something?'

'I'm not going to call you that.'

'Sir?'

'Mr Goldfish, that's your name,' I say, relaxing into the conversation the very instant the front door bursts open.

Jack strolls into the lounge.

Flustered, I switch off Mr Goldfish and hide him behind my back, but Jack is distracted by Jedi. He jumps up to put his paws on Jack's knees and for one crazy second I am jealous of my dog. His whole body wags, his tongue lolling out of his mouth as mine sits rigidly behind gritted teeth.

'Hello, boy. Hello. Hello, hello, hello,' Jack says, sounding happier than he has done for a couple of days. He sinks to his knees to scratch Jedi's ears. 'Ah. You like that. You like that, hey? That's nice, isn't it? Oh, which doggy loves their daddy, huh? Which doggy loves their daddy?'

It doesn't seem fair, the fact that Jedi is still Jack's dog and Mum is still Jack's wife but I am not Jack's daughter. Nothing about us is similar, not the way we look or the way we sound or the way we move. His body language is easy and open as he play-fights with Jedi. Mine's the opposite, awkward and closed as I lean back against the cushions, crossing my arms to make myself small. Not small enough though, because Jack notices I'm still wearing my uniform.

He pushes Jedi away.

'Have you forgotten the rules, Tess? School clothes off, homework out, as soon as you get home. That's not changing, you know. Just because of—' He waves his hand vaguely in my direction as a euphemism for my silence. 'Come on. I'm feeling positive today. I made a plan at work. I need to write my own stuff. That's the thing. I had an email from my agent saying he won't be able to make it to the panto this weekend. But that's fine. I get it. He's a busy man. But I'm going to take matters into my own hands now. Write my own scripts.' He beams. 'Come on. Let's do this, eh? I'll bring you up a cup of tea and then we'll both crack on with work.'

I slump further down the sofa.

'Up you get, Tess. I'm not having any more of this moping about nonsense. Get your work out of the way now then you're free to do whatever else you want this evening.'

Whatever else *he* wants, let's be clear about that. I might have got out of the pantomime on Saturday, but there's still tap class this evening. He signed me up a few months ago without even asking my permission, and it might be half a year too late, but tonight I am going to take a stand.

'Your old man was right, huh? You loved it, didn't you?' he asked when I climbed into the car after the first lesson. 'I did a bit of tap in *Singin' in the Rain*. First year of drama school.'

We drove through a summer evening the colour and texture of golden syrup. People were hot and sticky, spilling out of bars to sit outside with sun oozing over their toes. I watched them through the window, these alien creatures having fun on a school night.

'*Shuffle hop step, shuffle ball change and slide-to-the-left and slide-to-the-right. Shuffle hop step, shuffle ball change and slide-to-the-right and slide-to-the-left.*' Jack performed the routine in the car as we waited in traffic, thrusting a hand in my face. '*Left arm, right arm, stamp, stamp. Right arm, left arm, pick-up pick-up. Tap-spring, tap-spring, tap-spring, toe-hop. Tap-spring, tap-spring, tap* – all right, all right, I'm going,' he muttered when a car behind us beeped because the gridlock had cleared.

'Some people,' I sighed because Jack liked it when I said exactly what he was thinking. 'Rush rush rush. Caught up in the rat race, even on a nice evening like this.'

'Precisely.' He rolled his eyes and I rolled mine a second later, copying his expression, and then we both pretended to be scrabbling rodents with very sad faces until we started to giggle. I loved it, the way his lips danced as he nodded approvingly then patted my knee. 'Precisely, Tessie-T. No sense of fun. No sense of creativity. I couldn't live like that – a wage slave. Life's too short, Tess, I'm telling you. Do like your dad and take the road less travelled, eh? Robert Frost got it right. *I shall be telling this with a sigh, somewhere ages and ages hence: two roads diverged in a wood and I—*' He jabbed a finger at his chest before holding it out in the air to point at the mysterious path he had taken through life. '*I took the one less travelled by, and that has made all the difference.*' I'd heard the poem a thousand times before, but I squeezed Jack's hand in a show of false emotion. 'Inspiring stuff. A rallying cry to get off the treadmill and really – live, you know?'

'So why am I at school again?' I joked.

'You need your grades, Tess.'

'Yeah, I need my grades to get the career I am not going to have because life's too short to be a wage slave.' It was supposed to be funny, but Jack didn't laugh.

'Are you making fun of me?'

'No! Of course not.'

'Getting an education makes life so much easier, Tess. Trust me.'

Feeling wounded, I said, 'Well, you didn't get one.'

He didn't reply for ages, his thoughts travelling to some place I couldn't follow, returning in a sigh that sounded weary of the world and everything in it. 'I know I didn't.'

'Sorry, Dad. I didn't mean . . . Sorry.'

'Why are you sorry? I've done all right, haven't I?'

'Yeah,' I said, baffled by his tone. 'Yeah, Dad. You've done really well.'

'I know I have,' he snapped. 'I don't need you to tell me that. I could have got an education, Tess, but my parents let me drift. My head was too easily turned by what else was out there. I always knew I wanted something bigger, something better, but I should have knuckled down. My parents should have made me knuckle down. They were too lenient. That's why I didn't get my grades. There was no other reason. I was more than capable of it.'

'I know,' I said, which wasn't true. Jack rarely spoke about his childhood. He turned left, taking the corner too sharply, riding up onto the kerb as he swore under his breath. 'I'm sorry, Dad. I didn't mean . . . I just meant that sometimes school feels like a rat race. All the lessons. The homework. It feels like a treadmill that I want to get off, because, well, there is more to life. You were right. Like

[116]

those people outside the pub, having fun and–'

'Wasting time, you mean. You've totally missed the point, Tess. School is important. So is university. So is getting a job.'

'But—'

'But nothing. You misinterpreted me. Take the road less travelled sometimes. And other times stick to the path that will lead you to success and a decent career. That's what I meant.' I nodded as if this made total sense. 'You need to listen to what your old man is saying, eh? Anyway, did you enjoy the tap lesson? Tell me about that. You loved it, didn't you?'

'Yeah. It was great.' We grinned, relieved to be back on solid ground. 'It was brilliant.'

'You're going to stick at this one?'

'Definitely,' I say somewhere in my memory as somewhere in the lounge Jack nudges me with his foot.

'Earth to Tess. Are you in there?'

Well, no, actually, because I am Pluto, thousands of miles away in my own dark orbit, inaccessible and in awe of the change that is occurring right now, I can feel it. I hold Jack's gaze and it isn't even difficult anymore. I stare into his blue eyes with my eyes the same colour as Mr Richardson's. He could be sitting in his lounge, wondering if he has found me after years of searching because why else would he choose to be a supply teacher going round different schools is what I am asking myself without listening too hard to the answer.

I don't want to hear the voice of reason so I block it out and focus on our meeting in the classroom. Something more than graph paper passed between us today, I am absolutely sure of it. Okay, I am only about sixty percent sure of it, but all of a sudden I can't wait for period six on Thursday to see him again.

'Come on, Tess. It's time to do your – *No boy! No! That's not yours!*'

He's off in a flash as Jedi savages something in the kitchen. It's a furious tussle because the dog is not giving it up without a fight. Jack swears and Jedi growls and Jack tugs then finally grabs whatever it is and holds it high above his head. He returns to the lounge, panting and victorious, waggling the Sellotaped skull.

'Got him back! Yorick will give us the luck we need, eh, Tess?' He thrusts it in my direction as if the mascot might work some peculiar magic and make me talk. 'Let's get to work. We've got a lot to do tonight and not a lot of time to do it in. We'll have to set off early with those road works on Chorlton Road. For tap,' he says, in case I've forgotten.

I don't make any move to get up. The skull falls to Jack's side and he stares at me staring into the space forming between us, getting bigger by the second.

CHAPTER 17

Isabel isn't in the library on Wednesday morning. I look around, crestfallen – the straight rows of desks, the neat signs, the organised shelves. There is order here. Everything has its place according to the Dewey Decimal system. I take mine at a desk by the window, trying not to care that I am the only person sitting in the category 1.0 LONER.

'Charming,' Mr Goldfish says when I open my school bag. 'What about me?'

'No one else can see you. To the rest of the world I do look like a loner.'

'Get me out then. Go on. It's not like Isabel's going to come and sit with you.'

'She might. Not that I care either way.'

'Oh, really?'

I ignore him, taking out my English essay, not even glancing at the library entrance to check for Isabel. Okay, maybe glancing at it a little bit. The door opens and two boys walk in, deep in conversation about something definitely rude that makes them snigger. It opens again to reveal three girls. Then a couple holding hands.

Where the hell is she I try not to wonder because, let's face it, she chose to side with Jack and she chose to sit with Patrick in Maths rather than share a desk with me. I refocus on my *Othello* essay, writing a conclusion with more passion than I normally show in English, full of sympathy for Othello, who was betrayed by his friend, Iago. Finishing with a flourish, I declare that Othello was in no way responsible for his own downfall because he was an innocent victim of Iago's deceit. He trusted his friend because you're supposed to be able to trust your friends is the point I make at the end with a very determined biro, throwing in a couple of quotes before dropping my pen to flex my left hand and stare up at the sky.

It's completely white. The bit of world I can see through the window looks simple, just a brown rectangle of school above a square of grey playground that stops at a straight line of black fence beneath an expanse of blank sky. Maybe it looks simple because it *is* simple. Othello is good, and Iago is bad, and I am in the right, and Isabel is in the wrong, and anyone who was analysing us in an essay would no doubt come to this conclusion after a couple of paragraphs on one side of A4.

Somehow there's still fifteen minutes to kill before registration. Time drags without Isabel, no doubt about it. Period one today seems a week away. Period six tomorrow may as well be next year. It's thirty long hours until I see him again.

Mr Richardson.

Mr Richardson.

Mr—

'Goldfish?' comes a voice from my bag. 'There's more than one mister round here, you know.'

'Not according to the dream I had last night.'

I was searching for my dad in Chorlton, looking in the park and on the tram and down Nell Lane, staring into every car that passed. There were just women at first, so many women, but then I spotted Mr Richardson across the road where the Jehovah's Witness had been. He was shouting *I am your father* into a megaphone the size of a satellite dish and the words were booming out into space. My heart exploded. I tried to run, run, run, but a hand was holding me back. I spun round to see another Mr Richardson, clutching my wrist. *I am your father,* he said, and then a third Mr Richardson shouted out of a van, *I am your father,* and then hundreds of Mr Richardsons appeared all over the place, in the shops and buses and walking down the street, yelling the same thing. *I am your father. I am your father. I am your father.* I didn't know who to believe so I stood in the middle of a thousand potential dads, screaming at the top of my voice.

'I am your father,' Mr Goldfish whispers in the voice of Darth Vader.

'That's not funny.'

'Sorry.'

I check my emails on my phone, but there's nothing from the HFEA. I've got a good mind to march down to London and storm into Finsbury Tower on Bunhill Row, demanding a better service. They'd hand me a file that I'd tear open, my eyes widening to discover my real dad is a Maths teacher in Manchester, currently on supply at Chorlton Grammar School.

'Well, hello there.'

I spin round, hoping to see Isabel, but it's Anna and Tara and five of their friends, put together in a Barbie factory by the looks of it. Only Anna is different, pale and dark.

'Tess,' she says in a slow, quiet drawl like she's got all the time in the world to say my name. There's a sense of ownership in her gaze as well, lingering on my legs, taking in the fact I've abandoned my skirt. I threw it away in the outside bin on Sunday, distancing myself from the memory, double-wrapping the moment outside the canteen in two bin liners before chucking it out of sight.

I steel myself for the next attack.

'How are you, Tess?'

This is so surprising, I'd be speechless even if words weren't banned. Anna's smiling and so are the rest of the girls, but they look dangerous, elegant as swans but with something ugly paddling just beneath the surface.

'Oh sorry. I forgot. You're not talking, are you? Your poor voice.' Tara stifles a giggle. 'Mr Holdsworth told us about it yesterday in detention. Said you might need a bit of support over the next few weeks.' She taps her nose. 'Don't worry. We'll look out for you.'

The swans bob their sleek heads in unison and then they're gone.

I'm unnerved though nothing really happened. They were nice. Sort of nice. The sky is still blank and the school is still brown and the fence is still a straight line of black, but the world suddenly feels less simple. The playground is full of people now, Isabel on the periphery, sitting at a new bench as she scribbles in her notepad. I want to call out that I'm here, just up here, because the anger in my chest is tiny compared to the size of the Miss in my heart. I'd wave and she'd wave, maybe both of us flags of surrender. But I don't do anything. I *can't* do anything, and for the first time I feel frustrated by my silence. Patrick appears out of nowhere and sits next to my friend. Isabel shows him something on her phone that makes them laugh, and then they talk, and I watch, my heart hurting and beating, hurting and beating, counting down the endless seconds until registration.

I'm first to arrive at my form room in the Art block. Miss Gilbert is washing out an old jar of black paint that she fills with water before chucking in some pink flowers.

'Orchids,' she tells me, taking them to her desk. 'Saw them on the way to work. I'm going to get my Year Sevens to paint them.' She perches on a three-legged stool in front of the computer, looking sublime as always in green Dr Martens, dark blue tights and a black dress with flared sleeves that dance around her skinny wrists. Chunky silver rings glitter on her fingers and her dyed red hair shines with a funky halo because she is an awesome angel of darkness in the body of a school teacher. For some reason I think of Mum, marching through market stalls with a flower-stud in her nose.

Miss Gilbert bashes a button on the dusty keyboard as people start to arrive.

'Right. Here we go. Actually, no,' she says. 'I am not going to call out the register today, dudes. Want to get through it quickly. What can I say? I am very busy and important. In fact, don't tell Mrs Austin I told you this, but she's just the front man. I rule this school.'

Miss Gilbert's eyes find it hard to be sensible. There is a flash of green as she winks at me then turns back to the computer, checking off our names without reading them out, no doubt to save me the embarrassment of not knowing what to do when mine is called.

Like I say, she's awesome.

Isabel isn't in my form and neither is Anna or any of her friends, so I can relax. I shut my eyes to see Mr Richardson's face. His brown eyes are burning with curiosity because he's waiting for period six on Thursday too. *Twenty-nine hours and forty-five minutes*, he whispers in my ear, making my skin prickle with goose-bumps.

'That's the bell, dudes. The day is upon us. Off you go, everyone. Apart from you, Tess.'

Miss Gilbert beckons me forward and I stand awkwardly in front of her desk. It's messy, piles of students' work mixed in with her own pencil sketches, drawings in biro and half-finished paintings. In the middle of the chaos are the pink flowers.

'Gorgeous, aren't they?' she says, but that's not what I'm thinking. I feel sorry for them, trying to flourish with no real roots. 'I just wanted to check in with you, Tess. I know it isn't easy, being at school. Period. Ha, no. We all love it, don't we? But yeah. I suppose I just wanted to reassure you. Mrs Austin spoke to everyone this morning in staff briefing. No one's going to ask you to contribute in class, so don't worry about that. We're here when you're ready to talk, but there's not going to be any pressure from your teachers. And if it all gets too much for you then come and find me in here. We can hang out.' She squeezes my shoulder. Her rings feel nice against my bones. 'You'll be okay, Tess. I promise. Isabel can help you out in the lessons you share, right?'

'Er, no,' Mr Goldfish says. 'Not exactly.'

It's terrifying, how much things have changed in the space of a few days. A week ago I was an ordinary girl with parents that I loved, a home where I belonged and a friend who I adored. But I was blooming away under false pretences, and it was only a matter of time before everything fell apart.

Now I'm alone.

Mr Goldfish clears his throat.

Almost alone. I slip my hand into my bag and hold him tightly.

CHAPTER 18

At lunch, I dash to Dining Room Three, deciding once and for all to make amends with Isabel. I take my place by the menu and wait.

And wait some more.

If she turns up, I'll make an exception to the no-speaking rule, tell her I'm sorry till I'm blue in the face.

'Accept it,' Mr Goldfish says, after a while. 'She's not going to come.'

I study the desserts for two more minutes, just in case. *Chocolate pudding. Ginger sponge. Jelly.* And then I give it another thirty seconds because, who knows, the pickle-loving dinner lady might have made another mess of Isabel's sandwich. The double doors burst apart and I expect to see my friend, purple with outrage at the incompetence of the kitchen staff, but it's a group of girls in Year Ten I don't really know.

'Are you sure?' Mr Goldfish asks. 'They seem to know you.' They're sneaking glances at me, talking in low voices as they huddle in a circle. Mr Goldfish leaps out of my pocket. '*Hey! What are you gawking at? Yeah, that's right. DO ONE!*' he calls as the girls disappear, but three boys are staring now, nudging one another as they pass. 'What is everyone's problem?'

I hurry outside, the air cool on my hot cheeks.

'I'm the weird girl who's stopped speaking, aren't I?' I catch sight of my lonely reflection in the drama studio window. 'I'm not exactly doing myself any favours with this silence.'

It's getting harder to maintain, but I don't have a choice. I can't start speaking without saying why I stopped. Mum and Jack will ask questions. My teachers too. The speech therapist, who no doubt I'll have to go and see even if I do miraculously regain the ability to talk. Let's face it, becoming mute for three and a half days isn't exactly normal behaviour. Everyone will want to know why I've been acting so crazy and I will have to tell them the truth.

All six hundred and seventeen words of it.

No.

It's too big. Too scary. I'm safer here, behind my wall of silence and also my hair that falls in front of my face as I wander past the science block. Our bench is empty. I can't stand to sit on it alone so I keep walking. Somehow I find myself outside my Maths classroom, but Mr Richardson is nowhere to be seen. His stuff's here though, an old grey jacket draped over the back of the teacher's chair. A black rucksack I don't recognise is propped up against the desk and Mr Holdsworth's green marker pens have been replaced by a pot of red ones. There's not a coffee mug in sight.

I sit on the steps, checking my emails once more with a casual flick of my thumb. It freezes mid-swipe because for once there's something in my inbox.

I inhale sharply.

A reply from the HFEA.

'Open it then!' Mr Goldfish says, darting out of my pocket to stare at the screen. 'Come on! What are you waiting for?'

I expect it to be personal, written specifically to me by some woman with a lovely name like Summer or Joy because her job is to spread light and happiness to people in darkness. But this is a standard email from a man called Paul Beckett. It's a dull name for a dull man who's pretty much copied and pasted a paragraph off the website to send to me, a girl who spilled out her heart on a contact form, crying as she begged for information about her real dad.

At age 16 a donor-conceived person can complete and submit the application form found here www.hfea.gov.uk/113.html to apply for non-identifying information on the donor(s), the number, sex and year of birth of any donor-conceived siblings and find out if the donor(s) have re-registered as identifiable (i.e. if they have chosen to remove their anonymity).

'Donor-conceived siblings?' Mr Goldfish says. 'Does that mean brothers and sisters? Well, that's quite nice, I suppose.'

'I don't think so. There could be millions of them out there. Total strangers I'm related to without even knowing it. There could be some in this school,' I say in a panic. 'Oh my God!'

'Yes, my child?'

'That boy I kissed in Year Nine. The one at the party with the blond, spiky hair. He might have been . . . do you think he was . . . *Jesus!*'

'Do I think a thirteen-year-old boy with overly-gelled hair was Jesus?'

'That's not funny.'

'Sorry. Look, I don't think it's very likely that you were related.'

'But we could have been,' I say, dropping my phone and burying my head in my hands. 'We could have been related. There's a chance. You have to admit that.'

'Well, yeah, I suppose there is a very, very small chance that he might have been your brother.'

'Holy Crap!'

'Half-brother! *Half*!'

'That doesn't make it any better. I kissed him for ages. He put his hands – *places*. Oh my God. Oh my GOD.'

'Calm down,' Mr Goldfish tells me, like it's even possible, like everything's going to be okay if only I can breathe deeply. Hatred stronger than I've ever known it burns in my veins for Mum and Jack who are stripping me of everything – the family I used to have, the home where I grew up, and the memory of my first kiss with a boy whose spiky hair gradually flattened as we snogged outside in the rain. The lights of a disco ball shone in a puddle and the world was red and purple and green and beautiful, but now it's fading to nothing.

'How much sperm does the average male produce, anyway?' Mr Goldfish asks. 'You might have been the only fertilised egg from that particular batch.'

I picture it in a science lab inside a test tube with an indecipherable label. 'I'm never going to find him, am I?'

'Don't say that.'

'Have you seen the email? *Re-registered as identifiable.* It's a choice, isn't it? He could still be anonymous and I don't even get to find that out until I'm sixteen. How is that fair? How am I supposed to live for the next few months, wondering if he's left a name? And if the answer's no, what then? I never get to find my real dad?' Angry tears prick my eyes like hot needles. 'Is that how it works? That sons and daughters never get to meet their proper parents? How is that even legal?'

'You could try Googling it,' Mr Goldfish replies, 'because I don't know. I really don't. It sucks.'

'Yeah, it does,' I say, shakily. 'I tell you what, I should write my own blog for that stupid website, tell everyone how it feels to be a *donor-conceived person*. What does that even mean? I'm human, aren't I? Not some science experiment. I'm somebody's daughter. That means somebody's my dad. You can't just donate sperm and be done with it. It doesn't work like that, does it? I belong to someone!'

I don't want to break down, but I can't help it. The sound of my grief echoes round school, round Manchester, round the whole goddamn universe. I'm Pluto, but I don't want to be right now, and I cry out into the blackness of space, searching for meaning. Connection. Life.

It appears in the form of two brown eyes.

'Hey,' Mr Richardson says in his soft, soft voice. 'Hey, now.' He crouches down, putting a hand on my back. I look up at him as he smiles a lovely smile – lovelier, even, than Mr Darling's. 'You're Tess, aren't you?'

My heart leaps out of my body then slam-dunks down my throat. He remembers me. He helps me to my feet, picking up my bag and phone. I can't even begin to describe it, how much I love the sight of my belongings in his hand. Yet again he's dressed all in black, and I feel too colourful in my white shirt and green trousers.

'Come on. I'll walk you to your form room. You're one of Miss Gilbert's, aren't you?'

That's how it feels in Art One when she gives me tissues and pats my arm.

'I'll leave you two ladies to it,' Mr Richardson says.

'Thanks, Sir. It was good of you to bring her down here. You're the new Maths teacher, right?'

He holds out his hand. 'Mr Richardson.'

'Miss Gilbert.' They shake and she laughs. 'Very formal. I like it, Sir.'

He blushes as easily as I do. 'Sorry.'

'No! No, no, no! Don't be! It'll be nice to have a gentleman around here for a change.'

'I've never been called that before.'

'Well, now you have.' Miss Gilbert winks then falls serious. 'I wish you could tell me what was wrong, Tess. I might be able to help.' *She's the one*, she starts to mouth at Mr Richardson, but I catch her in the act. She grins at me, unashamed. 'You are the one, aren't you, Tess? Silent and mysterious.' She shakes her head. 'I couldn't do it. It must take an extraordinary amount of discipline. It's impressive, in a way.'

I've never thought of it like that.

CHAPTER 19

Mr Goldfish pops his head out of my bag as I walk across the bus park on Thursday morning.

'It's happening again, Tess. People are staring.'

'Thanks so much for pointing that out.'

'And at their phones. What's that about?'

'How would I know?' I have the funniest feeling they're all looking at the same thing. Fixing my gaze on a telegraph pole, I stride with more purpose. A crow settles on top of it, its wings fluttering to a stop as it coolly surveys the scene.

There are black phones. White phones. Orange ones. Blue. Three girls with pink phones giggle at me as I pass, pointing at something on their screens.

I pull up short. 'Tell me they haven't found Jack's blog.'

'They haven't found Jack's blog.' Pause. 'I mean, I can't possibly know that for sure but if it makes you feel better . . .'

The groan in my head is so loud I'm surprised the girls

can't hear it. 'Do you really think that's what they're looking at?' The six hundred and seventeen words suddenly appear in the sky, darker than the clouds, blocking out the sun.

Revulsion . . . I didn't love . . . Peculiar creature . . . I didn't love . . . Resentment . . . I didn't love . . . I didn't love . . . I DID NOT LOVE

I jump as a bus squeals to a stop. Mr Goldfish tugs me out of the way.

'Did the blog mention you by name?'

'No. No, I don't think so. But it might have done. I don't really remember.'

'You don't even know if Jack posted it, do you? He might have got cold feet.'

There's only one thing for it. I've avoided it so far, been far too scared to look, but I get out my phone and punch in the address of the Donor Conception Network. Thumb quivering, I click on *Personal Stories*, the words swimming on the screen. I blink and try to focus, but a boy from my year is leaping from the bus to land on both feet, directly in front of me.

Connor Jackson.

I don't like him and I really don't like the expression on his face. He shuffles to the right then hops to the left as I step from side to side, trying to get past.

'All right, Balls,' he says for some strange reason. 'How's it hanging? Go on. Give us a clue. Do you dress to the left or the right?'

'Hey, Balls,' Adam joins in, appearing next to Connor. 'I'm hungry. You got any nuts I can have?'

'Nice one!' Connor shoots imaginary bullets over my shoulder making a *brap brap* noise that sets my teeth on edge.

'Why are you calling her Balls?' comes a voice in the crowd. A small boy emerges, half-hidden behind a large pair of glasses. Damian, I think he's called. A Year Seven.

'Because she—'

'You mean *he*,' Adam corrects him.

'Well spotted. *He* has stopped talking, hasn't he? And everyone was trying to work out why. And then someone set up this anonymous Twitter account and tweeted that it's because *she* is actually a *he* and he's been hiding it all this time. But he can't now, can he? Puberty's made that impossible. There was even a picture. Would you like to see it?' he asks me in a gleeful tone. 'Spoiler alert: you look like a dog.'

'Hey, that's offensive,' Adam says, 'to my Doberman.'

Connor snorts then snatches my phone, fiddling about with it for a few seconds then holding it up so I can finally see what everyone else has been looking at. Someone's taken a picture off my Facebook page and posted it on Twitter with the hashtag #SheIsAHe

'No!' Mr Goldfish cries.

The photo's from the summer and I look big and bulky and boyish, hair scraped back off my face. I'm on holiday and I'm bursting out of a pair of blue shorts that are bulging at the front. It's my money belt, the one Jack forces me to wear when we're abroad, not that you can tell that from the picture.

Mr Goldfish cringes. 'So that's why people have been sniggering at their phones.'

'Including Isabel.' The words thud unexpectedly into my mind, followed by an image of a bench on the edge of the playground. 'Isabel and Patrick were looking at something on Wednesday.' My throat constricts at the thought of my friend being involved. She's always on Twitter. All the time. Of course she must have seen it.

'Easy now. Easy does it,' Mr Goldfish says, and that's funny because he sounds just like Mum. 'You're okay, Tess. You are. Just breathe.'

'Have you seen the comments too?' Connor scrolls and scrolls. And scrolls and scrolls. *Freak. Trannie. He-she. Man beast.* He tosses my phone in the air and catches it neatly. 'So that's why we call her Balls.'

'Because she's grown a pair of testicles,' Damian clarifies.

'No, dickhead. Because the pair *he* has already got has suddenly dropped. His voice has broken, hasn't it? That's why he's silent. He can't talk, not without revealing he's a bloke with gonads and a shed load of testosterone racing round his massive—'

'Ha! Testosterone!' Adam shouts.

'Boom! I love it!' Connor yells, firing his finger-gun at

my face like he's just hit the bull's-eye. 'Tess-tosterone. Brilliant!'

'Rude, you mean.'

Anna is standing a few metres away in a bright white shirt with short sleeves that expose her bare arms to the cold, November weather. She isn't shivering though. She's impervious, taking in Connor with cool, cool eyes and a pulse that doesn't seem to flicker.

'Leave her alone.' I stare at her, hardly daring to believe my ears.

'Leave *him* alone, you mean. She's a he. You've said so yourself loads of times,' he replies and that's true, a reminder that I should be wary of this girl unexpectedly coming to my rescue. 'Man Skull?'

'Man Skull was obviously a joke. You know that, Tess, don't you?' I'm glad no one's expecting a reply. 'What you're saying is—'

'The truth. She's a he. A man. A boy. A bloke with a massive—'

'It just looks massive in comparison to yours,' she sighs, sounding almost bored by the conversation. 'Yeah, that's right, Connor. Her non-existent penis is twice the size of the thing hanging between your legs.'

She waves a dismissive hand, white and elegant, drifting through the icy air.

'Jog on, Connor Jackson,' she mutters, and he actually does, and I can't believe how easy she made that look.

Maybe Mr Holdsworth did me a favour in that detention. Changed Anna's mind.

'Careful, Tess,' Mr Goldfish warns, but I turn to her with shiny eyes and lips very tempted to do something forbidden.

Maybe she senses it, the corners of my mouth twitching up towards the sky. Yeah, definitely she does, because she gives me a rare smile before disappearing inside.

CHAPTER 20

It's here at last. Period six. The door is hanging half-open, not a clear invitation to enter the classroom or an explicit message to stay out either. I hover for a few seconds on the boundary, peeking through the glass at my hopefully heaven-sent miracle eating a Blue Riband biscuit.

Mr Richardson throws the wrapper in the bin then writes something on the board – with his left hand I realise with a great leap of joy because here it is, yet more proof that we could share the same DNA. His fingers are short, just like mine, and he isn't wearing a wedding ring. He holds a pen the same way I do, and I copy his actions as he scribbles a sum while chewing the inside of his cheek. It's not something I do, but I give it a try, and wow it feels totally natural, as if this bit of flesh is meant to be nestled between these two molars. My cheek's found where it belongs, and maybe I have too I think to myself with growing exhilaration, pushing my face harder against the glass.

'You can come in, you know.' I'm embarrassed and so is

he, rubbing the back of his head. As always, he's wearing black trousers and a black shirt and a black tie.

'Perhaps he used to be an undertaker,' Mr Goldfish giggles, but I think he looks incredible, this man the colour of night.

'It's nice to see you looking happier, Tess. I've heard good things about you. Mr Holdsworth spoke very highly of your ability in this subject.'

I have an irresistible urge to work out the sum on the whiteboard, shouting out the answer maybe even in French to show off my language skills.

'Ce n'est pas une bonne idée,' Mr Goldfish says as people enter the room, Isabel among them, just one in the crowd for everyone but me. She avoids my eyes, pretending to be deep in conversation with Patrick. It hurts, how easily she's moved on in a matter of days. I ache for how things used to be. In the library. On our bench. Talking endlessly about everything and nothing. *Lord of the Rings*. Isawynka. Mr Holdsworth's mugs.

'The fact that she thinks you're a lesbian,' Mr Goldfish says dreamily and then, 'What the hell is your problem?' I'm gripping him hard. 'Strangling me, more like. Get off!'

'You don't think it was Isabel, do you? She wasn't the one who put up the picture?' A cold chill creeps down my spine. 'She knows my Facebook photos better than anyone. In fact, she's probably the only person who's ever looked at them.'

'I don't think it was her,' Mr Goldfish wheezes, but I'm not so sure.

Tara plonks herself on top of the table next to Mr Richardson's desk, swinging her legs as she opens a packet of chewing gum, seeing what she can get away with.

'What're you up to this weekend, Sir? Anything nice?'

Mr Richardson fiddles with the wallet on his desk, no doubt full of all sorts of personal information. I'd be able to work out where he shops. Where he lives.

'What the inside of a prison cell looks like when you're arrested for theft,' Mr Goldfish whispers. 'Get real, Tess.'

'Well,' Mr Richardson replies. 'I'll do a bit of marking. Play chess.'

Tara gnaws away at the gum. 'Who do you play chess against?'

'I play in a league. But this weekend I'll just be practising. Me versus me.'

'How's that even possible?' Tara asks, chomping the gum. 'How do you play with yourself?' She pretends to gasp, clapping both hands over her mouth. 'I didn't mean it like that, I swear!'

Mr Richardson has no clue how to respond. I try to come up with a witty answer to transmit to his brain, but I am equally flummoxed. Of course I am. The Richardsons are not people of snappy retorts.

'Are you allowed that?' he says at last. 'Because I don't—'

'This?' She points at her massive gob then beams. 'Yeah.

Yeah. Year Elevens are allowed gum, Sir. It's one of our privileges.'

Everyone has arrived apart from Anna. We're all waiting for the lesson to start. Trying to make a point without having to make a point, Mr Richardson removes the lid of a red marker then holds it up to the whiteboard, but Tara doesn't budge.

'You're okay, you are, Sir.' It isn't really a compliment. 'You know how to talk to us. More than Mr Holdsworth. He's too strict. But you're sound. Maths is going to be a right laugh now. Like, you really get teenagers, I can tell. Okay, this might be totally wrong, Sir, but I bet you have kids, don't you?'

Mr Richardson opens his mouth to reply as everything stops. The time. My breath. My heart.

'One son, yes.'

Still nothing moves, not the hands of the clock or the air in my lungs or the blood in my veins. Everything is waiting for some mention of me that surely is about to emerge from his lips, but no. He just points at the board with the wrong end of the pen.

'Okay, everyone. If you just have a look at what I have written on—'

'I knew it! How good am I?' Tara asks the room at large, oblivious to the mood of growing impatience, and how do you get to be like this, just so wrapped up in yourself that you don't sense the awkward atmosphere because I would love this particular type of immunity. 'You can always tell the teachers who have kids. Mr Holdsworth – obviously not a dad. I mean, he has no idea how to talk to teenagers, you know? How old is your son, Sir? Our age, I bet.'

'Seventeen. He's at sixth form college,' Mr Richardson says of this boy who could be my half-brother.

I want to get excited about it, like I really try to imagine hanging out with my older sibling, watching *Star Wars* with popcorn placed directly between us on the sofa, but I can't. It's too obscure and I find that, deep down, I don't believe it's true. Any of it. The wave of anticipation that has been building over the past three days comes crashing down then retreats, leaving a vast expanse of absolutely nothing.

'But anyway, if you wouldn't mind taking a – the lesson did start ten minutes ago and—'

'What's his name?'

'That's not important right now,' he snaps.

About time too. He needs to take some sort of control because this is getting embarrassing. I miss Mr Holdsworth and also, with an unexpected pang, Jack. Jack, who takes charge of any situation and makes people laugh and holds court like he's the judge, not the one being judged as completely and utterly incompetent.

'Oh, go on, Sir.'

He sighs. 'Henry.'

'Henry . . . Oh my God, not Henry Richardson?' The

hand clapping over Tara's mouth is genuine this time. 'You're Henry Richardson's dad?'

'Henry Richardson?' Sarah gasps from the back of the room where she's sitting at the only table with two empty spaces, one for Tara and the other for Anna, who still hasn't arrived. The doorframe is waiting for her to fill it; that's how it looks as it stands, empty and yearning, calling out into the corridor. 'You're Henry Richardson's dad? Oh my days. *Tara!*'

'*I know!*' she replies in an equally high-pitched voice, spinning round to look at her friend, who's craning her neck to return the blazing gaze. This is something incredible to them, something unexpected and brilliant and truly thrilling, and I catch a dazzling glimpse of their shiny life outside the black school gates.

Excitement fizzes in the air between the girls as the rest of us breathe oxygen the equivalent of flat Coke.

'Sir, I actually cannot believe this.' Tara's tone is different, enthralled and reverent. Mr Richardson senses the change, abandoning the marker pen entirely. 'You're so different to him.'

'I take it that's not a compliment.' He laughs, and she does too, and also Sarah, because, oh look at that, she's standing up at the back of the classroom and racing to join them at the front.

Part of me wants to too, but the other part sides with Isabel, angrily making a point of starting the work on the board. She turns to the right page in her exercise book with a very fierce finger-flick. She wants to be overheard, and she gets her wish, because they turn to stare at her in unison – three pairs of eyes versus one, and she wins because they look away first.

'Well done,' Mr Richardson says with a cough that's not as embarrassed as it should be. 'Look at that, everyone. I'm glad to see someone's showing some initiative. There is stuff on the board for you to be getting on with, you know.'

A mood of silent resentment settles over the classroom like black fog.

'I still can't believe it, Sir.'

'So, you know Henry, do you?' he says, giving the girls his full attention as I watch from a distance. 'Dare I ask how?'

'Everybody knows your son,' Tara replies. 'He's a hottie, Sir. Everyone's in love with him.'

'Tara!' Sarah squeals. 'You can't say that!'

'I'm just telling you the truth, Sir. Honest. He's, like, the hottest boy in Manchester.' I gouge the date into my book. My so-called brother sounds nothing like me – a Mercury, sizzling close to the sun. 'Probably the hottest boy in the north of England.'

'Well, that's – well. I don't quite know what to say. Thank you, I guess.'

Tara grins. 'Thank *you*, Sir. For producing him. *Anna!* You will never believe this,' she says as her friend finally strolls in, taking ages over it, in no rush whatsoever.

'Where have you been?' Mr Richardson tries to ask, but Tara and Sarah are talking over him.

'Sir's son! Guess who he is!'

'You will never guess!'

'Henry,' Anna says, and it's a statement not a question, as if she thought of the connection ages ago.

'Can you believe it? They're nothing like each other, are they? Like, Sir plays chess. On his own. How weird is that?' Tara looks dazed that two such opposite creatures could be in any way related. It makes me think of Isabel and her mum and how different they are. Okay, I've never met her in the flesh, but I have seen a photo and it's pretty obvious to anyone with eyes that Isabel is ninety nine percent her father's daughter.

The wave of anticipation swells once more. It's possible. Of course it is. I mean, some siblings look nothing like each other, especially ones who only share half their genes. Whoever this Henry is, perhaps he's more like his mum and I'm more like our dad, so we only have a couple of things in common – the same nose and the same freckles that appear in Spring then fade in Autumn, unlike our bond that, once formed, will stay strong all year round, I just know it.

Above the classroom, the fog thins to a grey wisp then disappears completely.

I have to meet him.

It's pure, this feeling, ringing out in my body like a brand new church bell on an unusually clear day.

[147]

'You play chess on your own,' Anna says, sauntering to her place. 'That sounds fun.'

'Oh, it is,' Mr Richardson replies, ignoring her tone or maybe failing to notice it altogether. No offence to maybe-my-dad, but he does seem pretty clueless when it comes to dealing with teenage girls. It's something I can help him with, just as soon as he invites me round for tea with Henry in their house that's probably crying out for a woman's touch. 'I don't mind it, really, being on my own. I suppose you could say I am bit of an introvert. Right, shall we get on with some work, girls?'

The lesson begins at last, but I don't pay any attention to it, just secretly look up 'introvert' on my phone because it seems important to read the official definition. The words glow on my lap.

A person who turns inward, retreats mentally.

I grin before I can stop myself. Another word for a Pluto, then.

CHAPTER 21

Tomorrow we're taking Gran out for tea because it is her birthday, but I don't want to miss a week of cleaning so I head to her house even though it's only Thursday, stopping at *Tesco* to pick up supplies.

'Won't Jack be annoyed?' Mr Goldfish asks. He puffs out his chest. '*Have you forgotten the rules, Tess? School clothes off, homework out, as soon as you get home.*'

'He's going shopping after work and Mum's got a meeting so no one will even know.'

Normally I'd let myself into Gran's house and shout that I'd arrived. I ring the doorbell instead. It chimes like a glockenspiel in a fancy orchestra.

Mr Goldfish chuckles. 'This is a bit formal.'

'I can't just burst into the lounge unannounced. Gran might be doing something private.'

I ring the doorbell one more time. Gran doesn't appear so I have no choice but to step into the hall, banging around a lot in the hope that she will hear me before I knock on the lounge door.

'Tess! Well, this is a nice surprise.' I drop some Eccles cakes into Gran's lap then squeeze her hand with all the love I can muster. 'Or is it Friday?' She scratches her head, looking worried.

I can taste the words I want to say. They're comforting, like the warm milk Mum used to give me when I was small that would fill me up and settle me down and make me feel safe. I grab the newspaper off the coffee table and show Gran the date.

'Thursday. I thought so. I'll make us some tea, dear. This is a lovely surprise. I don't normally have any visitors on a Thursday. Barbara used to come, before she went into the home.'

It takes Gran three attempts to get out of the chair, so I'm suddenly fascinated by the newspaper, hiding behind it as she hobbles into the kitchen. Definitely I am not going to get that old when I grow up is the decision I make as I crouch down on the floor. It isn't Gran's fault, the fact that she doesn't notice these crumbs, or that bit of thread, or the fluff by the fireplace. I have to be on all fours to see it myself. Checking she's still in the kitchen, I polish the ornaments with my sleeve, giving the lion a little stroke.

There's a rattle of cups and spoons as Gran reappears in the lounge. She doesn't ask why I've stopped speaking, and there's no mention of the pantomime. I curl up in front of the fire, watching the elaborate dance of the flames as I sip tea, giving thanks for Gran who's not afraid of silence. For the first time since the play, it is a joint thing, a shared thing, something to cuddle up in, like a blanket.

'I'm sorry. I will cheer up. I'm just not in the mood for a party tonight,' Mum says as we approach *La Dolce Vita* where we're celebrating Gran's birthday.

It's only six o'clock but it's already dark. I loll back, trying out how it feels to be Anna. I walk tall. I saunter. I take my time on each step, feeling my heel then my toes melt into the ground.

Manchester is big and booming, exploding in all directions for miles around. There must be thousands of streets. Millions of houses. It would take years to find out where Mr Richardson lives . . . unless I checked inside his wallet for a driving licence.

'No Tess!' Mr Goldfish hisses, just like he has every time this thought has entered my mind in the past twenty-four hours. 'It's madness! A crazy idea! And what would it achieve?'

'I could go to his house. Have a look at his son.'

'And then what?'

'See if I belong there,' I say because to me it's simple. 'Gut instinct. Intuition. Whatever you want to call it.'

'Insanity? Lunacy? Psychosis?'

Mum stops by the steps leading up to the restaurant, actually quite impressive with a big glass entrance. 'You know I'll put on a brave face. You don't need to worry about that.'

Jack rubs her elbow. 'It'll be nice tonight.'

'Hard work, more like. It's far too much for Mum at her age.' They start up the steps, the rhythm of their bodies perfectly in sync. 'I don't know what Susan was thinking, booking it here. But that's her, isn't it? Always has to be the one to do something extravagant. Doesn't get involved in the nitty-gritty, the boring day-to-day care, though that has felt easier recently. Mum seems to be coping better.' I smile at this as I follow up the steps. 'But organising this for tonight! Mum doesn't even like Italian food. It's ridiculous, don't you think?'

'We're here now. Let's just try to enjoy it, eh?'

'Fat chance. It's going to be—' She pauses, pressing her temples. 'Sorry. I'm tired, that's all. It's been the shittiest week, and that's swearing.'

That is swearing, and I am not used to hearing it come out of Mum's mouth. It sounds toxic, like she's been poisoned with unusual thoughts and feelings, emerging from her lips in acrid green smoke. I can barely see the old Mum through the smog and I want to apologise and waft it away, to make her clean and wholesome and smiley again, but I don't.

'Come on, Hels. Let's not think about it tonight.'

'Fine.' She doesn't sound convinced so Jack whispers something in her ear that makes her laugh and then they kiss at the top of the steps, this golden image of love bathed in the soft lights of *La Dolce Vita* as I skulk beneath them in the shadows.

The door's one of those rotating ones. Mum and Jack squeeze into the same quarter, leaving me out in the cold. I gaze at the moon, this segment of silver watermelon, its pips scattered across the sky. It seems wrong, so I mentally reassemble it, lifting each star and dropping it back into the moon where it belongs.

Jack bangs on the glass. 'Tess? Get in here. It's freezing!'

I don't move. Fixing the universe is a whole lot easier than dealing with what's about to happen on planet Earth in the next two hours, two and a half if everyone has dessert and coffee. I haven't seen Aunt Susan or Uncle Paul since I gave up speaking. There will be questions. Lots of them. Mr Goldfish glows in my pocket, warming the tips of my fingers.

'And you won't have to face them alone.'

'I won't tell you again,' Jack says, but he does, twice in fact when I still don't move because things are on my terms now, let's be clear about that. I only go through the revolving door when he's given up trying to get me to come inside. I slow it to a stop by pushing back on the glass so I'm suspended between the night and the restaurant, looking out on both but not a part of either.

'I could live like this,' I tell Mr Goldfish.

'You sort of do live like this.'

I walk into the restaurant without fully joining the scene. I don't speak to the girl taking my coat and I don't acknowledge the man leading us to a table and I don't smile at Uncle Paul or Aunt Susan, who beam at me as I sit next to Gran. My heart fills with pride because she looks beautiful in a lilac blouse and matching brooch. I put her present under my chair, excited about giving it to her later.

'Good to see you, Tess,' Uncle Paul says as I reappear, catapulting his hand across the table to squeeze my own. I hide mine in my lap so he's forced to swerve in the direction of the bread basket, grabbing a brown roll as if that was always his intention. He tears some off then throws it in his mouth. 'Really good to see you.'

'Great to see you,' Aunt Susan says, upping the ante as usual. 'How're you feeling, sweetheart?' She tilts her head to the right. 'Gorgeous girl.' I want to laugh as she takes in my face with a pained expression on her own. 'So brave. How is she doing, Jack? How're *you* doing?'

'Oh, I'm fine.' He shows his teeth to the whole table, this dazzling display of white, flickering in the candlelight. Reaching for the bottle of sparkling water, he starts to pour everyone a glass. '*Elsie,*' he says, talking to Gran in the patronising tone that gets on my nerves, '*can you manage something fizzy?*'

'It will make her gassy,' Mum replies and I almost giggle.

I feel giddy. Alive. Full of hope because at last I have a plan, even if it does involve snooping inside a teacher's wallet.

'Give her the still water instead.'

'Okey-dokey. Still water for you, Elsie. Susan, sparkling? Yeah, like I say, I'm doing well. Hating this weather, though. Perishing out there, isn't it?'

'How are you really?' Aunt Susan asks. She tilts her head the other way now. 'And you, Hels? You look tired. I hope you're looking after my little sister, Jacko.'

Jack's teeth disappear. 'We're fine thanks, Susan. Has it been the easiest week of our lives? Well, no. Of course not. But we're getting there. We'll crack it. Tess will be fine in a few days,' he says as I vow to be silent for the rest of my life.

'Of course she will,' Aunt Susan replies. 'She's a battler.'

I study the Specials board to see if there's anything with goats' cheese. I'm hungrier than I've been for weeks because I've got work to do, haven't I, a man to track down and a boy to meet to check for signs that we could be related. My mouth waters as I take in *Garlic bread with mozzarella* and *Asparagus wrapped in prosciutto* and – but no, I can't see the other starters because a massive head is blocking my line of vision. 'We all believe in you, Tess,' Aunt Susan breathes in my face.

'Yeah,' Uncle Paul says, appearing briefly over the top of a large menu. 'Totally. Is anyone having a starter or are we going straight onto mains?'

A waitress in a smart black dress appears. Telepathically I communicate my desire for something with goats' cheese, but she scribbles down the dish that Aunt Susan orders for me, the same thing she picks out for Gran.

'Everyone likes spaghetti carbonara. You don't mind do you, Hels? Me ordering for that girl of yours? Thought it would be better than putting her on the spot.'

Mum seems distracted and lets it slide.

'Was it stage fright or something, Jack?' Uncle Paul asks in a low voice. I straighten up, intrigued to hear the answer. 'Is that what caused it?'

'We're not sure,' Mum mutters as Jack says, 'Definitely. No question.' He takes a packet of breadsticks and tears it open. 'I mean, it happened on stage, just as she was about to say her line, didn't it?' We share a glance. 'She looked straight at me and – nothing. I gave her a shake and – nothing. She froze out there. That's how it feels, as if her voice box is frozen. But we'll find a way to thaw it, eh, Tessie-T?' He pats my shoulder like it's a dog. It growls angrily, a rumble of warning, deep in the bone. 'We'll get there. It might take a while, but we'll—'

'It might not, though, Jacko. Miracles happen all the time. You just have to believe. Have a little faith,' Aunt Susan says. She smiles too widely, the thermostat of her face turned up high because she wants to be the one to dissolve my silence. I can see it in her eyes – ice to water, that's what she's picturing, a curious gurgle deep in my throat, a

[156]

miraculous *thank you* dripping from my lips when I realise that I'm cured.

No one seems to understand that it's a choice. I could speak right now if I really wanted to, stand up in the middle of the restaurant and open my mouth to let out a blizzard. That's the kind of winter in my voice box. There's nothing solid about it. Nothing rigid. They might not be able to hear them, but there are words, thousands of them, flurrying about beneath the surface like flakes in a snow globe, hurling themselves noiselessly against the glass.

And I won't shatter it. Not for anyone. And especially not for Jack.

CHAPTER 22

'I do have faith in Tess, as a matter of fact. I have complete faith in her to get over this little—' Jack clears his throat '—blip.'

Mr Goldfish chuckles. 'Now's probably not the best time to reveal you're conversing inside your head with a goldfish.'

I smirk behind my curtain of hair. 'No.'

'I know that, Jacko. Of course I do. I only meant that it's important for you, for everyone, to—'

The arrival of the drinks prevents Aunt Susan from building up a head of steam. A lemonade I don't want is put in front of me. Everyone else is having something alcoholic, apart from Gran, who's been given an orange juice with a stripy straw meant for a child.

Jack holds up a glass of red wine by a long thin stem. 'To Elsie.'

'To Elsie.'

'To Elsie.'

'To Elsie.'

'*Happy birthday, Mum,*' Aunt Susan bellows as the glasses are returned to the table. '*Are you having a good time?*'

'*Of course she is,*' Uncle Paul shouts back.

'*Out past your bedtime, eh, Elsie?*' Jack yells and everyone laughs, except me and Gran. 'Well, if you can't misbehave on your birthday, when can you? Eighty – *years young, Elsie! That's it, isn't it? Eighty years young!*'

'This was a good idea,' Aunt Susan congratulates herself, gazing insistently round the table so we have no choice but to nod and agree. 'Just a shame that Dad can't be here. *Your grandpa would've loved this, Tess,*' she tells me in a similar voice to the one she just used on Gran. 'He liked a party.'

Jack takes a long sip of wine, kissing his lips together. 'How long were they married, again? Fifty-five years, wasn't it, Hels?'

'No, fifty-six,' Uncle Paul says. 'Impressive.'

I give Gran my full attention to show I'm only interested in her response, but Aunt Susan butts in before she can reply.

'Fifty-eight, I'll think you find. Dad died a couple of years before their diamond wedding anniversary. They'd have received a congratulatory note from the Queen, as well.' She touches Gran's frail wrist then shouts in her face. '*You would have liked that, wouldn't you, Mum? A note from the Queen?*'

'If anyone deserved it, they did,' Uncle Paul says, helping himself to another bread roll. 'Childhood sweethearts.' He starts to laugh. 'They used to finish each other's sentences. Remember, Hels? Sue? Mum would start saying something and Dad would complete it. *Don't forget to – get your car serviced, Paul. Make sure you – take a coat with you.*'

'To Mum and Dad,' Aunt Susan says, raising her glass once more. 'The perfect couple.'

'The perfect couple,' Uncle Paul agrees.

'The perfect couple,' Jack repeats.

'The perfect couple,' Mum says with a small smile. 'They really were.'

Everyone drinks, except me and Gran.

'*So, what's the secret then, Elsie?*' Jack asks. '*You must know, after fifty-eight years of happy marriage. What's the key?*'

'The bedroom,' Gran replies, without missing a beat.

For once, Jack is speechless. Uncle Paul examines the seeds on top of his bread roll and Aunt Susan takes a huge swig of wine as I cheer Gran on, pumping my fist beneath the table.

'Shall we do presents?' Mum asks eventually.

Gran receives a jigsaw of a steam train, a set of pink handkerchiefs, some lavender bubble bath and, best of all, a tea cosy in the shape of a lion's head that I found in a craft shop in Manchester.

'Thanks, dear. I love it,' Gran says and I glow.

'Apart from the obvious, did it go okay, then, Jack? The first night of the panto?' Aunt Susan asks. 'Sorry I couldn't make it in the end. It was one of those weekends.'

'For me as well,' Uncle Paul says, too quickly. 'You know how it is. Something always comes up that gets in the way at the last minute.'

'It's fine, it's fine. We sold out, anyway. I was worried you were going to turn up to find there were no tickets left.' Jack pretends to laugh, biting the end off a breadstick, and I wonder if his lies are obvious to everyone, or if I am just unusually good at spotting them these days. He twiddles the breadstick between long fingers that wrote those six hundred and seventeen words. Even now, it's hard to believe.

'Especially as there's no evidence of the blog on the website,' Mr Goldfish says. 'Unless you missed it.'

'Not possible,' I reply because last night I spent two hours scouring seven pages of stories and found nothing from Jack.

'Did your agent come in the end?' Aunt Susan asks. 'Hels said on the phone there was a chance he might travel up from London.'

'Nah, there was never a chance of that. He knows I'm in the play because, well, I have to keep him informed, don't I? He is my agent. But I told him not to bother with something so local. I'm writing my own stuff now, anyway.'

'Sounds good,' Uncle Paul says, pulling a breadstick out of the open packet. He taps it on the table then points it at Jack. 'I like that attitude. Got to make your own opportunities if there aren't any coming your way.'

'Crikey, there's plenty coming my way,' Jack replies, pointing his own breadstick at Paul, and I have the clearest image of two men circling each other, about to clash swords made out of dough. 'That's not why I'm doing it. I've got irons in the fire, some that are red-hot actually, but I've always loved writing. Got a lot buzzing about up here.' He jabs his head with the breadstick. A little bit snaps off, scattering crumbs over his shoulder. 'It's good to get it out on paper, you know? And it's going well. Four thousand eight hundred and seventy-one words in – not that it's about word count, of course. That's crass. But still. I've written almost five thousand words in less than a week. That isn't bad, is it?'

'What's it about?' Aunt Susan asks. 'Are we allowed to know?'

Jack is delighted to be asked. 'It's set in a garden shed and the characters are tools.'

There is no response from anyone whatsoever.

'I know it's abstract, but that's how my mind works, I'm afraid.' He lets out a sigh heavy with the burden of being blessed with such an almighty imagination, then rests his left elbow on the back of his chair and stretches his legs. 'Here we go. Okay, there's a rake and a spade and a bucket and they're all waiting to be used, you know? Every morning they think that something's going to happen, that this man referred to only as 'The Gardener' is going to give them purpose – a job in the vegetable patch where they can be put to good use. But he never turns up. Gradually, they fall into disrepair. At the end of the play, when The Gardener does finally open up the shed and light shines in from the outside world, it only reveals the tools' rust, rather than the skills they used to have.'

'How does it end?' Uncle Paul asks.

Jack covers his mouth with his fingers, clearly moved. 'The Gardener has no choice but to drive to *B & Q* to replace them.'

'*B & Q*,' Aunt Susan repeats. 'Right.'

'It's very Beckett-esque. Not for everyone.'

'No, no, it sounds . . . So, will you be in it?'

'That's the plan. I'll get a couple of the cast members from *Peter Pan* to have a crack at it too. Mr Darling, and maybe Nana the dog.'

'But not you, I'm guessing, Tess?' Uncle Paul says with a sneaky squeeze of my arm, creeping his hand round the side of the table this time. 'Like we said before – the limelight's not for everyone.'

'Tess takes after me, though.'

'Do you think so, Jacko?' Aunt Susan asks.

'Yeah, definitely. That's the funny thing about her reaction on stage. I thought she'd relish it. She's a real chip off the old block in many ways.'

Maybe I imagine it, but Uncle Paul and Aunt Susan exchange the tiniest of glances, gone before I can double check that it was actually there. My pulse quickens as I

[163]

replay it in my head, and yes, I think I did see it, the truth passing between them. It hits me hard, the realisation slamming into my chest, forcing me back into my chair with no air in my lungs.

'*They know*,' Mr Goldfish whispers, and he's right.

I mean, of course he's right because Mum's their sister, and there's no way she wouldn't have told them how I was conceived even if they don't exactly get along. It's too big, too important, not to share with family. I stare around the table at all these dishonest blue eyes. I don't belong here. I don't belong anywhere, and I start to drift away. I float above the restaurant with the chandeliers, tingling with them, jittery and precarious, before bursting through the ceiling, just another lost star in the big black sky.

'I don't think you're similar,' Gran disagrees. She touches my knee with a hand that's surprisingly firm and steady, and it's an anchor, drawing me back down to Earth. Her blue eyes are different from the others. She might know the truth, but she's on my side, that's what they seem to say as they gaze at me behind glasses that glint with something warmer than candlelight.

'They've known the truth my whole life, and they've let me believe a lie!'

It's dark in my bedroom, the only light coming from Mr Goldfish, who's perched on my desk as I yank off my clothes and chuck them in the wash basket. I cling to the memory of Gran's hand on my knee, but then I see Uncle Paul's traitorous one shooting across the table, and Jack's deceitful one, touching my shoulder. I shudder, pulling on my onesie, staring in the mirror at the bold orange stripes.

Tonight I am all tiger, burning brightly, feeling fierce with extra-sharp claws.

'I'm going to get that wallet.'

I seize Mr Goldfish off the desk and pace up and down my room that's not my room because I don't belong here anymore. The feeling was stronger than ever when we arrived home tonight and Jack put the key in the lock. He stepped onto the *Welcome* doormat, kicking off his shoes and sliding into his slippers. The slippers. I stood on the pavement in my silver boots next to a silvery tree, jealous of its roots.

That's how bad things have got, like I'm envious of a tree where Jedi has definitely peed six thousand times at a conservative estimate. At least the tree knows where it stands. It has a sense of place. It's fixed. Attached. And I am lost.

I belong to nothing, and no one, but that's all going to change.

'How, though? By stealing Mr Richardson's wallet?' Mr Goldfish asks, his light shining on the window then my cupboard then my window again as we hurtle back and forth.

'Borrow his wallet. There's a difference.'

'To you, maybe. To anyone who catches you, it will look like the same thing. It's a terrible idea, Tess.'

'It's the only one I've got.'

'It's dangerous.'

'I have to do this.'

'It's too risky.'

'But he's out there somewhere!' I charge to the window, flinging it open to let in a rush of cold, black air. 'I have a dad. A real one. I have to find him. And you have to help me,' I say, only vaguely aware that I am talking to a torch. Light pours from his mouth like a search beam, scouring the darkness for clues. It picks out the slate roofs of terraced houses and a ginger cat on a mossy wall and three cars stuck at a traffic light, waiting for the go ahead.

They get it, eventually, and so do I.

'Fine,' Mr Goldfish says at last. The word shines from his lips, illuminating the night sky.

PART THREE

CHAPTER 23

The December sunshine peps me up, the clean light bouncing off the windows of cars and buildings as I walk to school. It makes the world seem fresh and full of possibility.

I give Mr Goldfish an excited squeeze. 'We'll do it today. We'll get the address.'

'You've been saying that for two weeks.'

'Today is different.'

'You've also been saying that for two weeks.'

'But this time I mean it.'

'You've also been saying that for—'

'Okay, no offence or anything, but can you please be quiet? That isn't helping.'

Normally, Mr Richardson leaves the black rucksack in his classroom at break then goes to the staffroom to meet Miss Gilbert. It pleases me immensely, the fact that Mr Richardson so clearly has Miss Gilbert's stamp of approval, like he might be a terrible teacher, but he's a pretty great human being is what she seems to say every morning by accepting half the Blue Riband biscuit. Sometimes they chat. Other times they drink tea. Mostly they do the crossword in the newspaper that Mr Richardson brings to school when he arrives at nearly always quarter past eight.

He's a man of routine, leaving his classroom between ten thirteen and ten fifteen every break, returning on average thirty-seven seconds before the bell rings for period three is what I have learned from days of close surveillance. I've made notes, writing down his movements in a table I've drawn next to the one about Mr Holdsworth's mugs. It might sound odd – 'It does sound odd,' Mr Goldfish mutters – but I need to know his habits in precise detail if I am going to be successful in *Operation Wallet*.

'Let's just call it *Operation Tess Has Lost her Mind*, okay?'

'That's not very supportive.'

'I'm not very supportive,' Mr Goldfish replies as we approach school.

I avoid Conor and Adam and the staring eyes and the black crow that's been there every time I've decided to risk walking across the bus park, the bird circling above my head, its beak getting sharper and its claws more deadly as the comments get worse. Well, not anymore. I don't need to hear them out loud, thank you very much. I'm fully aware of what people think because I check Twitter every night before I go to bed, cursing the anonymous @BlaiseOfGlory for posting the picture in the first place.

Tess-tosterone got changed for PE in a toilet cubicle today. What's she trying to hide? #SheIsAHe

Anyone else notice that she's got a moustache? #SheIsAHe

I saw a bulge today. That's all I'm saying. #SheIsAHe

I don't want to read them, but I can't stop reading them, like it's an addiction or what have you, and I scroll endlessly, my eyes stinging in the bluish light. So far @IsabelBaggins hasn't commented and neither has @DarkAnna.

'That's because she's the mysterious Blaise,' Mr Goldfish says.

'Who?'

'Anna, obviously,' he replies, but I'm not so sure. Anna smiles at me in the corridor while Isabel marches past with her nose in the air. Anna stood up for me against Connor and promised to look out for me on Mr Holdsworth's orders, but Isabel has completely cut me out. It hurts to read the messages we used to send when we missed each other like crazy if we were separated even for a day.

How dare you be ill on a Monday when we have Maths, Tess? PythagorARSE. Apparently $a^2 + b^2 = c^2$. Well, now I know that I am ENLIGHTENED. Truly. Get well – by tomorrow.

I will. I need you like a hypotenuse needs a right angle. Translation: a lot.

The sandwich bar has run out of ham. HAM. What kind of sandwich bar has no HAM?

Jewish ones? I'll Google it and get back to you.

You do that. On a side note, the mug was yellow today.

Now we've gone days and days without talking. It doesn't even seem odd anymore, and that's the saddest thing of all.

'It doesn't make her Blaise though,' Mr Goldfish says, and I want to believe him, but I can't forget the way she giggled on the bench with Patrick. On that Wednesday morning, she showed him something on her phone. A few hours later, the picture of me on holiday had been posted on Twitter.

I reach the route that cuts across the playing fields. They're wet and muddy but it's still the best option. I squelch and I sink and I swear a lot and also cheer up a little bit too, because no one in their right mind would walk this way after last night's rain. Just to be sure, I glance over my shoulder and see nothing but a blue tit singing chirpily in a tree. I am safe for a few minutes at least. It's just me and the bird, the bird and me.

'And me,' Mr Goldfish says, flitting about in my coat pocket.

'Not really.'

He leaps out into the open as the bird takes off so there's a flutter of orange fins and blue wings. 'That's not very nice.'

'Are you going to get behind the plan?'

'Absolutely not.'

I shrug. 'Then you're dead to me.'

'But it's crazy, Tess! You're crazy!'

'Please stop talking about my sanity,' I say. I'm still a little sensitive after the speech therapy session in the too-neat office with the too-neat woman who pretty much called me a lunatic.

In a very careful voice with very clear consonants, she asked Mum and Jack a few questions about how my silence started, and whether I had any long-standing problems with communication. Then she leaned back and crossed her legs. 'I'm sorry, but there is nothing I can do.'

'What do you mean – *there's nothing you can do?*' Jack repeated, gripping Mum's arm as she gripped the strap of the Mulberry bag. It was empty apart from her phone and keys. Her normal bag was at home at the bottom of the stairs, stuffed with used tissues and pens with no lids and a bulging diary and a brush full of hair and a bruised banana and loads of other imperfect things that made up Mum's life. This bag was for show, nothing more than a prop clutched in her manicured hand, jutting out of the sleeve of a perfectly ironed blouse. I didn't recognise it so it must have been new, and it made my heart ache, how hard she was trying to convince this woman, this stranger, that she was good enough to be my mum.

'It isn't a problem with speech. Not a physical one, anyway. If, prior to the so-called mutism, Tess could talk perfectly well in a variety of contexts and has never had any developmental issues where speech is concerned, I am afraid this sort of thing is out of my remit. A sudden silence in an adolescent who has never had any language difficulties is highly unusual to say the least. The best course of action is to refer her to a psychologist,' she said, the last *t* hitting me in the face like a bullet.

Jack swore and Mum gasped and I winced, sitting between them on the too-firm sofa, desperate to tell the woman with the too-square fingernails that I'd made a huge mistake.

'Obviously I can speak!' I wanted to shout, but nothing came out. The therapist was dressed in a crisp, white uniform with the type of stiff collar you just don't mess with. It had gone too far. I couldn't say a word without getting into serious trouble so I kept quiet as she filled in a form that looked scarily official.

'You'll receive a letter in a few weeks' time from *CAMHS*.'

Mum went pale. 'What's that?'

'Sorry. Child and Adolescent Mental Health Services. They have a unit in South Manchester. It's a great place. Welcoming and supportive,' she explained as I made a ferocious vow never to find out for myself if this was true.

'In the meantime, here are some leaflets you might find useful,' the speech therapist continued, passing this huge great big stack to Mum, who started to cry into a yellow handkerchief. It stayed out for a week, drying on the radiator in between Mum's breakdowns. Every time I came downstairs to see it twisted in Mum's hands, I almost caved, all these words pinging against my silence, harder and harder, until I was scared it was going to crack.

'Look, I'm sorry I said the c-word, okay?' Mr Goldfish says, diving back into my pocket as I reach the library.

'Not *the* c-word.'

'You know what I mean. You're not crazy, Tess, obviously.'

'Says the talking fish that only I can hear.'

I'm early, so I have the place to myself, at least that's what I think until Isabel pops her head up over a table where she's crouched down by her bag. The library elongates to twice the size then shrinks as the awkwardness slams us together. Our movements seem massive. She gets out her notepad with arm gestures that fill the room as I walk to a desk by the window on feet bigger than the floor. They boom as she breathes and I blink as she coughs.

She coughs again, like maybe she's clearing her throat to speak is what I am hoping with all this Beat in my wrists. But no. She buries her hot face in the pages of her notepad. I take some work out of my bag and try to focus because the words are back, a blizzard of them, hurtling themselves against the glass. I want to speak. I want to speak so much I can taste it on my tongue, feel the shape of the words in my mouth, but I wait for the storm to pass. It does eventually, the words melting like snowflakes, trickling back down my throat.

I sneak a look. She's writing furiously.

Freak. Trannie. He-she.

'Paranoia. Paranoia. Paranoia,' Mr Goldfish says, spelling out the word with his light so it glows in my pocket. I hope he's right.

Next time I check, Isabel has gone. I pack up and make my way to my form room. Miss Gilbert waves as I walk in.

'What a beautiful day, dude. A day to make things happen, don't you think?'

I agree. By break time I'll have that wallet.

CHAPTER 24

Mr Richardson's room might be empty, but it feels alive, the air quivering and the walls watching and the lights murmuring some sort of judgement. I tiptoe towards Mr Richardson's desk, but no one intervenes. No one shouts or tells me to stop as I bend down by the rucksack on the classroom floor.

It's almost too easy. The bag is here, and so am I, and the zip is open, inviting me to look inside. I peer into the black depths. There's a bunch of keys, a new teacher's planner and an old book of Sudoku. Of course there's an old book of Sudoku. If he really is my dad, we're going to have all sorts of things in common.

'Stop fondling it and get a move on,' Mr Goldfish whispers so I move the book to one side and go deeper, deep as I can. If he came back now, I would be in so much trouble, definitely suspended and maybe even expelled. My mind plays it out – Mr Richardson appearing in the square of glass, his cheeks draining of colour as he finds me elbow-deep in his rucksack. *THIEF* he'd cry at the top of his voice. *THIEF!*

'Hurry!' Mr Goldfish says because I've stalled, my hand freezing as I glance at the door to check it is still closed.

Click

Heart hammering, I jump to my feet but it's just – 'The radiator,' Mr Goldfish says. 'Just the radiator.'

Squatting down on wobbly legs, I take a deep breath to calm myself, or try to, because let's be clear I am way past that point. I am noise and sweat and fear, jangling nerves and tight muscles and wild eyes looking at the bag which becomes a monster, a living, breathing monster with menacing jaws waiting to bite off my hand.

Mr Goldfish nudges his nose against my leg. 'Come on! It's twenty-five past ten.'

I swirl my arm one way then the other, my fingers scouring the objects in the beast's belly.

'It isn't here!'

'Side pocket!' Mr Goldfish shouts, beside himself now, a flash of crazed orange. 'It must be in a side pocket!'

I twist the bag to face me and make a start on the left. The noise of the zip echoes around school, the sound quite possibly of my sanity ripping in two. This is madness. Mr Goldfish was right. This is crazy and so risky and completely futile because I am never going to find it – except that I do.

A wallet.

A brown leather wallet hiding at the very bottom of the

side pocket. I pull it out with a clammy hand. The contents take my breath away, my lungs swooning against my ribs.

This is his stuff. Bank cards and receipts and a photo of a toddler and a woman with auburn hair – his late wife, it must be, because no one would keep a picture of an ex in their wallet. He's a widower who plays chess at the weekends to fill the lonely hours, and I feel so sorry for him as I gaze down at a young Henry beaming up at the woman beneath a blossom tree that will always be in flower in Mr Richardson's mind, I just know it.

'For God's sake, the driving licence!'

'Sorry, sorry!'

I turn my attention to the cards jammed in the narrow slots, four stuffed in each one making it difficult to pull them out. It's painstaking and I am panicking because there's more noise now, people starting to make their way to their next lesson on feet that rumble in the corridor below because somehow, unbelievably, school is carrying on as normal outside this room.

'Abort mission! Abort mission!' Mr Goldfish cries, but I carry on, the wallet shaking as I go through the cards in the first slot and the second slot and the third slot – and there, at the back of the very last slot, is something pale and pink and oh so promising. I tease it out.

The licence.

It contains everything I need to know. Mr Richardson's full name. His date of birth. And his home address.

[179]

There's no time to study it now, but I do register the fact he's called Jack, which makes me laugh out loud, the first noise I've made in days. It sounds odd to my ears, brash and abrupt. Pulling out my phone, I take a picture of this Jack, my Jack, staring up at me from the licence with eyes so like my own.

'You're on. You're totally on. A horse drawing competition it is. But you'll regret it.'

'What?' I ask Mr Goldfish, who stiffens in my pocket.

'I didn't say anything,' he whispers.

The voice didn't come from inside my head. The voice came from outside the classroom door.

'Farmyard animals are my speciality,' Mr Richardson says as I shove his driving licence back into his wallet in the wrong damn slot.

'That's the wrong damn slot!' Mr Goldfish shouts.

I try to rectify my mistake but the card is jammed and my fingers are too slippery so it stays where it is.

The door handle rattles as if Mr Richardson is about to turn it, but he carries on chatting to someone not in view.

'Farmyard animals are your speciality? Why? Were you a sow in a former life, or something?'

I'd recognise her voice anywhere. It's Miss Gilbert, and she's giggling, too high-spirited to be a teacher. Wild, that's how she seems, with a personality that gallops in a place where people trot.

'You do know a sow is a female pig, not a male one?' Mr Richardson asks, cantering now, trying to keep pace. I can hear it, his spirit rising on hind legs before throwing caution to the wind and making chase, maybe even for the first time since his wife passed away.

'Since when?'

'I can't believe you don't know that a sow is a female pig.'

'You're having me on, right?'

'We can Google it, if you like?' Mr Richardson says. 'My phone's in my bag.'

'No!' Mr Goldfish shouts as the handle moves, descending in a slow arc as I plummet to my knees. I throw the wallet into the pocket but it ricochets out again, spinning away from me in the worst possible direction. It stops about a metre from the door, which opens only a fraction then stays where it is. 'Grab it! No, leave it! No – get it!' Mr Goldfish cries, swimming about in my head with my thoughts, bouncing off in all directions.

'You're just trying to get out of the art contest,' Miss Gilbert says, sounding louder now, her voice travelling through the gap in the door. 'I'm right, aren't I? You know I'll win, even if farmyard animals are your so-called speciality.'

I lurch after the wallet on my hands and knees, pretty much like a farmyard animal myself. I am a sheep, bleating in panic, and a cow—

'Crapping yourself stupid,' Mr Goldfish says, which is not that far from the truth. I reach out for the wallet, dangerously close to Mr Richardson's shoes. Two slivers of mismatched socks are just about visible beneath the hem of his trousers. It takes me by surprise, these splashes of colour in an otherwise all black outfit.

'It's because of my sister,' Mr Richardson explains as my fingers make contact with the leather. 'The youngest one. I've told you about her?'

'The vet?'

'Yeah, Katie. Well, she was always asking me to draw animals. Pigs. Cows. Horses in particular,' he says as I reverse, wanting to move quickly but scared of making any noise. The result is a semi-fast backwards crawl while holding my breath, as if somehow this will make me lighter and more silent. 'I've had years of practice, that's all I'm saying.'

'And I've had years and years of practice, that's all I'm saying.' I make it to the bag without being noticed. 'I am an art teacher, Mr Richardson, so if we're having an art contest then of course I am going to win.'

'Not necessarily.'

'Oh, please. You teach Maths, the least creative subject in the school.'

'But I can draw.'

'Well, we'll see about that,' she says.

'Yes, we will – right now, if you like?'

'I do like.'

'Come on in then, Miss Gilbert.'

I shove the wallet into the pocket then leap away from the bag without doing up the zip, panting as if I've run a marathon. The bag is back where it belongs, but it's facing the wrong way I realise with a jolt of panic that explodes down my spine with the force quite possibly of lightning. My legs cave so I pretend to sit down on a table and do my best to breathe normally. I count it out – in for two, out for two – and brace myself for whatever is about to happen next because there's nothing I can do now apart from pray.

'*Our Father, who art in Heaven,*' starts Mr Goldfish, '*hallowed be thy name. Thy Kingdom come, thy will be—*'

'Tess?' Mr Richardson says. 'What are you doing in here?'

I am absolutely not allowed to look at the bag.

'So why are you looking at the bag?' Mr Goldfish whispers.

'Did we have an appointment I've forgotten about?'

'Tess, it's so nice to see you,' Miss Gilbert says, glaring at Mr Richardson.

'Yes, yes. Of course. So nice to see you.' The words are right, but the tone is wrong. He looks at me, and then at his desk, and then at his bag. Mr Goldfish plays dead in my pocket.

'Oh my God oh my God oh my God. He *knows*.'

'A real treat,' Mr Richardson says, his eyes on the open zip.

'I think it's a compliment, actually. I told Tess that she could come and hang out in my room if school gets a bit much for her, but she's obviously chosen to come here instead. Says a lot about you, that does, Sir, given that you've only been here five minutes.'

'What can I say? We do get on rather well.' I'm breathless for an entirely different reason now. 'Very well, in fact. I've been keeping an eye on her. She's obviously going through something difficult. I suppose you could say I've taken her under my wing.'

'Cock-a-doodle-doo,' Mr Goldfish crows as I look at Mr Richardson in disbelief. I am under his wing and I never even realised it, and when did that happen and how long can I stay here are the questions fizzing in the champagne of my mind.

'That's really nice.'

'You've got a good one here, Miss.' My head turns into a Catherine wheel, spinning madly, emitting thousands of sparks of bright white joy. 'She'll be fine in my class.'

Miss Gilbert touches his arm with gentle fingertips that stay too long on his elbow. 'I know she will.'

CHAPTER 25

'It was brilliant! Brilliant! *Operation Brilliant!*' Mr Goldfish says when I've floated out of the classroom and through the rest of the day on feet that barely touch the ground.

'I told you it was a good idea.'

'And I should've listened!'

It's already getting dark. I waited half an hour to make sure Connor and Adam's bus had left before venturing out of school. I'm not in a rush. Jack's going to the dentist after work and Mum's staying late for Parents' Evening at her school so I'm free for one more hour. It shines before me, a whole circle of time, the size and shape of a full moon, all silvery and spectacular. 'We got it. We actually got it. The address!'

Mr Goldfish's light seems to brighten as I point him at a street name.

'Beech Road. We're getting close.' I refer to my phone, open on a picture of Mr Richardson's driving licence – a photo card with two lines of tiny black words that let's be clear I will never tire of reading. Tapping the screen with my

[185]

thumb, I zoom in on his address then flick to my map. 'We want Reeves Road. I think it's just up here. Near Gran's house, actually.'

My stomach lurches because this makes total sense. Gran's lived in this part of Manchester pretty much her whole life and maybe Mr Richardson has too. He might have known Mum when they were younger, back when she had dyed red hair like Miss Gilbert's. Perhaps they even dated and that's why he offered to donate his sperm when she was having trouble getting pregnant.

'It's possible,' I say defensively, expecting Mr Goldfish to contradict me, but he salutes.

'Whatever you say, boss!'

He darts ahead, weaving between streetlights the same colour as his skin. I follow, hurrying past a row of red semi-detached houses, flushed with pleasure, like definitely they have been waiting for me to walk down this street is the exact feeling I get from their smart front doors and neat lawns, trimmed in preparation for my visit. A few Christmas trees are twinkling in porches and lounge windows.

Mr Goldfish spins round a lamppost then returns to me with a neat backstroke. 'What's the plan when we get there?'

'Peep through the window.'

He smacks his fin against my palm. 'Genius. Pure genius.'

'As soon as I see Mr Richardson, it will be obvious whether or not I belong in there with him. And then there's

Henry. If there are similarities between us, that will be proof, won't it? That we share genes? That Mr Richardson is my dad?'

'Absolutely. Concrete proof. Bravo, Tess. It's an excellent plan.'

Nothing can go wrong, that's how it feels in my body so powerful and strong as I stride down the road. I am Tess the Almighty, Tess the Conqueror, Tess of Getting Things Done and Making Things Happen and Taking Risks That Absolutely Pay Off.

The first left passes in a blur, and the second, and then the third appears, this opening to a street that is about to become extremely significant in my life, I just know it. On feet that have never been so nimble, I speed along the pavement until I reach number twenty-four, larger and more impressive than the other houses on the street. In a row of red, it's the most red, and its Christmas lights shine brighter and more magical than any others for miles around.

'There it is,' Mr Goldfish says.

'Let's do this.'

I set off up the drive.

I am a quarter of the way there.

Half-way there.

Almost there – and with an injection of pace I weave round two plant pots then flatten myself against the house.

I duck beneath the windowsill before peeping over the ledge, straightening my legs slowly.

'The fruit bowl?' Mr Goldfish suggests. Hiding behind it, I peer through a space between a tangerine and a banana. I can see it at last through a tiny gap, the amazing world of Mr Richardson's kitchen, basking in the light of a cosy lamp.

Something finally clicks into place, or maybe I click perfectly into *this* place. Yeah, that's what it is. I belong here. I fit. My awkward edges feel smooth and a weird sense of calm washes over me, even though I'm spying through a teacher's window and could be caught quite easily. I'm serene. I know without question this is where I should be.

There are maths magnets on the fridge and a Sudoku mug on the draining board and an actual goldfish in a tank by a comfy armchair where I could curl up and tell Mr Richardson about my day as we drank tea and shared Blue Riband biscuits.

'How about the bush over there?' Mr Goldfish asks. 'Is that the perfect place to do a wee because—'

'Yes, I'm desperate. Thanks for pointing it out.'

'It's all part of my stellar service as your—'

'Ssh!'

'—I was going to say *imaginary friend*. As in, someone who talks inside your head. As in, someone who doesn't make any sound so doesn't need to be told to—'

'*Ssh!*' I say more urgently, tying to quieten my mind and focus because the house is suddenly alive with noise.

A TV has been turned on, or someone has opened a door to let the sound of it out into the hall. That must be it, because I can hear voices too – one male, one female – getting louder by the second. I can't make out the words, but I know who it is from the tone. The unusual cadence. The cool, slow drawl.

It could only belong to one person, and sure enough Anna walks into Mr Richardson's kitchen, accompanied by the best-looking boy I've ever seen in my life.

'What's she doing here?' I mutter, definitely not as surprised as I should be. For some reason, I am just not that shocked to see Anna stroll into the place I want to be more than anywhere else.

She's standing in the middle of the kitchen as if she owns it. Tara and Sarah appear next, and then two other boys. It's the girls' first visit, I can tell by the way they're looking round, taking in the unfamiliar surroundings before carrying on chatting, like they've just entered any old room in any old house rather than the most incredible kitchen of all time.

Mr Goldfish tugs my sleeve. 'Let's go, Tess! This is too risky.'

He's right, but I can't seem to move. The boy who must be Henry stoops to open the fridge and a hungry look flashes in Anna's eyes for something other than food. She wants him, no doubt about it. It's written all over her face, normally so unreadable – and then it's gone, deleted, the sizzling letters of her red hot DESIRE disappearing the instant the boy stands up with a six-pack of Coke. It's impressive, how cool she is when he offers her a can, shaking her head as if thirst is beneath her, something that affects lesser mortals with weaker throats.

He shrugs, chucking cans to everyone else. He really is the best-looking boy in the entire country, never mind Manchester, tall and blond and—

'Maybe also your brother,' Mr Goldfish reminds me. 'You're supposed to be looking for clues that you're related, not lusting after someone who might be—'

'Don't say it again!' I squeal, horrified with myself and my incestuous thoughts in no way appropriate. Henry takes some crisps out of a cupboard, reaching up to the top shelf so his T-shirt lifts to reveal abs that make me blush. Putting on my most rational head, I pull him apart, divide him into arms and legs and face and hair, performing a post-mortem because he's dead to me as a romantic option.

Our hair's the same colour when mine's not dyed.

He's broad-shouldered, and I'm broad-shouldered.

And we have the same strong jaw.

And similar noses.

And also our skin is pretty much the identical shade of beige.

I duck beneath the windowsill and press my back against the wall, needing it for support.

'Woah,' Mr Goldfish says. 'That's uncanny.'

'I'd love want to see his eyes.' In case there's any confusion, I add, 'Just to check the colour. Not as he leans in for a kiss or anything. I would hate that.'

Mr Goldfish says nothing.

'Honestly. It would be totally wrong and disgusting. Horrid. I can't think of anything worse.'

Still nothing.

'It makes me feel sick just thinking of it. Yuck,' I say, my mind lingering on an image strictly forbidden before I can banish it out of sight. 'I am not into that kind of thing.'

'I hope not, Tess. I wasn't wearing a *My Friend Loves Incest And I Am Proud Of It* T-shirt last time I checked . . . What?'

'Nothing. It's just – nothing.'

'I know,' he says. 'You miss her. Come on. Let's go before they realise you're here.'

'*We're* here,' I correct him. Holding him out, I slip down the drive and follow his light all the way home.

CHAPTER 26

Except it isn't my home. It's more obvious than ever as I step into the kitchen, blinking three times when I turn on the light. It's too stark, the complete opposite of cosy. Jedi scampers down the stairs and bounds up to me, ears flapping and tail wag-wag-wagging at top speed.

'I wouldn't leave you behind, boy,' I tell him in my head. He rolls on his back with his paws in the air so I give his belly a good scratch.

'Do me!' Mr Goldfish cries, bursting out of my pocket to lie on his back too. 'Do me, not him!'

I stroke Jedi's whiskery chin. 'When I move in with Mr Richardson, you're coming as well.'

The sooner, the better. It's suffocating in this house. Jack is everywhere, in the order of the shelves and the precision of the dishwasher and the neat stack of post from the past few days. I check it quickly but there's no letter from CAMHS.

'Hello!' Jack calls, opening the front door. 'Good day?'

He takes off his shoes and pads into the kitchen. 'Have you only just got in, Tess? Where've you been? Why aren't you upstairs making a start on your homework?'

I feel it more acutely than ever, the distinct lack of shared DNA as I stare into his cold blue eyes. He's a stranger to me and I don't have to do anything he says I tell myself firmly because part of me wants to run upstairs like a good little girl who's still keen to impress her dad.

Onto the counter, Jack drops a paper bag stuffed with food from the organic shop.

'I'm sick of having this conversation with you, Tess. Please just do as you're told, eh? This is a big year, isn't it? Exams? You can't afford to take your eye off the ball.' He points upstairs. 'Go on, now.'

I move to the kettle to make a cup of tea. I slink over to it, channelling my inner-Anna, making my skin tougher and my pulse slower and my feet firmer as I stand in the kitchen as if I own it and look at Jack like he does not own me.

The kettle takes forever so I play with Mr Goldfish, twisting him in my hands.

'For crying out loud, Tess! Stop messing about with that stupid kids' torch and do something productive for once in your life!'

I flare up because he's gone too far this time. No one bad-mouths Mr Goldfish in my presence and gets away with it.

'Yeah, Jack,' Mr Goldfish cries, making a fist out of his fin as he hides behind my shoulder.

'I mean it, Tess.' I take a clean cup out of the dishwasher and a teaspoon out of the drawer. 'Are you listening to me?' I get a teabag out of the silver pot. 'You're really trying my patience, you know that?' I drop the teabag into a cup, a plain white one with absolutely no pigs to speak of. 'I'm warning you,' he says through gritted teeth. 'If you make that tea, you will be going without food tonight.'

I make the tea.

And I take a couple of biscuits out of the tin and stuff them in my mouth. Chocolate and caramel ooze over my tongue as Jack's lips tighten.

'That's not going to help, Tess.' I grab another biscuit. 'Comfort eating is not the way forward.' I grab two more. 'For God's sake, you're already big enough as it is!'

He's never articulated this so explicitly before, and he hangs his head in shame. This is the closest we've ever come to being honest and I silently dare him to say them out loud, all six hundred and seventeen words of his blog.

'Look. I'll make you something healthy, okay? That's all I meant. Something nutritious.' He gestures at the bag of food. 'I've got some courgettes.'

I love courgettes, but not as much as chocolate. I take one more biscuit then walk to the table. Jack tracks my every move, his eyes narrowing as I sit down and grab the remote. We both jump at the sound of the TV because neither of us expected me to turn it on. I choose the most irritating programme I can, something loud and brash and American then make a big show of settling down to watch it, cradling my tea in both hands.

'Fine. Fine. It's your life you're ruining, Tess. But just so you know,' he whispers, holding up his finger and thumb, deathly pale in the stark, white light, 'I'm this close to giving up.'

He sweeps out of the kitchen.

'You can't give up on something you were never on board with in the first place!' I bellow behind lips that burn with how much I want to scream the words out loud. 'I saw your blog. I know how you feel so stop pretending that you care! You don't love me and you never have!'

Tea sloshes everywhere as I slam down my cup then dash into the study. Jack's desk stands against a teal wall dotted with silver frames – his certificate from drama school and a poster from *Hamlet* and a review from his episode of *Lewis* that doesn't even mention him by name. They're bunched up on the left, nothing but empty wall to the right.

'Please tell me you're not looking for the blog,' Mr Goldfish groans when I turn on the laptop.

'It's not on the Internet. I'll have to find the file on here.' The shower comes on upstairs. 'He'll be busy for a while.'

'It's going to hurt you.'

'That's the point.' It would give me a savage sort of pleasure to be confronted once more with the extent of Jack's betrayal in undeniable black and white.

'How long does it take to have a shower, though? Ten

minutes?' Mr Goldfish flits nervously about the desk, circling Yorick and the framed poem by Robert Frost. *Two roads diverged in a yellow wood* it starts, and that sounds about right to me. I'm at a crossroads, aren't I, with Jack on one side and Mr Richardson on the other. There's no doubt in my mind which path I should take. 'Five minutes? No, one minute, apparently,' Mr Goldfish squeaks because Jack's footsteps are thundering down the stairs.

'Look at the tea on this table! Who are you? Gran? Would it have killed you to wipe it up?' I can hear Jack rummaging in the bag of shopping. He charges into the study in a stripy dressing gown, holding a new bottle of shower gel. 'What are you doing in here, Tess?'

I've got as far as opening up Microsoft Word and typing the first three letters of the file name into the search bar.

DCN—

I try to delete them, going for the button but missing it completely because my eyes are on Jack watching me fumble with hands definitely up to no good.

'Why can't you use your own laptop?' He sounds irritated because this study is more his domain than even the dishwasher. Everything has its place – every book on the shelf with its spine not at all broken, and every pen in the pot with its lid not at all chewed. Jack gives me this look like I don't belong, a biro that has run out of ink or a book with tatty pages and a story not worth reading.

'What are you trying to do? Homework, is it?'

[196]

The search bar on the screen winks at Jack. *DCN*, it says, over and over again, *DCN*. It's flirting with him, daring him to fill in the other letters. The screen flickers. I wait for the penny to drop. I can almost see it floating high above Jack's head, a coin that contains my face instead of the Queen's, the date of my conception engraved clearly on the metal. It doesn't fall, and that's a shock, how much I wish it would.

He sighs. 'Is it the printer you're after? It's not hooked up.' He messes about with a couple of wires. 'There you go.'

He's going to stay and watch me do it, so I go to Google and randomly type in *Othello*, copying and pasting a couple of paragraphs into a new Word document.

There's a whir and a wheeze and then the printer begins with a mechanical *jjj – jjj – jjj*.

As the paper emerges, I grab Mr Goldfish and shine his light on the ceiling, writing the letters I was too afraid to type.

DCNETWORK BLOG
DCNETWORK BLOG

The words gleam above Jack, even if he can't see them.

I don't stop there. In my room, I shine Mr Goldfish out of the open window, using the stars like a giant join-the-dots puzzle. They glow as the beam makes contact, the words I can't say out loud twinkling over Manchester, brighter than the car headlights and the cats' eyes and the Christmas trees and the streetlights and a million TVs flickering in a million homes with a million ordinary mums and dads with absolutely no secrets.

I love you, Gran, I scrawl across space. It reflects in her eyes as she looks out of her lounge window, pouring herself another cup of tea from the pot covered in a lion's face. It purrs to the one on the mantelpiece, who purrs right back.

If I have to, I will buy every bottle of polish in the supermarket to keep Mum and Jack off your back.

'That's sweet,' Mr Goldfish says, opening his mouth even wider to project the words into the sky. 'Nothing says I love you like a bit of dusting.'

When Mum comes home, she asks Jack if I'm okay.

NO I write, again and again, the word getting bigger, my arm swooping more madly until the only thing in the universe is my cry of protest.

I AM NOT OKAY
I AM NOT
I AM NOT
BECAUSE I KNOW THE TRUTH

The words are jagged, tearing apart the sky with their ferocious lines and sharp angles and spiky edges.

I write to @BlaiseOfGlory and everyone on Twitter, posting replies in my very own cyberspace, hanging half out of the window now so I can stretch further, shining Mr Goldfish from one side of the black horizon to the other. I own this night. It is my World Wide Web, my forum, and I tell everyone what I think of them and Jack too, scribbling my response to his blog in stars that have never shone more fiercely.

'I don't mean to be a kill-joy or anything,' Mr Goldfish pants, 'but I could use a break. I'm exhausted.'

I place him on my desk next to my Sudoku book, but I haven't finished yet. No way. Picking up my phone, I open Twitter, my vision blurred from the dazzling display in the night sky. The screen's hazy, moving in and out of focus as I invent an anonymous name.

@FishOfGlory

I feel as tough as my friend, as bright and bold, my heart thumping wildly in my chest as if powered by the world's biggest battery.

'Now what?' Mr Goldfish asks. I scan the endless words that have been written about me in the past few weeks.

I grin. 'Revenge.'

Tess-tosterone got changed for PE in a toilet cubicle today. What's she trying to hide? #SheIsAHe

Her disgust at your vanity and the way you pout in the mirror.

Anyone else notice that she's got a moustache? #SheIsAHe
Who? Your mum?

I saw a bulge today. That's all I'm saying. #SheIsAHe
Could have been that spot on the end of your nose.

I don't stop for fifteen minutes, replying to old tweets and new ones that keep pinging through. I have an answer for everyone, typing quickly with two thumbs that find the perfect words without effort.

'It's beeped again!' Mr Goldfish cries. 'Look, look, look! It's Blaise-Of-Glory! What did she say?' He swims up to my phone, flattening his nose against the screen.

Who is @FishOfGlory anyway? Is it you, Tess-tosterone? What, are you so pathetic you even have to hide on here?

'What a hypocrite! Anna's hiding, isn't she?'

'We don't know it's Anna,' I say. 'Or even if it's a girl for that matter.'

'Ask. Go on. What've you got to lose?' I type something all in a rush – *Says @BlaiseOfGlory #potkettleblack* – then press *send*. 'Brilliant,' Mr Goldfish says. 'That will have her quaking in her boots. Talk of kettles.'

I wait, the pulse in my neck beating so hard, my head feels as if it's throbbing.

I haven't hidden my identity, Tess-tosterone. It's here for all to see.

'Well, that makes no sense,' I mutter, before writing a quick reply.

If you say so.

I get a response immediately.

You have to be clever enough to see it, unfortunately for you.

'See what?' Mr Goldfish asks. I study the avatar of the mysterious account – a cartoon image that gives nothing away. 'Blaise. Blaise. *Blaise.*'

'Stop saying Blaise!'

'*Blaise.* It's weird though, isn't it? Who calls themselves Blaise?'

CHAPTER 27

'How do I look?' I ask the following day.

'Cheep.' I frown. Mr Goldfish jumps onto the lid of the loo in the girls' toilets. 'Not cheap as in cheap.' He makes wings. 'Cheep as in little chick. You know, cute little feathery thing.' We stare at each other as he clucks. 'Never mind.'

'What about this?' I fiddle with the hem of a jumper I found in the back of my drawer. 'It's not too frumpy, is it?'

He holds up his fin to make an 'okay' sign. 'It's ideal. Plain as plain and black as black can be. The perfect plumage because you're a—'

'Bird underneath Mr Richardson's wing. Yeah, I get it. And these?' I pull up my trousers to reveal two colourful, mismatched socks.

'You look great, Tess.'

It feels pretty great, like I'm pledging allegiance to the only person who I can trust.

Hiding Mr Goldfish in my pocket, I make my way to the sink and study my reflection in the mirror. I do look like

Mr Richardson, if you ignore my dyed hair and the fact I have no dimple. We are carbon copies, cut from the same cloth, black as the night at the very end of the solar system, swirling round Pluto, the planet of introversion. Black as silence. Black as—

'Tess?'

'Crap,' says me or Mr Goldfish as Anna and Tara and Sarah crowd round me in a tight semi- circle. I turn on the tap, glancing at the trio in the mirror, wondering how it feels to be them, these girls with glossy hair and confidence to match, who hang around with older boys in teachers' kitchens.

'You off up to Maths?' Anna asks with a dazzling smile. She's stunning, no doubt about it, the type of girl Jack would love me to befriend. I picture it, sitting with Anna at lunch, and walking with her out of the school gates, and following her maybe even into Mr Richardson's house. 'We're going that way. You can join us, if you like.'

I do like.

I think I like.

Actually I'm not at all sure that I *should* like.

Man Skull's wearing a skirt. I didn't know they made them in man sizes. How does she fit her fat legs inside it?

'Precisely,' Mr Goldfish whispers. 'You're speaking sense at last. She can't be trusted!'

Something else comes back to me – a white hand drifting through the icy air as it dismisses Connor Jackson. *Man*

Skull was obviously a joke. You know that, Tess, don't you?
I'm still not sure of the answer to that one, so I carry on washing my hands.

Soap. Bubbles. Rinse.

'Maths?' Anna turns off the tap.

She links me. I want to enjoy it, like this is a really good thing I tell my arm very clearly, but it stays completely rigid. Anna pulls me out of the toilets into a corridor full of not that many people because lessons started two minutes ago. Mr Richardson will be pacing round the classroom, yearning for his favourite student.

I'm here. I'm coming.

We start to walk, the four of us together, and I can't quite believe it, how I appear to be sort of in their gang. Just as I'm relaxing into the arm-link, Anna ends it, shoving her hand into her bag and pulling out her phone when it beeps.

'It's Finn. They've finished for the day.'

'God, college is easy,' Tara mutters. 'They have more free periods than lessons.'

'The boys are going into Manchester,' Anna says casually as I swallow a firework that explodes in my stomach. 'Shall we go and meet them?'

'And what? Skive school?' Sarah replies. 'We can't do that. It would look too obvious if three of us were absent.'

'Four of us,' Anna corrects her, nodding at me. 'Maybe meet them later then.' Texting as she walks, she starts up the steps. I follow, my head spinning in delirium of the most delicious kind. It is effortless, this climb. I am light. Airy. Full of helium as I bob after Anna, my head shiny as a foil balloon, somewhere near the ceiling.

Anna stops abruptly when we reach the top. 'Damn. I've forgotten it.'

'What is it, Anna?' Tara asks. 'What have you forgotten?' It sounds rehearsed, like a script.

'My homework, Tara. That worksheet we had to fill in.' She turns to face me, a couple of steps below. The sun burns its way through a cloud and sets her outline on fire. I have to squint to gaze up at her. 'Did you do it, Tess?'

'Did she do it?' Mr Goldfish scoffs. 'She only spent two hours on it last night, triple-checking her answers to make sure they were absolutely right.'

'Shut up!' I tell him because I don't want to hand it over.

'Do you mind if I copy it quickly? Sorry. Shouldn't keep asking you questions when you can't reply. Still, I know the answer to this one.' She holds out her white, white hand with all this Expect that I am just going to obey.

And I do.

Of course I do. It's Anna, and she gets whatever she wants.

'Thanks so much,' she says when I pass her the worksheet. 'That's so good of you.'

The classroom door swings open. 'What time do you call this, girls?'

'Hello again, Sir,' Tara replies, bold as anything,

bounding up the steps to greet Mr Richardson. Sarah crowds round him too, but I hang back with Anna, hoping that he'll notice my black jumper. 'Remember us?'

'You're late.'

'How could he forget?' Sarah replies. 'We're his favourite students, aren't we, Sir?'

'Not right now, no.' He's trying hard to remain cross but a hint of amusement has crept into his voice. 'I prefer pupils who are a tad more punctual.'

'Boring, you mean,' Tara replies. 'We're full of surprises. Good ones, right, Sir?'

'Oh, delightful.'

'I bet it was the best surprise,' Sarah says, quite seriously. 'Us lot, in your house. I bet you couldn't believe it.'

'I was – how can I put it? Overjoyed. Yes. There is nothing I like more than getting home from work after a particularly tough day to find pupils in my house, eating my food, watching my television.' His tone is exasperated but his eyes are shining as he takes in Tara and Sarah and also Anna, but not me or my black jumper. 'Right, ladies. Time's ticking. I'll take your homework off you here and then we can go and get on with the lesson.'

Tara hands in her worksheet, and Sarah hands in her worksheet, and Anna hands in my worksheet, without so much as a glance at me. A cry of outrage echoes round the cavern of my mind where no one but Mr Goldfish can hear it.

'Tess? No homework? Well, that's disappointing,' he sighs, but the air from his lungs is warm on my face. I am visible at last, one of the girls, standing in front of him in disrepute. I love how he's shaking his head, taking in all four of us now.

'You lot. You'll turn me grey. I'll have to keep you behind after school, I'm afraid, Tess. Fifteen minutes in here at the end of the day.' He sounds apologetic, but he needn't be sorry because actually this is the best news I've had for ages.

A hush falls as we enter the classroom. It's a spell we're casting as we walk. Only Isabel is unaffected by our magic, rustling about in her pencil case, getting out a protractor so she can start work. Isabel. Isabel. *Isabel.*

'Stop saying Isabel!' Mr Goldfish whispers.

'*Isabel.* Oh my God!'

'What is it?'

'What did those tweets say last night? *I haven't hidden my identity. You have to be clever enough to see it, unfortunately for you.* That's why it's spelled in such a weird way. I mean, why not blaze as in b–l–a–z–e, right? The letters are important.' I scribble them down then rearrange them to form Isabel's name.

'No!' Mr Goldfish cries.

'Yes,' I reply, my stomach twisting into a knot. Blaise is Isabel. Isabel is Blaise. I watch her calculating the size of an angle, radiating anger that the lesson has been disrupted.

Her jaw is set. She's determined. Furious. Ruthless, when she wants to be.

Mr Goldfish shakes his head. 'I don't believe it.'

The knot tightens. 'Well, I do.'

CHAPTER 28

I don't wait outside Dining Room Three at lunch, and I avoid our bench by the Science block.

'It's easy to lie online, Tess,' Mr Goldfish says, again and again. 'There's no proof that it's her.'

The nausea is proof, the churning in my gut. I kill time trying to find Anna, hoping that she might link my arm again and whisk me off on an adventure. I'd happily skive the rest of the day as long as I could be back for Mr Richardson's detention.

Fifteen minutes alone with my teacher. A delicious slice of time, good enough to eat.

Somehow, the hands of the clock drag themselves to half past three. Two minutes later, I'm bursting into Mr Richardson's classroom as Mr Goldfish groans, holding his head between his fins.

'You dashed up those steps with no regard for me whatsoever.'

I drink in the sight of my teacher. My dad. Maybe my

dad. Probably. The tension between us is tight as string, like I feel as if I could reach out and pluck it, make us both quiver more than we already are. He's been waiting for this too. It's a big deal for him. It's a big deal for both of us.

'No regard for my comfort,' Mr Goldfish goes on. 'My safety. My head was smashing against your thighbone.'

'Ssh.'

'Repeatedly.'

'Please be quiet.'

'No exaggeration about forty-five times.'

'I'm trying to concentrate.'

'And I'm concussed!' he moans so I slip my hand into my pocket and turn him off. I have to focus. This might be my only chance to have some one-on-one time with Mr Richardson. Some father-daughter time. That's the connection between us, I am almost definitely sure of it, and I have the funniest feeling that Mr Richardson realises it too.

It's in his eyes. Or maybe his smile. Or maybe his hands, fiddling with the sleeve of his black jumper just like my black jumper. He throws a piece of chewing gum into his mouth, needing to freshen up his breath for what he's about to say. The words are new, shiny, never uttered before this moment of confession that's about to happen any second now, I just know it.

'Thanks for coming, Tess.' He is more than welcome. I go to sit down, but he says, 'Don't. We've got an appointment in Art One with your form tutor. We need to let her know what's going on.'

The tension in the air sags a bit. I love Miss Gilbert, but I don't want to see her right now. I don't want to see anyone, or go anywhere. I like being in here with Mr Richardson.

'Tess?' he says, because I appear to be staring intently into his truly remarkable brown eyes. He chuckles. 'You are funny. So intense. You remind me of my son.'

It's a throwaway comment, but I pounce on it with the hunger of a wild scavenger. I am a fox, running off with that sentence. A vulture, spreading my black wings as I soar with his words into the white, white sky. I do a loop-the-loop, perch high on a branch and crow with delight.

'Miss Gilbert will be waiting. After you.'

I step out of the classroom and start down the steps with all this Aware of his eyes on the back of my neck, prickling with goose-bumps. I wait for him at the bottom. I'd wait for him forever, but he's at my side two seconds later and we walk together to the Art block on feet perfectly in sync, no doubt precisely the same size. When I glance over my shoulder, I can see them, our identical footmarks stretching back down the corridor, back through the years and months of my life to the day of my conception.

'Well, hello there!' Miss Gilbert shouts over loud music, something with a lot of electric guitars. She's working at an easel and she's done a twisty thing with her hair, tying it in a messy red knot at the back of her head where it's held in place with a paintbrush. I am not the only one gazing at it in admiration. Mr Richardson can't take his eyes off it, or the loose strands of scarlet at the base of her neck where the silver clasp of a necklace catches the light. She glitters. Even in the darkest room, she would glitter. 'To what do I owe this great pleasure?'

I wait for Mr Richardson to remind her of the appointment, but he says nothing. His eyes are still fixed on those soft red tendrils. Miss Gilbert rubs the back of her neck, like maybe goose-bumps are prickling her skin too.

'Is everything okay?' Two crescent moons swing from her earlobes as she jumps off a stool. Her green Dr Martens squeak on the floor. A radio's lying on its back among a pile of paper, its wire tangled with the leg of the easel. She bends down to turn it off. 'With Tess, I mean?'

'That's dangerous.' He doesn't sound annoyed at her disregard for safety, more amused by it if anything. 'A radio down there. Beneath that. I'm guessing you have water on it?'

'On it? That's my easel, I'll have you know. My beloved easel. And yeah, I do have water on it as a matter of fact. But it's cool. I'm careful.'

'I have never met anyone less careful in my life.'

'Ha. Okay. But you love it.'

If I could sigh then I would sigh as the clock in Art One hits three thirty-seven. Miss Gilbert must sense my growing impatience because she says, 'So, what can I do for you, Sir?

Something to do with Tess, I'm guessing?' She pulls up two stools then sits back down at her easel. 'Make yourselves comfortable. And don't judge me, dudes. It isn't finished yet.'

We catch sight of the painting – a dolphin leaping out of an ocean as dawn breaks. There's nothing cheesy about it though. The sea is choppy and the sun is the smallest pinprick of white. The beach is stark, an ordinary stretch of sand briefly transformed into something spectacular by the appearance of the dolphin.

'Wow,' Mr Richardson says, and oh God I long for that type of reaction. Maybe if he could see how fast I can do a Sudoku puzzle, he might shake his head at me in all that wonder. 'That's quite something.'

Miss Gilbert looks at him hopefully then pulls a face, a childish one, sticking out her tongue. 'Not really. It's rushed.'

'It's incredible.'

'Dashed off in a double-free.'

'Even more impressive in that case, then.'

'Thanks,' Miss Gilbert says in a funny little voice. 'That's kind of you.'

They stare at each other with tingly eyes. Miss Gilbert blushes the same colour as her hair. She turns to me quickly with the air of wanting to talk about something safer and definitely more boring.

'Why are you here, Tess? Not in trouble, I hope?'

Totally in trouble is what I shout with my eyes, very sulky and rebellious as I tilt my chin to the floor but look up at an extremely edgy angle. *I am off the rails* my rock star pout seems to say. *Out of control.*

Mr Richardson waves a hand. 'Oh, it's nothing serious. A missed piece of homework.'

'Er, Tess? Did Sir say you could leave?' Miss Gilbert asks because I'm standing up. I've had enough.

'It's fine. She's done her time.'

I almost cry out in dismay. It isn't true. There's still five minutes of my detention left, three hundred precious seconds he's willing to throw away. I hate him suddenly, all my love turned inside out to loathing. There's a valley, plunging into darkness, where there used to be a mountain. But then he smiles at me – properly, fully – and the world shifts again, like I can actually feel it happen, the plates of the Earth moving beneath my feet.

'No need to come down on her too hard. She's a good student.'

'I know she is,' Miss Gilbert replies.

'The best student in my class, actually. The others are quite chatty. It's great to have someone so quiet and focused.'

I revel in my silence.

CHAPTER 29

'Watch where you're going!'

Connor sticks out his foot and I stumble, but just about manage to keep my balance. My bag's not so lucky, clattering to the ground where it bursts open and spews out my stuff in a spectacular vomit. It's not the school books I'm bothered about. It's the Sudoku one I filled in last night, every single page of it as I imagined Miss Gilbert walking down the aisle to marry Mr Richardson. Obviously their favourite student was a bridesmaid, unconventionally beautiful in a big black dress and sparkly silver boots. We had champagne. Danced all night. And then we moved in to our new home with a kennel for Jedi and an annexe for Gran.

Adam laughs. 'Trip over them, did you? Are they affecting your balance now they've dropped?'

'So, come on, Balls. Fill us in. Have you touched it yet?' Connor asks in a dirty whisper, moving closer to stand over me as I shove my books in my bag with frantic hands. 'Bet you exploded all over your bedroom ceiling, didn't you?'

'Bet you took the roof off your house.'

Connor snatches my bag. Before I can even process what's happening, he's pulled out the Sudoku book.

'No!' Mr Goldfish gasps.

If he flicks through the pages, he will see it, grid after grid filled with nothing but my teacher's name because definitely Mr Richardson is the answer to every question in the universe, let's be clear about that.

'Puzzles? Who brings puzzles to school?'

'Someone with no friends, that's who,' Adam says.

'You're right about that, mate.' Connor shakes his head at the front cover then chucks the book on the floor. As I go to grab it, he kicks it out of my hands and it flies down the corridor and falls open. I lurch after it, doubled over. 'Ad, get a picture of that! Amazing! Like a rhino or something!' Connor races past me and kicks the book again. There's the click of a phone and a shout of laughter. 'Get it up there now!'

'Maybe he's Blaise,' Mr Goldfish says, but I don't have time to worry about that. The Sudoku book has spun to a stop at a pair of black shoes.

I'd know them anywhere – and the left hand that picks up the book.

Two brown eyes widen in surprise. I must have written Mr Richardson's name over five hundred times.

Mr Goldfish hides his face, writhing in agony. 'I can't watch. It's excruciating.'

I can't either. Connor and Adam run off and then there is silence, ten seconds of silence that I feel in my throat, each tick like a thump of pulse.

'Well,' Mr Richardson says, rubbing the back of his head. I watch his fingers pull awkwardly at his blond hair. 'I think this is yours. A few of the answers are wrong, though.'

He's smiling. My heavy pulse becomes a flutter, the lightest flutter of butterfly wings as I begin to emerge from the darkness. He can see me. He knows why I wrote his name. He's been looking for me too, ever since he helped out Mum, the girl with the bright red hair and flower-stud in her nose who bewitched him as a teenager. It all fits.

'*Erm*,' Mr Goldfish says, but I turn him off because I don't want to hear it.

'Want to get lunch, Tess?' Anna asks when she finds me wandering the corridor. 'My treat to say thanks for the homework. It was good of you to man up and take the detention on the chin like that.'

Tara snorts and Anna glares and Tara regains her composure so quickly I might have imagined her losing it in the first place. I switch Mr Goldfish back on, needing his support.

'What was that?'

'I need your support.'

'Yes, you do, because this is a terrible idea,' he says as I follow the girls, who float into Dining Room Three in spectacular formation.

'Sit,' Anna says.

'Your name's Tess, not Jedi,' Mr Goldfish mutters, but I take my place at a large circular table in the very heart of the dining room. The girls chuck their coats and bags into the middle of it, chatting loudly. They own this space, that much is obvious, here at the centre of the action beneath a light shining brighter than the sun. The heat of it is intense, beaming down on me because I am here too, slap-bang in the middle of things, a Mercury at last.

I try hard not to feel out of place, but I am red-faced and sweaty and uncomfortable in the glare.

'I'll get you something,' Anna says. 'You man the table.'

I wait for a laugh that doesn't come. The girls join the queue and suddenly I'm alone in pretty much the most conspicuous spot in school. I feel ridiculous, painfully aware of the stares and the confused glances in my direction because I don't belong in this room, never mind at this table. I tap my knees then fiddle with my phone then play with a napkin, but as it turns out I am hopeless at origami. The graceful white swan I was attempting looks more like a plump turkey, pretty much how I feel among this elegant flock.

I chuck the napkin to one side, trying not to worry where Anna has got to.

'I bet I know.' Two suspicious black eyes peek out of my pocket. 'It's a hoax, isn't it? Blaise strikes again.'

'I thought you said it was Connor.'

'I said it could be Connor. It's more likely to be Anna. I bet she's spying on you through a window or something. Taking photos to put on Twitter. Laughing her head off because you're still waiting for her to return like *hashtag-the-world's-most-gullible-idiot*.'

Just then, Anna comes back, handing me a plate of food.

'Thank you,' I say in my head for Mr Goldfish's benefit. 'Thank you for doing exactly what you said you would.'

Anna sits down next to me. 'Everyone loves a burger, right?'

It smells incredible. As the other girls glide back to the table, I lift it up, my mouth watering, my lips parting to take a big bite that never happens because—

'Yeah,' Mr Goldfish whispers. 'Your new friends are giggling.'

'Sorry!' Tara gasps. 'It's just this joke that Sarah told us earlier. We can't get it out of our heads.' She collapses over her salad. I stare around the table. They're all eating it – seven small plates of crisp, green lettuce. 'That one about the er, the er, the—'

'—pig that crossed the road,' Sarah says as I go cold all over. 'Yeah, it's a good one.' They explode again then look back at me, still clutching the burger, meat juice dripping down my fingers.

'Shut up,' Anna says. 'No one wants to hear about a pig crossing a road. Tess is trying to eat.' She nods at my huge plate of food. I'm wary now, chilled to the bone. 'You're hungry, aren't you?' I don't reply, but that doesn't seem to matter. 'I thought so. Come on, then, Tess. That burger won't eat itself now, will it?' She smiles sweetly. 'Have a bite. Go on.'

I am not going to do it.

Definitely not.

So I have no idea how it ends up in my mouth.

'Keep eating. Go on. Very good.' Anna pats my arm. 'I thought you'd like it. So, Saturday night,' she says, and the feathers of her swan-like friends quiver in anticipation as the fat turkey tries not to keel over with painful indigestion. 'Finn suggested the bar we went to before. *The 312*. About eight.'

'Is Henry going to be there?' Tara asks, waggling her eyebrows, but Anna's feathers will not be ruffled.

'I dunno. Probably. You fancy it, Tess?'

I keep my face impassive, but my heartburn rages out of control and sets fire to my cold bones.

CHAPTER 30

Mum and Jack talk in the lounge as I hover on the landing. The lamp-lit glow of their conversation travels up the stairs, brighter at the bottom and petering out towards the top where I stand in pretty much darkness.

'So it went well, then?' Mum asks as Jack sits down on the sofa. I picture it, same as every evening – Mum sprawled against the cushions, feet curled in Jack's lap like a purring cat. 'They liked the idea?'

'They seemed to.'

'I knew they would.'

'They haven't seen the script yet.'

'It's brilliant.'

'You haven't even read it!' Jack laughs, and Mum does too. I turn my hands into puppets that guffaw on the wall.

'Call it blind faith.'

'Or blissful ignorance.'

'No,' Mum replies. 'I've read some of your stuff before. You can write.' The puppets stiffen, waiting for some mention of the blog that doesn't come. No doubt Jack is holding his finger to his lips and pointing upstairs as Mum cringes at the near-miss and nods. 'So, are they going to do it? Mr Darling and Nana, is it?'

'Yeah. Pete and Daniel. I think so, anyway – if it works around job and family, that sort of thing. But they seemed keen.'

'That's good.' I can hear the smile in Mum's voice.

'It's such a relief, Hels. To be in control of the material. To be in control of my own destiny. I know we've talked about money but, I don't know, I've been thinking. Now I've finished at the Volvo place I might take some time off before getting another temp job. Focus on the script?'

'Okay,' Mum says, simply. 'If that's what you want to do.'

'I'll work hard, and it will only be up until Christmas while I get the first draft finalised. It's just . . . I don't want to tempt fate, or anything, but – oh, I don't know.'

'Go on.'

'I've got a great feeling about it, that's all. Like it could be the start of something big.'

'That's brilliant, darling. We could use some good news, that's for sure.' There's a long pause. 'A psychologist, Jack. How did we end up here? That letter still hasn't arrived, you know.'

'I'll chase it up next week if we don't hear anything.'

There's silence again, and then Mum says, 'What did we

do wrong? Where did we mess up so badly? I miss her.'

'I know.'

'I miss her voice so much. Her laugh.'

'Her laugh most of all,' Jack says, and it sounds genuine, which takes me by surprise.

I miss them too, Mum and the dad I thought Jack was before I found out the truth. I move closer, but I haven't done up the laces of my silver Dr Martens so my tiptoe turns into a tumble as I clatter down the stairs.

'For God's sake, Tess. What are you—' Jack's words die as I appear in the lounge. The expression on his face blows me away, like have I actually got my outfit right for once is what I am asking myself in wonder. 'Tess!'

'You look gorgeous,' Mum says, leaping off the sofa with a glass of wine in her hand. She puts it down on the coffee table where a halo of red appears on the wood. It surrounds Mum too, this tipsy fuzz that makes her glow. 'I can't get over it. I love the dress. I absolutely love it.'

I bought it ages ago from a charity shop. It's flattering, pulled in under my chest and flaring over my stomach in a dramatic A-line with sequins that glisten on the hem and the halter neck. It's a vintage dress from the nineteen fifties, and yeah it might smell a bit foisty from the different cupboards it's lived in for over half a century, but it makes me feel good, like the combined power and beauty of all the women who have ever worn it is embedded in the silky black material.

'You look stunning.'

'Door,' Jack says, unnecessarily, because we can hear it for ourselves – an unusual knock, just two, slow taps.

'So you're actually going to go through with this?' Mr Goldfish asks, swimming about in my black handbag.

I steel myself. 'It looks like it.'

I received a text from Anna yesterday afternoon when I was at Gran's. *Henry's giving me a lift into Manchester so I'll call for you around seven thirty if you give me your address. Wear jeans okay? It isn't a dressy place.* Well, I didn't fall for that one now, did I, Googling *The 312* to check it out myself.

A swirl of cool wind announces Anna's arrival.

'Hi.'

'Hello,' Jack says, taken aback. She looks incredible – black shiny hair and purple vampy lips and a nose ring I could never pull off. She's wearing tight leather trousers and a full-sleeved blue top with an asymmetric neckline, coolly off kilter. She takes in my lack of jeans with a flicker of irritation that makes Mr Goldfish whoop in triumph. 'Sorry, I don't think we've met.'

'Anna.'

'Anna,' Jack repeats, sounding surprised but delighted. 'Anna, hey?' Despite everything, I bask in his admiration, flushing the colour of Mum's wine and feeling as alcoholic as it too. I'm twelve point five percent drunk on this moment. The rest of me is sober.

[224]

'You ready?' she asks. The answer is no, but I need to get closer to Henry if I'm going to get closer to Mr Richardson. I pick up my phone from the coffee table and drop it in my bag.

Mr Goldfish yelps. 'Are you trying to knock me out?'

'Where are you going?' Mum asks.

'Into Manchester,' Anna replies.

'To do what?'

'Go to a bar.'

Mum laughs, but she isn't amused. 'That's ridiculous. You're underage.'

'Let them go, Hels,' Jack says. 'This is a good thing for Tess.'

'Wrong!' shouts Mr Goldfish. 'She's walking into some sort of trap!'

'A really good thing.' He grins at Anna. 'Have fun.'

'Jack, have you lost your mind?' Mum says as I make to leave. 'Tess isn't going anywhere.'

'Don't embarrass the poor girl.' For once I agree with him. Anna's looking from Mum to Jack, a smirk on her face. 'Let her go. She's practically sixteen.'

'She's only just fifteen, actually. And you have to be eighteen to go to bars. She's staying right here. At home. With us.'

Anna shakes her head just once. 'No.' The cold wind blows into the lounge and whistles through the hollow O of that word, hanging in the air.

'What do you mean, no?'

Anna changes tack immediately, giving Mum a beautiful smile. It scares me, how easily she can turn it on, and I think back to a similar grin in a bus park after she had dismissed Connor.

'It's an underage night. At the bar we're going to. No alcohol or anything, so you don't have to be eighteen to get in. Everyone from school will be there.' She says this last bit to Jack because she's got the measure of him, all right.

Sure enough, he snaps his head towards Mum. 'Hear that? Come on now, Helen. It's such a positive sign that Tess wants to go out. With other people. To integrate with her friends. Let's not deny her the opportunity, eh?'

'Deny it!' Mr Goldfish urges, peering out of the bag. '*Deny it!*'

Mum blows out her cheeks. 'Fine. How're you getting home?'

'My mum will pick us up at eleven.'

'Okay then, Tess. You've got your phone, haven't you? Don't wander off out of that bar. What's it called?'

'Visage,' Anna replies.

'Lie!' Mr Goldfish bellows. He swims up to Anna and thrusts his fin in her face. 'You'll get found out.' She won't though. I bet if I looked, or Mum for that matter, there really would be a bar called *Visage* hosting its very own under-eighteen disco this evening because Anna is that good.

I pass over the threshold, stepping out into the grey fog of

[226]

the night. It's fierce and wolf-like, biting my skin, grabbing me by the scruff of my neck and making me shudder.

'Jacket!' Mum hurries after me with a brown duffel coat, not exactly suitable for this type of evening. 'Keep warm. And safe. Safe most of all.' She pulls me into a hug.

'I'll look after her, Mrs Turner,' Anna says.

'That's what I'm worried about.' There's a glint in Mum's eye that for once Anna seems unable to return. She uses Henry's car as an excuse to look away, nodding at the blue vehicle parked in the only empty space about thirty metres down the road. 'Come on, Tess.'

Mum lifts a hand that she doesn't wave. Her fingers are outstretched, sort of pressing against the night, like maybe she's trying to ward off all its dangers for as long as possible before I disappear out of sight.

CHAPTER 31

Even the back of Henry's neck is divine.

'You just used the word *divine*,' Mr Goldfish whispers as we pull into a depressing car park surrounded by iron fences complete with signs shouting out in big red letters that we are leaving the vehicle at our own risk. They don't need to tell me that. I know it's dangerous to step out of the safety of this back seat where I've been hidden away for the past thirteen minutes. Anna and Henry have been talking in the front, and a boy who I think is Finn has pretty much ignored me in the back. There were no formal introductions, just a nod of two heads as I climbed into the car.

'I know I did.'

'You sound about forty years old.'

'I know that too,' I say, but I can't seem to help myself. The back of his neck *is* divine, muscles I didn't know existed rippling above the collar of his T-shirt – the black collar of his black T-shirt.

'Like father, like son,' Mr Goldfish says in a warning tone that more than kills the mood.

In the car park, I stare determinedly at my feet, trying hard not to notice the musky scent of Henry's aftershave as he appears at my side.

'Nice boots.' He lights a cigarette and the world shrinks to the size of that fiery dot.

Mr Goldfish tuts. 'Lung cancer, that's all I can say.' Smoke drifts from a pair of perfect lips and joins the fog of this misty night. It swirls around me, clinging to my hair and my face and my body, seeping into every crevice. I blush. 'You won't be blushing like that when he's hooked up to a ventilator. And did you know that smoking makes men impotent?'

We wait for Henry to move because he's in charge of this evening, not Anna. I've never seen her like this – quiet, sort of cowed by someone else's presence. He lazily points the cigarette in the direction we need to go.

'Shall we?'

Anna buys cocktails for the girls but a pint of beer for me.

'I thought you looked quite thirsty.' She rubs my arm in the *oh so considerate* manner of a very good friend as she holds out the pint. 'Hope you like it.' I stare at the drink without moving. Maybe it's the dress shimmering with the strength of one hundred women, but I feel different. It might have wrong-footed me at first, this little dance between sweet and sinister, but I've got Anna's moves nailed now.

The sequins on my dress glitter dangerously, all these glinting eyes watching Anna watch me with a new expression on her face. She's on her guard. The silky black material hardens like armour against my skin as she puts the pint on a tall circular table in the middle of our group. Henry watches the whole thing, studying me closely.

The girls buy a second round, and a third, but the beer remains untouched.

'Lemme take a photo of you, Tess,' Sarah says, slurring her words. It takes her a while to find her phone even though it's just in her bag. Clumsily, she pulls it out then waves it above her head. 'Photo time! Just because you're really pretty. Everyone, tell Tess how pretty she is because she must feel so uncomfortable in that dress.' She points at my face that doesn't go red, and then at my feet, which stand their ground. 'Boots.' She giggles then hiccups. 'Very girly.'

'You are such a girly girl, Tess. You are. Totally. The picture of femin . . . femim . . . femiminity. That's why you should hold this for the photo,' Tara says, lurching for the pint and sloshing beer over Anna's blue stilettos.

'Watch it!' She snatches the glass out of Tara's hand then tries to force it on me. We're back here again, but this time it feels more threatening. She's drunk now, careless and aggressive, shoving the glass towards my chest. 'This drink cost me four quid, you know. Don't be so rude. Take it.'

Henry's still staring. I'm not the only one to notice the intensity of his gaze. Anna's tuned in to his frequency, same way I am, like we're both able to read his micro-expressions, the slight shifts in his mood, the irritation evident only in his knuckles as he grips his drink more tightly. He's angry, and I don't think it's with me.

Anna shoves the glass into my hand then glares at Henry.

'Look at you, staring at him. I mean her.' She pretends to gasp. It's an ugly movement, a palm flattening against pretty much her whole face. Swaying a bit, she picks up a cocktail glass smeared with purple lipstick then clinks it against mine. 'Cheers, Tess. *Chin, chin.*'

The girls collapse.

'Chin!' Tara cries in delight. She leans closer, studying my face. 'It really is massive, Tess. No offence.' The girls giggle. 'And look at that! She actually does have a moustache!' Three pairs of wild swan eyes fix on my upper lip. It takes more will-power than I knew I possessed to hold my head aloft. 'There, in the corner.'

Anna points at her own mouth, smearing her top lip to one side. 'If it was me, I'd wax it off, but then, that's the difference, isn't it? I'm female. Not like Balls, here.' It's a shock to hear her call me this, because even now, even though it's completely ridiculous, I want to believe that she was on my side against Connor in the bus park.

'When are you going to accept the truth, Tess?' Mr

Goldfish whispers. 'It's all been a game. She's Blaise, isn't she? It's so obvious.'

I think he might be right. Anna pats my cheek and tweaks my nose so hard I take a step back, splashing beer over my boots.

'Hey, hey, hey, where are you going?'

'Getting away from you,' Mr Goldfish snarls, but Anna has taken hold of my arm, her nails digging into my flesh.

'We love you, Tess, even if no one else does, okay? And we know you're a girl. We're on your side, right? Tara? Sarah? It's not us writing stuff on Twitter. It's the other freak. Isabel, in case you haven't worked it out yet.' Their nods are so exaggerated, I'm surprised their heads don't topple off their necks. I don't believe them, and the knot in my stomach eases slightly to think that Isabel might not be involved. 'We don't call you Tess-tosterone, do we girls? We know you're – what's that female hormone called again?'

'Say again? That female what?' Sarah asks, pointing nowhere near her ear.

'Hormone!' The quiet, slow drawl has vanished now. Anna's voice is out of control. 'Tess is full of that female hormone. What's it called. East – something?'

'Oestrogen.' It's Henry who says it.

Anna wheels round. 'Trust you to come to Tess's rescue. If you think she's so full of oestrogen, why don't you do something about it?'

[232]

'You're drunk, Anna.'

'I'm sober, to be honest with you. I can hold my alcohol better than any man in this room. Actually, I was making a very good point if you would just let me speak for once,' she slurs, stumbling on her stilettos. 'What I was saying was – if you think she's so special then go for it. That's your bag, isn't it?' She necks the last of her cocktail, the ice clinking against her teeth then smashing to the bottom of the glass. 'You're welcome to her. Him. It. Why don't we find out once and for all?'

Discarding her drink, Anna clutches my dress and starts to pull it up, exposing my knees. My thighs. I try to push her away but she's strong. People are looking. Some are laughing. And then Henry grabs her by the arms and practically lifts her away.

I smooth down my dress with trembling hands, my heart thumping against my ribs.

'Fat bitch.' Anna glares at me with an expression of pure loathing, her true feelings revealed at last.

'You don't have to listen to this,' Mr Goldfish urges. '*Go!*'

She rounds on Henry. 'If that is your type then go nuts. With her nuts. You know the rumour about her, right? That's she's got balls? There's photos and everything.'

'And who started that rumour?' Henry asks, sounding almost weary. 'You?'

'High five!' She holds up an unsteady hand that he ignores. She looks at Henry hard as she can when her eyes won't exactly focus. 'Go on, then. Take her. I dare you.'

She doesn't think he's going to do it. Neither do I, so it's shock for both of us when Henry puts down his glass. It taps softly against the table in a matter-of-fact sort of way, like it's no big deal, how he's walking away from his friends towards the luckiest girl in the room who just so happens to be me.

'Fancy getting out of here?'

'All right, you've made your point,' Anna says, and she tries to laugh with Tara and Sarah, but they're staring at Henry in disbelief. 'You don't have to take her anywhere. I wouldn't subject you to that. Talk about an—'

Henry puts one hand on each side of my face and kisses me suddenly.

CHAPTER 32

'I'm guessing now isn't the time to remind you that he could be your half-brother?' Mr Goldfish asks as Henry pulls away.

Our hands are still touching. There is nothing in this bar apart from the tips of our fingers and the heat passing between them.

Mr Goldfish clears his throat. 'There is also me. I am in this bar. Right here. Talking to you.' He appears over Henry's shoulder, waving a bright orange fin. 'Hello? Hi? Remember me?' He jabs a fin at Henry. 'Remember him? Your maybe relative? Your quite-probably half-brother?'

My fingers go cold. Unbelievably, I am the one who breaks contact, but Henry doesn't seem to mind. He nods like together we've made the decision that it's time to go. I am dazed, disembodied, gazing down at a girl leaving a bar with the best-looking boy ever to have set foot inside it.

I can't resist glancing back at Anna and Tara and Sarah,

who haven't moved since Henry put his hands on my face where I can still feel them burn. The girls are completely still, mouths open – three horrified swans and one triumphant turkey, strutting out of the door. It's foggier than ever, as if the essence of Henry has thickened in the atmosphere because this boy, sighing at the murky sky, is the opposite of bright and clear and simple. He's no Mercury. He's cool and dark and mysterious. A Pluto, if ever I saw one, just like me.

'This is getting really weird,' Mr Goldfish mutters. I almost turn him off. I reach into my bag to flick his switch but stall at the last second. I need him, because yeah this is all becoming a little bit confusing, like I want to run away from Henry and also stay by his side forever, and these two competing forces go to battle in my limbs that freeze as he disappears down the road.

I follow.

Of course I do. I'm human, high on adrenalin, and Henry is impossible to resist.

I don't know what I expect to happen when I catch him up, but it's something incredible. Henry doesn't take my hand, even though it's readily available, swinging at my side. He doesn't look at me either, or speak, just trudges to a food van to get a hotdog.

He asks for fried onions and plenty of ketchup. I try to find the romance in this, but it's impossible when red sauce is splurging out of the bap onto his chin.

'Want some?' He holds it out, half-eaten, the sausage glistening with fat and spit.

It takes Henry precisely two minutes and seventeen seconds to finish eating, and I know this because I counted it out, the agonising passing of time where nothing happened apart from that mouth, chewing that hotdog. He wipes his hands on a napkin, screws it up, and drops it in a bin.

'I didn't even want that. But that's consumerism, for you. Capitalist bastards making us buy things we don't need.' He kicks at a polystyrene box. 'So much unnecessary packaging. Drives me insane. It's no surprise the planet is dying, right? You want a ride home?'

I glance at *The 312* in the distance, wondering if Anna is expecting me to return, loving the thought of vanishing into the night.

'You're going back in there?' Henry asks, misinterpreting the reason for my stare. He pulls a packet of cigarettes from his back pocket. 'Why are you friends with those girls, anyway?' His face glows orange in the flame of his lighter. 'Same reason I am, I suppose.' He laughs sardonically. 'They're fit, aren't they? Nice to look at? Popular? At least that's what Finn keeps telling me. He's into Anna for some strange reason.' He inhales deeply then blows smoke at the sky. 'Superficial bullshit. None of us is immune. It's pervasive, the sickness at the heart of our society.' He stoops over the bin, and for a second I think he might vomit, but then he reappears with something held delicately between his thumb and forefinger. It's a brown half-eaten apple that he spins like a globe. 'There is something rotten at the core of our world.'

'Is this what they call foreplay?' Mr Goldfish whispers, sounding uncertain.

'Something broken at the heart of everything, on every level. Think about it. The planet – broken. Society – broken.' Henry points at the apple, roughly where the United Kingdom might be. 'And us—' he glances at me '—the individuals, two little specks of nothing in all this madness . . .'

'Broken?' Mr Goldfish guesses, filling the long, strange silence.

'Totally and utterly screwed.'

I wouldn't speak in the car even if I could speak in the car. There are no words. Henry doesn't mind the silence. In fact, I think he quite likes it, driving along with even an engine that seems muted. It purrs quietly as we trundle at forty miles an hour down a road where the speed limit is sixty. He almost touches my knee every time he goes for the gearstick, which is a lot, because he can't make up his mind whether to stay in fourth or fifth. We drive and we drive and we drive and then we stop at a red light.

Mr Goldfish crosses his fins then nods at the clock on the dashboard. 'Good job we're not in any rush. Walking would be quicker than this. Does he realise it's gone green?'

Evidently not, because we don't move. The van behind us revs its engine to make a point that Henry ignores. He's fixated on a stray dog running down the street, tail between its legs. That's how he looks too – woeful and lost and defeated by something, I don't know what. He would no doubt say *the world* but I wonder what it is in his world, or who it is that's responsible. Let's be clear, no one has a face like that over too much polystyrene packaging.

The van beeps. Henry blinks so slowly I think his eyes have closed for good. They open eventually, the rims pink and raw as he yawns in the darkness then pulls away, in no rush to get home.

To our home, maybe. He isn't a good advert for it, and that's a surprise when I think about the smiling boy in Mr Richardson's wallet. Something's happened to him, and it comes to me in a great flash of realisation that almost makes me groan at my stupidity. Of course that's what it is. It makes total sense. I have to fight the urge to grab Henry's fumbling hand as it fiddles with the gearstick. He lost his mum, and ever since that tragic day he's been struggling to find direction – in this car and also this life that has no meaning, not anymore. There's a hole where his mum used to be, a black gaping hole that only a new sister could fill.

'Not a girlfriend, then?' Mr Goldfish asks. 'Well, I'm glad that weirdness is over.'

I am too, because it's a lot simpler to know where I

stand, which is firmly by the side of my new brother I say to myself, trying to erase the kiss from my mind. It was for show, very much a closed-lipped sort of kiss. A sisterly kiss, full of tenderness and support because he needs me, and I need him, two broken individuals who are totally and utterly screwed without each other.

'You're pretty intense, you know that,' Henry says, looking at me looking at him with no doubt the warm eyes of a loving sister. I just about refrain from touching his arm in a gesture of sibling solidarity. He feels it though, I'm sure of it, glancing at me and glancing at me and glancing at me as we drive down a black road. 'Will you quit staring?' He lets out an odd bark of laughter. 'Don't worry. I do it too, according to Mother dearest. She's always telling me to lighten up.'

'From heaven?' Mr Goldfish asks slowly.

I wait for Henry to correct himself with a sob of anguish, to change his last sentence to the past tense, however hard it is. *I have to face up to the fact she's gone*, says the Henry in my mind as he grips the steering wheel in torment. *I have to face up to the fact she's dead and not coming back.*

The Henry on the driver's seat says nothing of the sort, however. 'My dad too. They're always going on about it. I'm a little—' he pauses – '*dark* for their tastes. They find my conversation around the dinner table rather gloomy. But it goes both ways. They're far too sunny for my liking.'

He pulls up outside my house, but I don't get out. Mr

Richardson is married, but he can't be married, but he is married, but he can't be married, and these two things clash in my mind until my head hurts and I have to turn off my brain, just for a minute, and sit.

That's all I do. I sit and Henry sits, cutting the engine with a twist of the key. There's still some fog, but it's thinner, and there's a breeze now, pushing broken wisps of cloud past the frowning surface of the moon. The universe is sad and angry, clouds escaping I don't know what, hurrying madly to I don't know where, but there's a sense of bailing out. Letting go. Giving up.

All is lost, that's how it feels as I undo my seatbelt with fingers that barely function on an arm more weary than it has ever been in its life. He is married, but he can't be married, but he is married, but he can't be married and round and round it goes until I close my eyes, dizzy with it all.

I see Mr Richardson and Miss Gilbert and the auburn woman from the photo in the wallet.

I open my eyes to find Henry offering me his hand.

'Well, this has been fun.' Another odd bark of laughter echoes round the car. I take him in – his forlorn brown eyes and tragic face that a thousand girls will definitely fall in love with. But not this one. I grab his hand and we shake solemnly. 'Actually, it's been more interesting than my usual Saturday night. At least I got to escape that bar nice and early. And I won't tell them, my mates, or Anna. We don't have to lie, but they don't need to know that I ate a hotdog I didn't want, spouted some bullshit about the decaying heart of humanity and drove here in silence. Let them think that we had sex. In the car. And that it was awesome.' He grins and shrugs. 'Only if you want to, that is. I'm just saying. I won't contradict whatever story they happen to believe.'

He shivers. Without the engine to work the heater the temperature has plummeted. He blows into his hands, and I blow into my hands, and the windows steam up all around us. My house fades, and my street, and there is just this car and this peculiar boy and this peculiar moment of calm before quite possibly a storm.

PART FOUR

CHAPTER 33

'So there isn't going to be a storm?' Mr Goldfish clarifies as I lie in bed on Monday morning, preparing to be struck down by a sudden bout of flu.

I hold out my hand as if I'm checking for rain. 'Nope. No storm. I was wrong.'

'Are you sure about that?'

'Absolutely positive.' I shine Mr Goldfish at my Maths textbook that just so happens to be sitting at the very top of a pile of homework. Of course I still did it yesterday to the best of my ability, pages thirty-one and thirty-two, just like Mr Richardson instructed.

'You're deluding yourself, Tess.'

I fling him to one side. We've been having this argument ever since I traipsed through the front door on Saturday evening.

'Home for ten twenty-seven? Not exactly a dirty stop-out, are you?' Jack said, shuffling along the sofa, patting the emerging space with a hand that just for once I hadn't the energy to disobey. I sat down next to him, leaning back against the cushion still warm from his body. It felt good after the chill of the car. My goose-bumps faded, the temperature of my blood rising a few degrees as I came back to life – to my life, in my house, with this family and this Jack, maybe not quite as bad as I once thought.

Mum held my left hand and Jack squeezed my right, crushing my thumb with his wedding ring. His *wedding ring*. His WEDDING RING. A jolt shot through me, almost making me leap off the sofa. I studied the ring, marvelling at its presence, its undeniable existence, its unmistakable thereness because Jack is unmistakeably married. Mr Richardson doesn't wear one, and if I could have sung then I would have sung that glorious realisation from the rooftops.

I twist Mr Goldfish around to look him in the eye. 'Henry was lying, or maybe he's crazy with grief, but Mr Richardson isn't married.'

'You don't have to wear a wedding ring to be a husband. And you don't have to be a husband to be someone's partner. You're being ridiculous.'

'I'll prove it to you. I'll go to Henry's today and we'll see who's right.'

'You should be going to school!' I pull the duvet over my head but Mr Goldfish wiggles beneath it. 'You can't avoid Anna forever.'

'She pulled up my dress in a bar. What's she going to do at school?'

Mr Goldfish glows brightly as he puffs out his orange chest. *'The only way to conquer your fears is to face them.'*

'Or hide from them beneath a duvet until they go away. Isn't that a quote?'

'True courage is—'

But I never find out what true courage is because Mum pokes her head around my door and I start to cough, right on cue.

'Tess, are you okay?' She turns on the light, hurrying to my bed as the spluttering lump beneath the duvet hacks up a lung or two. 'I thought you were coming down with something when you went to bed so early last night. Aren't you feeling very well?'

'She's fine,' Mr Goldfish mutters as Mum pulls down the duvet.

'New pyjamas.' Actually, they're old ones – an old black T-shirt and an old pair of black jogging bottoms and two odd socks that I put on yesterday afternoon to pledge allegiance to Mr Richardson. 'This is for you, darling.' She puts the pig mug on my bedside table. 'Is it your throat? Let me take a look.' She grabs Mr Goldfish, whose eyes bulge in shock. 'Open wide.'

'Arrrrrrrgggggggggghhhhhhhhhhhhhhhh.'

'Not you,' I snap before doing as Mum asked.

'It doesn't look sore, to be honest. There's no redness,

but that cough does sound nasty. I don't know.' She beats the torch in her hand.

'Ow, ow, ow,' Mr Goldfish says in time with the *tap, tap, tap* of his head against Mum's palm. She turns him off and drops him on my bedside table. It's strange seeing him like this, an inanimate object next to my Sudoku book. It makes me feel strange for talking to him.

'I'll have a quick touch, shall I?' Mum finds my tonsils quickly because her fingers have done this a hundred times before. I'm familiar territory, a landscape she knows well. She leans over me, the ends of her long hair brushing against my cheeks. It scares me how nice it feels, how easy it would be to say something in the voice she misses so much. *I'm here, Mum. I'm still here.* I'd tell her about Anna and she'd march into school to put a stop to it.

Our eyes meet in the brown cocoon. She smoothes back my fringe and smiles.

'I think you are a little off colour. There's a nasty flu bug going round my school. Loads of kids have come down with it. Better to be on the safe side, that's what I say. I know just what you need.'

She dashes off, clattering round the spare room then racing downstairs to boil the kettle. She's back a couple of minutes later, holding something behind her back. I'm curious. I don't want to be, but I am, watching the smile on her face double in size as she reveals the hidden object.

'My heart is your heart,' she whispers, and wow that

takes my breath away, this line from my childhood that she always used to say whenever she handed me the hot water bottle. It's small and red with a distinct smell of rubber that I want to hate but sort of love with all this Confuse in my nostrils. She nudges my elbow and nods down at the bottle, holding it out a bit, and then a lot more when I don't move. She looks so vulnerable, standing there with maybe her actual heart quivering in her outstretched hands, and I really want to take it, which is the precise reason that I don't.

CHAPTER 34

There are four letters scattered on the *Welcome* doormat but only one of them stops me in my tracks. *FAO the parents or guardians of Miss Tess Turner*. Well, I know what this is, all right, so I slip the letter in my pocket then pull on my boots and step out of the front door, relieved to be leaving because Jack's at home, working on his script.

I chuck the letter from CAMHS into a bin outside a grocery store, and in no time at all I'm on Reeves Road. It's freezing so I pull up my hood then hurry to Henry's house on feet that feel as if they're being pulled. It's irresistible, and I'm on the drive before I know it, moving towards the kitchen without stopping to check if the coast is clear. Mr Richardson will be at work and Henry will be at college so the house will be empty, I am certain of that fact, so I get the shock of my life when I peep through the window to see a woman with auburn hair making a cup of coffee.

I gasp, flattening myself against the wall as Mr Goldfish coughs smugly.

'I don't want to say I told you so but – I definitely did tell you so.'

'She could be a cleaner or something.'

I peer back over the windowsill to look more closely at the woman who's grabbing the milk from the fridge, taking a sip out of the bottle.

'I don't think that's the cleaner, Tess. At least I hope not. No. That's Mr Richardson's wife. She's the woman from the photo. And she has a ring on her finger.'

It glints as the woman stirs the coffee. She returns the milk to the fridge then drops the spoon in the sink where my face is hovering above the fruit bowl. She screams as Mr Goldfish yells, 'Hide!' and I do my best, like I sort of duck behind a bunch of bananas, but I've already been seen.

'At least pull down your hood and smile,' Mr Goldfish hisses as the woman looks all around, definitely for a weapon to defend herself against the hooded hooligan staring blankly over the top of a menacingly bruised banana. 'You look mental.'

I feel it too. I have a terrible moment of clarity, gazing down at myself dressed in black with my nose pressed against Mr Richardson's window as I skive off school to avoid a girl who's angry with me for kissing a boy who could be my half-brother. I feel odd. Not here. Dizzy and distant as I float into the sky. The woman opens the window so I dive into the blue with Mr Goldfish, doing a furious front crawl all the way to the other side of Manchester.

On this side of Manchester, the woman peers out of a cautious crack.

'What do you think you're doing?'

I pull down my hood to show that, hey, I'm just a girl with dyed black hair, bad roots and three spots on my forehead because I'm not even grown up yet. I'm fifteen and stupid and struggling I suddenly realise with tears that prick my eyes.

'Can I help you?'

'She's here to see me,' comes a voice from somewhere on the drive. 'We hooked up on Saturday night. Not like that,' Henry sighs as his mum goes pale. 'Honestly, Mother. One track mind. We're friends.' I like how he says that. 'You coming in?'

He doesn't ask how I know where he lives or why I've turned up unannounced, just strolls to the front door as if he expects me to follow. And so I do.

Mr Richardson's hall is full of ordinary things – a pile of clothes at the bottom of the stairs, pictures on the wall, a radiator, a thermostat, a table with a phone on it – but they seem special, imbued with meaning, sort of hallowed with a halo-like glow. He's worn those clothes. Taken those pictures. Turned down that thermostat. And made calls on that phone quite possibly to the HFEA in London to enquire about his long-lost daughter.

'Or to ring Miss Gilbert when his wife's in bed,' Mr Goldfish says.

'They're just friends.'

'So why were you so keen for Mr Richardson to be single?'

The question swirls around my mind as Henry beckons me into the kitchen.

'Mother – Tess. Tess – Mother. Julie, if you prefer.'

'Lovely to meet you.' Now that she knows I'm friends with her son, Julie's eyes are warm and welcoming with flecks of gold brought out by an unusual necklace with a large amber stone. 'Are you at the sixth form college too?'

'College, Mother. Not *sixth form college*. No one talks like that. And Tess doesn't talk at all, which, you know, is pretty out there. There is already too much bullshit in the world, right, Tess?'

I say nothing, but I feel eloquent, like maybe I'm communicating something pretty damn impressive, just by standing here in silence.

'I wish you wouldn't talk like that, Henry. It's crass.'

'The world's crass, Mother. Filthy and shallow and meaningless. I'm simply reflecting the quagmire that is society in my own dirty diatribe.'

'Are you, dear? That's nice,' Julie says, half-smiling into her coffee. 'Given that you're battling an existentialist sense of ennui, I suppose you won't want a piece of that?' She points at a chocolate cake. 'Pity. It's your favourite.'

'It was my favourite when I was ten,' Henry says, but he sits down at the table and gestures at a chair, telling me to do the same. It's incredible, the fact I'm here at ten past one on a Monday afternoon when I should be in school. It's so absurd, I almost laugh.

'How was *college* then?' Julie asks as Henry shoves his finger into the top of the cake then licks off the icing. She taps his wrist. 'And where are your manners?'

'The same place as everyone else's. Lost forever in our dog-eat-dog world.'

'And college? I asked about *college*, didn't I? Can you at least give me a straight answer to that? Did you hand in your Maths project?'

'Yes,' Henry says, in a mock-serious voice. 'I handed in my Maths project.'

'Good boy.'

'I'm not a boy,' he replies, but there is warmth between them, even if Henry doesn't say what his mum wants to hear. He's a Pluto, unashamedly different, and Julie gets that. Likes it, even.

'Cake, Tess?' she asks and I take a piece feeling more at home in this house than I have done in my own for weeks.

CHAPTER 35

It isn't even odd being in Henry's room. He holds up a vinyl record, black except for a white bird trapped inside a silver cage. He grins at me, his blond hair falling into his brown eyes, and how can a boy look so mainstream but be so unconventional is the question I am asking myself in wonder. The two opposite charges meet with an explosive power, static crackling and sparks flying whenever Henry moves or talks.

'Careful, Tess,' Mr Goldfish whispers.

'I'm comforted by him, that's all,' I reply, and it's true, because this strange boy makes me feel less strange, and more strange, and generally at ease with the whole idea of *being* strange, same way Isabel does. She would love Henry, no doubt about it. She belongs here, with us.

Music drifts from the record player.

My heart is crying, my lips are burning, desire going up in smoke . . . I choke, on all the things I want to say and do and change, I choke . . .

'It's about you, right?' Henry's eyes are closed, his fingers interlinked behind his head as he lies on the carpet. 'Cahill's a genius. He makes every song feel personal.' He opens one eye. 'In this case though, oh silent one, the lyrics do seem particularly pertinent.'

I want to ask what the song is called, and Henry must sense the question in the way I glance at the record player that whirs and clicks and plays something else.

'*Settle for Less.* Good title, don't you think? That's what life is, if you ask me. Settling. Trying not to settle. A battle between the two.' He leans up on one elbow and looks at me through his fringe. 'Did you have that thing when you were a child? Yeah, you must've done, because everyone did, right?'

I have no idea what he's talking about, but his weary tone has disappeared, his bored demeanour replaced by something more agitated and real. He sits up, locking his hands around his knees, the sinews of his forearms tense beneath the skin.

'Six, seven, maybe all the way up to ten or even eleven, you think you can do anything, don't you? People tell you regularly. *You can do anything. Be anything. Rule the world. What do you want to be?* That's what you're asked, over and over again, and I bought into it, you know? The myth. The idea that anything was possible. But it's bullshit.' He shakes his head and laughs, though it's clear he's not finding it funny. 'It's even happening now. Same at your school too,

I bet. Like last week, there was a talk by some guy who works behind the scenes for Formula One. I'm not into cars but his job was objectively impressive, like I could see that, right – the fancy hotels and the girls and the money, all that sort of thing. At the end, he looked at us, three hundred seventeen year olds sitting on those deeply uncomfortable green school chairs, and says, *This could be you in ten years' time*. Even points at the spot where he's standing, like it's going to be easy to step into his shoes. Follow his path. It was irresponsible, and that's what I told Miss Baynard who organised the talk, and then I get into trouble for speaking the truth.'

He blinks in disbelief at the memory, but he doesn't stop talking, gripping his knees more tightly.

'They think it's what we need to hear, but it's the opposite. Inviting glamorous people into college, asking them to parade their glamorous lives on stage, getting them to inspire us with their message that anything is possible if only we *believe. Dream. Reach for the stars*. Well, no thanks. That's not for me. I'm not going to get there, and neither are most people that I know, and that's fine by me. It is. It really is. When did it stop being fine for everyone else? The normal stuff. Sunday roasts and, I don't know, taking a walk in the park and listening to music and working in an ordinary job for an ordinary wage that will allow you to maybe go on holiday once a year, and really look forward to it too because you're not a greedy bastard wanting more,

more, more, all the time. That's who should be doing a talk at college. Seriously. Show me someone happy with a life like that, because it's enough. It should be enough. All that other stuff is meaningless.' He lies back down and stares up at the ceiling. 'I dunno,' he says, sounding tired again. 'It just makes me sort of sad.'

I think of Jack working on his script in the study, of his half-empty wall waiting for frames that never seem to come, and I feel sort of sad too.

'And me,' Mr Goldfish mutters. 'I'm depressed after that, anyway. Jesus. Talk about a downer.'

I think of our neighbour, Andrew, and of Uncle Paul and Aunt Susan, and of the lies Jack tells to these people about the life he's leading, and of the poem he recites about choosing a different path when really he's on the same road as the rest of us. I think of Captain Hook and Hamlet and Yorick, and of Jedi who adopted the skull after the first show, and of Jack who took it back and placed it on his desk. It's the battle between settling and not settling, and actually I think Jack finds it hard.

'Was that sympathy?' Mr Goldfish asks, but I don't respond because I'm not entirely sure.

It's overwhelming so I close my eyes. Music fills my brain, soothes my thoughts and calms me down. Henry chats a bit every now and again but mostly we're silent, letting the lyrics talk for us because they feel significant, like we are part of everything, or everything is a part of us.

Maybe one or two or ten thousand hours later, the front door opens and a soft voice calls, 'Hello?'

I sit up, disorientated. My body's heavy. My head's all of a fuzz. The music has stopped and the room has gone dark, too dark, because too much time has passed. My feet tingle on the carpet, blood rushing back into my toes as I come to my senses. Mr Richardson has returned home from work, and I need to escape before he realises I am here.

'Too late for that,' Mr Goldfish says, because my teacher is peering round Henry's door.

'Julie said a girl called Tess was up here.' He frowns. 'I see you know Henry like the rest of the female population of Manchester. What are you doing? You weren't at school.'

I flush and panic and flush a bit more.

'Relax, Dad. She's obviously off sick, isn't she?' Henry says from the carpet where he's still lying down, wafting an arm in time with some imaginary tune. 'Music therapy. Can't beat it. Good for the soul – and maybe the common cold, as well. Who knows?'

'She should be at home if she's ill, not up here listening to your nonsense. Julie had no idea you were a pupil at my school, Tess. She thought you went to sixth form college with Henry.'

The arm wafting stops. '*College*, Dad.'

'But it is a sixth form college, as opposed to a teacher training college or an agricultural one or a – anyway, that's not the – what I am trying to say is Julie would never have

[259]

let you stay, Tess, if she thought you were absent from school.'

'Close the door on your way out, Dad.' Mr Richardson steps into the room. He's wrapped up from the cold in a black scarf and a pair of thick black gloves. 'Oh my God. *Get out.*'

Mr Richardson laughs at his son's outrage. 'Did you hand in your Maths project?'

'He did,' Julie replies, appearing round the door.

'What is this?' Henry splutters.

His parents grin, putting their arms around each other in a smooth, practised motion I see twice more in my head – reliving it, rejoicing in it. Their bodies tessellate, the grooves of Julie accommodating the bumps of Mr Richardson, and vice versa, so they touch from their shoulders to their ankles, merging as one.

'Look at that,' I whisper as Mr Goldfish peeks out of my pocket. 'They're happy, which means—'

'What? It's even worse that he's been flirting with Miss Gilbert?'

'Talking to her, you mean.'

'Romancing, I think you'll find.'

'Conversing.'

'Seducing, Tess, and you know it.'

'No!' I say firmly. Mr Richardson is a good man. An upstanding citizen. A Maths teacher, for God's sake, more interested in chess moves than romantic ones.

'Can you get out of my room now, please?' Henry groans.

'Fine, fine, we're leaving,' Mr Richardson says. 'And you should too, Tess. Do you need a ride home? I'm sure my son will be happy to give you a lift, chivalrous as he is.'

Henry agrees and that's nice of him, but I can't help feeling disappointed that Mr Richardson didn't offer himself.

We reconvene in the hall, standing in a tight circle not the slightest bit claustrophobic. I belong here, with this family. Mr Richardson's black rucksack is sitting on the hall table next to the phone where definitely he rings the HFEA on a regular basis. There's no *quite possibly* about it. He wanted to find me, and now he has, and the blood in our veins throbs in our wrists as our feet sink into the red red carpet of our home.

Next to the bag is a white box. Mr Richardson picks it up, lifting the lid to reveal three pink cakes.

'For you, Jules. Stopped at *The Cupcake Kitchen* on my way home.'

'Jack!'

I've never heard someone say his name before, and I like it, the familiarity of it, the sense that we're linked in some strange way by this name I've been close to my whole life, even if it has been attached to the wrong man.

'Best cafe in Manchester,' Mr Richardson tells me.

'Do you know it, Tess? It's in Didsbury, so I'm extra lucky because it's out of Jack's way. You should've told me you were going though. I baked a cake.' She kisses him. 'Not that I'm ungrateful.'

'You can never have too much cake on a Monday.'

'It's a motto I live by,' Henry says. 'Might get it tattooed on my chest.'

Julie rolls her eyes. 'I bet you'll still eat one.'

'Hell yeah.'

Mr Richardson laughs, putting down the box and removing the glove from his right hand and then his left, pulling each finger free in turn. Mr Goldfish stiffens as a thin gold band glimmers in the light of the hall.

'Ring!' he cries, swimming around Mr Richardson in a frenzy. 'Ring! *Ring*! Where was that ring at school, Tess? Why doesn't he wear it?'

Mr Richardson passes me a cupcake.

'Go on. You have mine. I don't mind forsaking it for my most conscientious pupil.'

'Oh, is she the one?' Julie asks.

'The *one*?' Mr Goldfish repeats.

Julie helps herself to a cupcake. 'I'm glad you're getting the help you need, Tess. I don't find it easy, either. Not a numbers person, which is strange, living with these two.' She points at her husband and her son as I try to work out what she means. I'm good at Maths, really good, so I am quite offended by the suggestion I might be struggling.

'She's getting there. Anyway, good to see you, Tess.' Mr Richardson ushers me towards the door. 'I'll see you at school tomorrow, unless you're still feeling off in the morning.'

'Something tells me you might be,' Julie says, giving me a knowing look as she takes a bite of the cupcake. I must look confused because she says, 'Parents' Evening tomorrow night.'

'And you call me on my manners, Mother. Talking with your mouth full.'

'Sorry.' It takes an age for her to swallow. I'm watching every muscle of her jaw, and Mr Richardson is too. 'In my day, you didn't have to go along with your parents. You could sit at home and hide, but that's not the case now, is it? Must be so uncomfortable. I wouldn't blame you for trying to get out of it.' Her smile fades when no one reacts. She fiddles with the silver chain of her necklace and for the first time I notice something unusual about it – a tiny insect trapped in the amber stone. She glances from me to Mr Richardson. 'It *is* Parents' Evening tomorrow night?'

Mr Richardson nods, and I see that twice more in my head too – reliving it, but not rejoicing in it, because it's a lie.

CHAPTER 36

A hand with a ring on the fourth finger waves as I charge down the drive.

'Look at that, Tess!'

I can't. I focus on the blue car, on ordinary things that make sense, like a wing mirror and a number plate and a windscreen and a door and a seat and a belt that I'm too shaky to click into place. I gaze at the silver buckle, trying to unsee the thin gold band, the symbol of Mr Richardson's wedding vows, strong and seemingly true on a finger that looks as if it never takes it off.

'But you know different,' Mr Goldfish bellows so loudly my teeth clench. 'You know he removes it at school.'

'Actually,' I reply in my most rational voice, fighting to stay calm despite the *thump, thump, thump* of my chest, 'people take off their rings all the time. To go to the gym. Wash up. Take it to the jewellers to have it cleaned or resized or what have you. He probably just . . . I think that . . . Yeah . . . That will be it.'

'*Tess!*' Mr Goldfish bursts through the windscreen and swims out into the night. 'He's a cheat!'

The words echo around the garden, around Manchester, around the whole world.

'Shut up!' I roar, and even though it's in my head, my lips jut forward as if I am saying it out loud. 'You don't know that. You don't know that at all. I don't want to hear it!'

'Why are you *the one*?'

'Shut up!'

'And why did he lie about Parents' Evening? What's he going to do tomorrow night instead?'

'Please stop!'

'Everything okay?' Henry asks, but his voice is polite, unconcerned, because nothing has changed for him in the last two minutes. He starts the engine and the clock glows red to show that it's twenty-seven minutes past six, later than I'd even imagined. 'Shall we?'

Mr Goldfish hurtles back through the windscreen, skidding to a melodramatic stop by the gearstick. 'What are you waiting for? Get her out of here!' I can see him, even though I know full well he's in my pocket, this outraged fish shaking a fin at the house as we reverse down the drive. Slowly, too slowly, we trundle back the way I came, passing the grocery store where I threw the letter from CAMHS into the bin. In hindsight, maybe that was a mistake.

I need help.

'Yeah, you do,' Mr Goldfish says. 'You need your

head examining if you think Mr Richardson is faithful to his—'

I turn him off with a jerk of irritation and sit in silence. It feels deeper. More profound. Sealed around me tightly, no longer at risk of cracking. I'm encased in amber like the creature in Julie's necklace. I can't tell Henry about his dad, and I can't tell Julie about Parents' Evening, and I can't tell Mum what I saw on Jack's computer.

My heart is crying, my lips are burning, desire going up in smoke . . . I choke, on all the things I want to say and do and change, I choke . . .

'Where have you been?' Jack follows me into my bedroom where I kick off my boots to stand on the carpet with socks odd as Mr Richardson's. 'How do you know that boy? Where did you meet him? What were you doing with him for six hours?'

His words can't reach me. I'm somewhere over here, and he is somewhere over there, and we stare at each other from opposite ends of a chasm growing wider all the time, filling with secrets we can't share.

'Well, I think that's pretty obvious,' Mum says, and I don't even blush.

Jack does though, snorting loudly. 'She's not that kind of girl.'

'Isn't she? How do you know?'

'I know my daughter, thank you very much.'

Mum raises an eyebrow. 'Oh, you do, do you? We don't know where she's been. Why she's silent. What she's thinking. But, you tell me Jack,' she says, stabbing her finger in the air. 'Given that you think you know our daughter so well, you tell me what's going on in that thick skull of hers because I'm at a loss.'

She rounds on me so quickly her hair flies over her shoulder and whips her spine. 'Or perhaps you would care to enlighten us, Tess. I'm guessing you've not forgotten how to speak. I mean, maybe you even do speak to people outside the house. That boy, whoever he was . . . I can't imagine you said nothing the whole time you were together. How did you meet him if you didn't utter a single word?'

She looks ferocious, like the animal part of her is hurting. I want to put her out of her misery but I don't know how. Too much has happened and I can't speak without causing more pain – for Mum and Henry and Julie with her kind, gold-flecked eyes.

'You're playing us for fools, is that it? Your teachers too? Pretending to be some sort of mute when all the time you're talking to everyone else, saying things to people who don't even know you when I, your own bloody mum, can't get you to open your mouth!'

She starts to sob. Jack goes to her at once. They clutch each other, their bond stronger than ever as ours stretches and stretches and almost snaps.

'Okay, Hels. Okay, sweetheart. We'll get to the bottom of it. We will. I promise you that. The letter's due any day now.' Guiltily, I picture it lying in the dustbin. 'We'll get some answers.'

'Not if she doesn't speak at the appointment. We can't make her, can we? She might never talk again! What then? What will we do? What can we do? I just don't understand it,' Mum weeps. 'What did we do wrong, Jack? Why would she stop speaking? It doesn't make any sense. She was doing fine. She was happy. What suddenly changed?'

The night of the burned spaghetti comes back to me in a flash. I look at Jack the precise instant he looks at me.

'I don't know,' he replies eventually, but there is something uneasy about his tone.

CHAPTER 37

Mum doesn't bring me any tea and Jack doesn't make me any porridge, but that's okay because I don't have an appetite. I'm not entirely sure I have a stomach.

I go through the bus park rather than using the route across the fields, but I'm not being brave. It takes no courage because I have no fear. Connor shouts, same stuff as always, but his words bounce off my skin about four times the usual thickness. Nothing can touch me. I have no feelings left.

I don't break my stride when I reach the playground. If I bump into Anna then I bump into Anna is my general disinterested vibe as I move through school. Taking a random left, I go up some stairs and down some others, wandering past classrooms and the library and two lots of toilets, making it as far as Dining Room Three before doing a u-turn. Still I dawdle, only half-aware of where I am and what I am doing, my brain lagging a couple of seconds behind my vision. The corridor is distorted, the door handle of my form room too, swimming in and out of focus as I go to grab it. I push open the door to find that I'm late, which is odd, because I didn't hear a bell.

'You're back!' Miss Gilbert cries. I stare at a Mars Bar wrapper on the floor. A table leg. A sink with a dripping tap. 'Good to see you, Tess. Sorry to hear you've been ill.'

'And who's she heard that from?' Mr Goldfish asks. 'Mr Richardson, when he called late last night to say he'd messed up? Given the game away?'

'Take a seat, Tess.' A bird lands on the skylight, a huge, dark thing with bulbous eyes that pecks at the glass with a sharp, sharp beak. It could be the crow from the bus park. Or it might be any old blackbird. Or a magpie. It's too much effort to try and work it out. 'Tess, a seat, please.'

I move slowly. People laugh. I barely hear it.

Miss Gilbert does the register and reads out the notices then tells everyone they can chat. She joins in as usual, leaning over our desks rather than sitting behind her own. It's background noise, nondescript and indistinct, but then out of the fog like a car appearing at the very last moment, I am hit by words I don't expect. The jolt is physical, almost sending me back off my stool and onto the floor.

'You don't know *The Cupcake Kitchen?*'

I'm dizzy as the moons spinning madly either side of Miss Gilbert's face.

'No, Miss. I've never heard of it!' Claudia giggles at Miss Gilbert's exaggerated look of horror.

'You are missing out, dude! It's immense.' Her eyes shine in a way that makes me nervous.

'Where is it? I've never even heard of it.'

'Didsbury.' I want Miss Gilbert to be quiet now, so I send my silence hurtling through the air to bung up her throat like a cork in a wine bottle. 'I went there yesterday afternoon.'

'I knew it!' Mr Goldfish shouts. 'Did you hear that, Tess? She went there yesterday afternoon!'

There's a name etched into my desk. I've never noticed it before. I lean forward to examine the *D* and the *E* and the *A* and the *N*, touching the letters, digging my nail into the deep grooves, harder and harder, until my finger throbs.

'Tess. Everyone's gone.' I look up to see an empty classroom. 'Are you all right? You seem a bit spaced-out.'

Miss Gilbert's feet tap across the floor. They don't normally tap. They squeak like mine because we both wear boots.

'Not today,' Mr Goldfish whispers as Miss Gilbert appears in front of me. Red dress. Red heels. She's dressed up for something. Someone. 'A date?'

The room goes massive then shrinks to the size of pretty much a coffin. I grip Mr Goldfish tightly, needing the power stored in his batteries as I fade and fade and almost faint.

'I don't suppose you could do me a small favour, could you?' Miss Gilbert asks. Her voice is too airy. No one talks like that unless they're trying to appear relaxed. 'Just a little thing. It will only take two minutes.' She scribbles something on a bit of scrap paper then darts back to her desk to grab an envelope, sealing it tightly. 'Take this to Mr Richardson, will you?'

She holds out the envelope, but I don't accept it.

'Come on, Tess. It's important. A room swap, period two. He won't know where he's going unless you give him this and – *look*,' she says, gesturing to the group of students congregating outside the door. 'I'd do it myself if my next class wasn't waiting.'

I take it.

I don't know what else to do.

'Thanks, dude. I'm much obliged.'

'Tess. Great. I'm glad you've come to see me.' Mr Richardson is sitting at his desk in front of a newspaper, holding a cup of tea in his left hand. I stand by the door, the note hidden in my pocket. 'Free period first thing on a Tuesday. Not bad, eh?'

I can't help noticing that his hair is unusually neat and a nicer jacket than the one he wore home yesterday evening is hanging on the back of his chair.

Mr Goldfish nudges his nose out into the classroom. 'Is he wearing the ring?' I crane my neck ever so casually in an attempt to see round the mug. The tips of Mr Richardson's fingers are visible, but nothing else. 'Damn it.'

'Look, Tess.' Mr Richardson's talking more to the Prime Minister on the front page of the newspaper than to me. 'I wanted to clear something up. Several things, actually.' He looks at me at last. 'Have you got a minute?'

I've got all the time in the world if he's about to say what I need to hear. He beckons me closer, but I'm already on my way. As I get nearer, my conviction that he's innocent grows stronger, this judge in a funny wig declaring it loudly as he taps a hammer in the courtroom of my mind. There is an explanation and I cannot wait to hear it, practically running the last two steps to Mr Richardson's desk where he puts down the tea to reveal that he's wearing the wedding ring.

'No!' Mr Goldfish cries.

'Yes!' I reply as the judge in my head throws off his wig and dances a jig of pure joy.

'Yesterday evening. My wife,' Mr Richardson starts, and I nod even though it's not allowed, my head too buoyant to care, too free and easy on my neck all of a quiver with delight. 'She confused you with someone else.'

It's irritating, how loudly Mr Goldfish snorts.

'I've been staying behind to give another student a bit of extra help after school. Someone without your talent for Maths, obviously.' I beam, my face out of control. I am drunk on relief, the delicious bubbles of it fizzing in my blood. 'When I said you were conscientious, she assumed

– wrongly, of course – that you were the girl I've been tutoring. Easy mistake.'

That does make sense.

'Does it?' Mr Goldfish asks.

'And as for the other thing. What she said about that, you know, that – the whole Parents' Evening malarkey.' His eyes are back on the Prime Minister, who looks up at him warily. 'I had to tell a bit of a white lie. I hope you understand.'

I wait.

The Prime Minister waits.

The whole country, maybe even every person on the planet, holds their breath as Mr Richardson opens his mouth.

'It's just, well, it's her birthday tomorrow so I'm going shopping this afternoon.' A huge exhalation drifts across the world, this soothing wind that blows any doubt from my mind. 'Romance isn't my strong suit, I'm afraid to say. Birthdays. Anniversaries. I usually forget, so I wanted it to be a surprise.'

He grins at me and I grin back, our brown eyes locking together.

'I knew you'd understand. We're on the same wavelength, you and I.' Our identical DNA emits an electric charge that crackles in the space between us. 'We get each other, don't you think?' My heart skips a beat then stops working altogether. 'Share more than just a love of black jumpers, that's for sure. Listen. I don't know why you're silent,

Tess, but I have to say I do relate. The impulse to be quiet. Withdraw. I understand it, that's all I'm saying.' He leans in close. 'I hear you, Tess. I hear you even though you're not saying a word.'

I flush the happiest pink of my life as Mr Goldfish remains steadfastly orange. I reach for the envelope because there's no reason to hide it anymore.

'No, Tess!' Mr Goldfish grabs a corner as I try to pull it out of my pocket. 'No. Don't do it. You don't know what's in there!'

I yank the envelope free and thrust it into Mr Richardson's outstretched hand.

'What do we have here then?'

He tears it open with his thumb and pulls out the note, reading it with a smile, half-biting his bottom lip.

Mr Goldfish shakes his head. 'That's quite a reaction for a room swap.'

CHAPTER 38

I don't get much done in my morning lessons because Mr Goldfish will not shut up, forecasting doom, which let's be clear is completely ridiculous when there is nothing but hope on the horizon. I luxuriate in its warmth, feeling myself melt, my emotions dripping back into my blood as they gradually unfreeze. There's happiness and excitement and optimism.

'And delusion and naivety and general pig-headedness,' Mr Goldfish finishes as I draw a diagram of a heart in Biology, labelling the chambers with Mr Richardson's name. Jack, I write, over and over again. *Jack.* 'What about that cafe in Didsbury? *The Cupcake Kitchen* place? He obviously went there with Miss Gilbert.'

'So? They're friends. Like me and Henry.'

'But you kissed Henry.'

'You know what I mean.'

'That's the whole problem, Tess. I don't.'

I ignore him, shoving him in my bag when the bell goes

for lunch. I still don't have much of an appetite, but it's different now. I'm full, not empty – sated and stuffed to the brim with all this Content that makes eating pretty much pointless.

Swiping my card, I enter the library, wandering up and down the neat rows, enjoying the quiet and the sense of order that cannot be disputed. If there was a shelf marked FAMILY, that's where I'd be, slap bang in the middle of it with Mr Richardson. *I hear you even though you're not saying a word.* I caress the wood, loving how cool it is, how solid.

'And that's the psychopath he chose, if you can believe it.'

Anna, Tara and Sarah must have followed me in here, and now I'm trapped, a wall behind me, shelves either side, the girls up ahead. Anna folds her arms slowly, back in control. I don't know what's more terrifying, a drunk Anna, or a sober one.

'If Henry wants you,' she says, her tone light but dangerous, 'I don't want him. Just so you know.' Her dark head tilts to one side and her black eyes don't blink. 'If he has a fetish for girls who are boys, he won't want me. You're welcome to him. I always thought he was a bit different. Looks pretty enough, I'll give him that, but he's clearly wrong in the head if he wants to shag someone as fat as you.'

'Shut up.'

'Thanks,' I tell Mr Goldfish because miraculously Anna has stopped talking.

'It wasn't me.'

Isabel appears around the corner, bag on both shoulders, notepad clutched in her hands. I can't believe she's here, and at the same time I'm not at all surprised. She juts out her chin, nervous but determined, and it's Isawynka she's thinking of, I just know it, as she stares Anna down.

'Leave her alone.'

'Or what?' Sarah asks. 'What are you going to do, Isabel? Hit us with your pencil?'

Tara snickers. 'Poke us with a pen?'

'Whack us over the head with that stupid little notepad you're always carrying around?' Anna turns her back on me and moves closer to my friend. That's the label Isabel would get in the Dewey Decimal system, no doubt about it – 1.0 TRUE FRIEND. Anna swipes the notepad out of her hand. It flies into the air, pages fluttering like a frightened bird, this rare, precious species, not often seen in public. It hits the floor, where it bounces twice then lies still. Anna reacts first, gliding over to it. Isabel's too scared to move. She's rooted to the spot, hands in tight fists, her mouth falling open in dismay.

'That's mine.' Her voice is smaller now. 'Give it back.'

'Oh, this is brilliant,' Anna says in genuine glee, rifling through the pages. 'This is – girls, you have to see this.'

'Give it back,' Isabel says again, and I go to her side,

crossing far more than a few metres of carpet. She looks grateful and I give her arm a squeeze.

Anna presses her heart, all touched by our reunion. 'Isn't that just lovely? I tell you what. How about this? Isabel, I'll give you the notepad if your friend here asks for it in a man-voice I can record on my phone. What do you think?'

Isabel's quiet for a few seconds. 'That's stupid.'

'It isn't. It's a fair trade. I love this notepad, but what I love even more is the idea of Balls giving us a little taste of his post-puberty voice. Everyone's dying to hear it, Man Skull. And I've promised people evidence.' She sniffs. 'Blaise has quite a following, as I'm sure you're aware. I don't want to let my public down. What do you say – in your deepest voice, if you please?' Her phone beeps as she points it at me, a white light appearing in one corner. 'I'm filming.'

Isabel looks from me to the phone.

'You can put a stop to this, Tess,' Anna drawls. 'You just have to say the word. Well, maybe more like ten words in the right sort of way, but your friend is worth that, surely? Come on. What are you waiting for? Don't be shy. Say hello in your new voice.'

I won't do it. No way. And Isabel would never ask me to.

The light of Anna's phone is dazzling. 'Come on, Man Skull. Ten tiny words.'

Tara clears her throat, getting ready to read from the notepad.

'Please, Tess.' It's so quiet, I think I might have imagined it, but no – Isabel is tugging on my sleeve. I stare at her in disbelief. '*Please.*'

'*And then the brave elf, Isawynka, wielded her sword, The Great Blade of Turner, and together the unconquerable pair, the formidable twosome struck down their foe, the foul troll Anspog Beltchum, known in* – oh my God . . .' Tara giggles '. . . *the foul troll Anspog Beltchum, known in the common tongue as* Anna!'

'Do you really think I care what some geek has written about me in a notepad?' Anna asks, but she thrusts the phone so close to my face it almost takes the skin off my nose. 'Smile, Man Skull. You're on camera.' I blink into the white light, no idea what to do.

Mr Goldfish wiggles out into the open. 'Radical idea, I know, but how about saying something?'

'I can't do that. I'm not going to talk like a man so Anna can put it on the Internet.'

'I'm not asking you to. But tell Anna no. In your own voice.'

I swallow. 'It won't work. I can't just – What, you think I can just open my mouth and talk? That it's that easy?'

'Yes, I do. Absolutely. Give it a go!'

Isabel shakes my arm. 'Please, Tess.'

'*Anspog Beltchum roared, its peculiarly long neck twisting and turning like a serpent, the black head of the ugly beast wafting through the air.*'

'I can't do it,' I tell them both. 'I'm sorry but I can't.'

'I'm getting impatient,' Anna sings.

'Come on, Tess!' Mr Goldfish cries.

'Leave me alone!' I bellow to Mr Goldfish and Anna and Isabel most of all because I can't bear it, the way her shoulders are drooping in disappointment. 'My silence is the only thing I have left and I am not about to sacrifice it. Do you hear me?'

Anna seems to.

'You're not going to do it,' she says flatly. 'Well. You got me. I really thought you would.' The white light vanishes. 'I guess we overestimated her, Isabel. I think we both thought she valued your friendship more than she obviously does. Well, no matter.' She takes the notepad from Tara and drops it in her bag. 'Sorry, Isabel – but a deal's a deal and someone failed to deliver.'

CHAPTER 39

I speed through the bus park at the end of the day, keen to escape quickly. There are things I don't want to see.

'You should wait for Isabel. Apologise,' Mr Goldfish says. 'You let her down at lunchtime, and for what? Mr Richardson? Because he said you're on the same wavelength? Is that it?'

'She let me down too, all those times she didn't meet me for lunch and went off with Patrick.'

'I know. But you hurt her, Tess.'

'And she hurt me. She betrayed me to Jack, telling him about the text.'

'You told lies! On purpose! You pretended you were friends with Anna because you were ashamed of Isabel, and then you suspected her of being Blaise. You're not exactly innocent, are you?' A blue car similar to Mr Richardson's roars past and I almost leap over a wall to avoid having to look at it.

'I wasn't ashamed.'

'Embarrassed then, nervous about Jack's judgement, and Isabel realised it. How awful is that?'

My stomach twists guiltily. 'About as awful as it's been to see her laughing with Patrick. It's . . . it's . . .'

'Understandable after you humiliated her?' Mr Goldfish says, gently.

'Maybe. I don't know. But I couldn't do it in the library, okay? I couldn't speak.'

'You *wouldn't* speak. There's a difference, Tess.' Another car that looks like Mr Richardson's purrs down the road. I flinch, and Mr Goldfish clocks it. 'Hang on a minute, you're scared!'

'No, I'm not.'

'Yes, you are!' He jabs a fin in my face. 'You're terrified. You don't think he's shopping for his wife at all.'

'That's crazy,' I reply too quickly.

'You're frightened of seeing him with Miss Gilbert,' he says, swimming in front of my eyes. I blink to get rid of him, but he stays where he is. 'That's it, isn't it? Admit it! You know they're meeting up tonight. You saw it too – the dress and the heels and the hair and the nice jacket. You know he's lying.'

'I don't,' I growl.

'You do.'

'*I don't!*' I snatch Mr Goldfish out of the air and thrust him in my pocket with a hand that maybe even does it for real.

[283]

'Prove it, then.' Somehow he's back in front of me. Right in front of me. I can't make out the pavement or the road or the trees or the shops so I swipe frantically and shove him back in my coat. 'I have to make you see, Tess,' he says with no irony at all as he reappears, blocking my view. I panic, swinging my arm in my imagination or real life, I can't be sure. 'Go back to school.'

That stops me in my tracks. 'What?'

'You heard me. Turn around and go back. Let's wait for Mr Richardson in the car park. If you're so convinced there's nothing to worry about, prove it. Come on. Let's go right now.' He pulls my arm. I can actually feel it, this insistent tug tug tug on my sleeve. I shake him off. He tugs harder. I shake him off again and a boy looks at me strangely so I pin my arms to my side and square up to Mr Goldfish, whose eyes flash dangerously as my own. 'You're a coward.'

'And you're a bully.'

'You know he's a cheat, Tess. You know it. You're not stupid and you're choosing to walk away. To deceive yourself. It's pathetic.'

'Oh, I'm pathetic? You're not even real. You don't exist.'

'So why can you see me?'

'I can't!' I snarl, but it isn't true. He's floating before me, bigger than ever, his body a fiery orange, his eyes a fierce black and the light from his mouth so blinding I have to shield my face.

'Is everything okay?' a man asks, pausing with a large

poodle on a lead. The dog sniffs at my feet but ignores the fish floating half a metre above his head.

'Look at that,' I say, more to myself than Mr Goldfish now. 'You're not even real. The dog . . . the dog would be able to . . .'

'Woah,' the man says as my legs buckle beneath me. 'I've got you.' He catches my arm and leads me to a bench, but that's the very last thing in the world that I want. I need to get away from this bit of road, not sit here and stare at it. There's a blue car. And another one. And two more trundling past with couples in the front who may or may not be my teachers.

'Check them,' Mr Goldfish urges, but I close my eyes. At first, there's nothing but darkness, but then a pinprick of amber flickers in the distance, moving towards me, getting larger and larger – the dot becoming a circle becoming a creature becoming a fish with determined fins, hurtling through the black choppy ocean of my mind. 'You have to face the truth.'

I fling open my eyes and race off, away from the man and the poodle who's straining on his lead, trying to follow.

'There, boy. Stay there. Good dog. She doesn't want to play.'

I do, actually, more than anything. I want to find out what he's called and really care about the answer. I want to delight in things again, like the soft fuzz of a poodle's ears and the cold tingle of drizzle on my cheeks and the reassuring warmth of a cup of tea that I could drink at the kitchen table all relaxed in my house because it was still my home.

'I have nothing without Mr Richardson!' My feet pound against the pavement, my hair whipping back off my face. 'He is everything now. Why can't you understand that?'

'You don't need him, Tess. You don't. You already have a—'

'Don't you dare say that,' I shout. 'Don't you dare!'

'But it's true. You have someone. He might not be perfect but he is still your—'

'THAT'S ENOUGH!'

I screech to a stop by a lamppost, my heart battering my ribs. My hand is clumsy with fury as I grab Mr Goldfish from my pocket, turn him off, and fling him into a dustbin with all my might.

'I don't have Jack. I don't have Mum. They lied to me for years. Do you know how that feels, to be let down by the two people you trusted more than anything in the world? You think I can forgive them? You think I can just forget that blog, the words Jack wrote about hating me, finding me disgusting, ugly? Are you even aware of how impossible that would be? The ridiculousness of what you're asking me to do?'

There's no reply because Mr Goldfish is lying between an old beer can and a polystyrene cup, small again, and lifeless, half-hidden among the rubbish.

The drizzle turns into rain that splatters against Mr Goldfish – the *torch*, I correct myself, because that's all he is.

A children's torch.

Made of plastic.

Not even dead to me because he was never alive.

I grab the milk from the fridge and splash some into a glass, spilling some on the side.

'You want a cloth?' Jack asks. It's dripping down the fridge so I snatch the blue rag and throw it on the puddle that's forming on the floor. 'Come on, Tess. You can do better than that!'

His tone is strange – half-reprimand, half-joke – trying to make his point but wary of causing conflict after I stormed into the house and slammed the door. I wait it out, daring him to pick a side because he can't be all things to all people now, can he, like he can't ask me to stand out and fit in, to take the road less travelled while keeping my nose to the grindstone, to ignore the rat race at the same time as trying to win it. It doesn't make any sense. He makes no sense, so yeah, I let the milk seep off the work surface and wait for him to make a choice.

A creamy swirl oozes over the tiles.

'Are you waiting for it to clean itself up?' Jack asks in the same odd voice but a knot has formed in his cheek where he's clenching his jaw. He stares at me. I stare at him. And then in pretty much the world's most perfect timing, Jedi trots into the kitchen, making a beeline for the milk. Lick goes his fat pink tongue. Lick lick.

On the floor.

Up the cupboards.

On the work surface as he rises on his hind legs.

'For crying out loud, get your nose out of there!' Jack says, finally losing it, giving Jedi a nasty tap. 'It's not hygienic. We still have standards, you know.' Jedi hops down and skulks away. 'Sorry,' he says to me or the dog, I'm not entirely sure. 'Sorry. It's just . . .' He sighs, too weary to talk is what I think at first, but then he gives me this look. Maybe I'm reading too much into it, but he seems burdened more than exhausted, breathing heavily under the weight of so many secrets.

I start to scrub. The tiles. The cupboard. Anything I can get my hands on. Jack opens his mouth as I go for my pocket, reaching for Mr Goldfish, my heart sinking when I realise he's not there.

Before Jack can say anything, Jedi barks loudly. He scampers to the patio door to see Bobbin, our next door neighbour's dog, leaping over our wall. Jedi howls in outrage then throws himself against the glass, and suddenly it's funny, how serious this whole thing should be and how ridiculous Jedi is making it, spinning round in a mad circle. I can't quite believe it, but I smile, and Jack does too. Our eyes meet for an instant, very bizarre and unexpected, then Jack walks across the kitchen to open the patio door.

CHAPTER 40

Miss Gilbert wears heels on Wednesday, but by Thursday her feet are back in her usual dark green boots, and why is that I wonder, as she stays behind her desk even after she's completed the register. She isn't working, or messing about with paint, or doing a sketch to add to her random collection dotted around the classroom walls. She's just sitting, hands in her lap, totally still.

Everyone else has noticed too, the weather of the art room very different without Miss Gilbert shining away in the middle of it.

'I know what you're about to say,' I tell Mr Goldfish. 'And no, I don't think Miss Gilbert's bad mood has anything to do with Mr Richardson. They're friends, aren't they? Good friends. Nothing's changed as far as I can see.'

I wait for a reply that doesn't come. It's hammering it down, so Mr Goldfish must be wet and cold and also lonely. I gaze at the glowering clouds, willing them to lighten up.

It's a moody kind of morning. Even the bell seems to screech more bad-temperedly than normal. Miss Gilbert lets us into the corridor, her expression vacant – until I pass, that is.

'Tess, wait a sec, will you?'

She leads me into the shadow of a large display cabinet containing rows of garden gnomes made out of clay. There's a sea of misshapen pink faces watching Miss Gilbert fiddle with her moon earring.

'It's just, Tuesday. The note.' Her winky eyes are unusually serious. 'I know you gave it to Mr Richardson, but how did he seem when he read it?' Again, I'm glad of my silence and the fact that there's no need to answer. I feel it, wrapped tightly around me, a thick winter coat against a wind of the most chilling kind. 'Sorry. I know you can't . . . Sorry. Can you nod?' She waits for me to move my head, staring at me so closely I get an itch by my eyebrow. 'Was he pleased? I don't know, did he smile or something? Was he happy to receive it?'

Yes, he was happy. Very happy. Maybe a bit too happy for it to have been a note about a room swap. I wait for Mr Goldfish to say *I told you so*, but nothing happens.

'I'm sorry,' she says again, and she sounds as if she means it. 'You can go. I shouldn't . . . Forget I said anything. Go on. You're free. I won't hold you hostage by these monstrosities any longer.' She rolls her eyes at the garden gnomes. 'Art, obviously. It isn't important – the note, I mean. Art is vital.

The lie that makes us realise the truth. Picasso said that. I love it, don't you? These gnomes, for instance: they reveal the truth that most Year Sevens can't do clay work for toffee, not that you heard me say that.'

She winks now, joking around, and then it's gone. 'Don't tell Mr Richardson I was asking about the note, will you? Not that you can. Sorry. It's just – the room swap.' My throat constricts as I realise she's about to lie. 'It didn't go all that well. He was – anyway. Details.' She flashes a smile that's all effort and pretence. 'Won't bore you with them. Have a good day, Tess.'

'You're in here too, Patrick. Did you know Isabel thinks you're an orc with the rancid breath of a stray dog?'

Anna peruses the notepad, leaning back in her chair at a casual angle, putting up her feet on the table. Mr Richardson is nowhere to be seen. I can't work out if I'm relieved or not, like I keep peeking at the doorway, wanting to see him and not see him, desperate for him to appear to alleviate my distrust, terrified of him walking into the room and saying something that will make it grow.

There's a war in my brain, all right, and the doubts are winning. I push them back, picturing it clearly, two hands driving back a black army of termites demolishing certainty and hope and joy and the only bit of security I have left. I preserve it, protect it, surround it with a moat and a barrier and a barbed wire fence because actually I believe in Mr Richardson.

I say it again in the silence of my mind.

I believe in Mr Richardson.

Anna scans Isabel's notepad, rocking her chair onto its back legs.

'I'll give you the exact quote, shall I, Patrick? May as well hear it from the horse's mouth. *Isawynka had led Patrock on* – that's you, obviously, Patrick – *duping the orc most horribly, and she wasn't proud of it; nay, she was ashamed most wholeheartedly of her actions, but saw in them a necessity if she were to be reunited with her sword, The Great Blade of Turner.'* I stiffen at this, glancing at Isabel, who's staring, white-faced, at Anna. *'She endured Patrock's dull talk and his rancid breath akin to that of a stray dog, comforting herself with the knowledge that her duplicity, though not kind, was—'*

Patrick's on his feet, kicking over his chair and swiping Isabel's pencil case off the table where it clatters to the ground.

'Hey!' she cries.

'I thought we were friends.'

'We are friends.'

Anna snaps the book closed. 'Some friend, Isabel. Dull talk, was it? Rancid breath? Not that I don't sympathise. He does stink.'

'Listen to me,' Isabel says, wringing her hands. 'That's fiction, Patrick. Fiction. Words. A story. And anyway I wrote that stuff ages ago before I got to know you.'

'Dull talk?'

'I'm sorry.'

'I thought you liked hearing about my pet lizard.'

'I do!'

'And my breath is not rancid!' He rounds on Anna. 'I floss!'

She lets out a whoop of amusement.

'Don't listen to her,' Isabel says. 'I'm sorry. I should never have written it, but that was before. Now we're friends I'd never say something like that. Honestly.'

I can tell it's the truth. She likes him, and she's upset that he's upset because they're symbiotic, no doubt about it, staring at each other with tears in their eyes.

'I can't believe you wrote those things.' His voice is strangled.

'Oh, Patrick. They don't mean anything, especially not now. Things have changed.'

'Yes, they have because this friendship is over.'

It's melodramatic and people jeer, but I wouldn't join in even if I could join in. My heart goes out to him, this boy who's been betrayed by words he didn't expect, written by someone he thought he could trust. I know how it feels. He packs up his things and moves desks, kicking Isabel's pencil case under Mr Richardson's desk, which beeps.

At least, the phone on top of it beeps.

'Sir's got a message!' Tara exclaims, racing forward

to have a look. She doesn't pick up the phone, just gives it a prod so the screen appears as two tiny squares in her pupils. 'He does have a friend, after all. Someone called—' she squints and I pray for *Julie* to emerge from her lips '—Laura.'

'Let me see!' Sarah says, darting to the front of the classroom too. 'Laura is not the wife we met at his house.' My gut twists painfully. I don't want to hear this, not now, not when my faith in Mr Richardson is already wavering. She takes the phone off the desk then chucks it to Tara who chucks it right back.

'Bloody hell, put it down!' Anna snaps. 'He's probably just gone to the loo.'

'Relax,' Sarah says. 'I can't open it. There's a password.' The knot in my stomach lessens then retightens when Sarah giggles. 'But there's a bit of message on the lock screen.'

'Read it then!' Tara squeals. She tries to peer around Sarah, who shoves her out of the way.

'Oh, it's good. It's really good.'

'What does it say?'

I charge towards Sarah, needing her to stop, but it's too late. The private words thunder in my ears – *I never want to see you again* – as I snatch the phone and Mr Richardson walks into the room.

CHAPTER 41

This is what he sees: me holding the phone while Tara and Sarah loiter a couple of metres away because they leapt to one side when he opened the door.

'What do you think you're doing?'

I drop the phone as if it's burning my fingers. It clatters horribly on the desk, lighting up to reveal the snippet of message. Mr Richardson stuffs it in his pocket.

'That is my private property, Tess.'

His eyes are a different brown now, a paler brown, hard and frosty like the ground in winter. We are on the same wavelength, but it's flat-lining in my chest that aches and aches as he shakes his head. Pushing back my hair, I try to tell him with no words that I was saving his phone, not stealing it, willing him to hear me once more.

I hear you, Tess. I hear you even though you're not saying a word.

Well, not anymore. My silent plea falls on deaf ears and he gives me this look, all too familiar, because I've done it again. I've disappointed another Jack.

'See me after the lesson. This is serious, Tess. I'll have to let your parents know about this.' That can't happen, no way, so I take a step towards him, willing him to realise that it was Tara and Sarah, not me, his favourite student, the girl tucked beneath his wing. He shoos me away. 'Go back to your place. We'll talk about this at the end.'

No one intervenes. Isabel doesn't come to my rescue this time. She's scared and upset, glancing from Mr Richardson to me to Anna, who's pulling at her shirt.

'Is it me or is it hot in here?' She fans herself with the notepad as her friends sit back down, looking dazed by their good fortune. 'I am boiling.'

'I'm waiting, Tess,' Mr Richardson says. I'm back at my desk, but I'm still standing up because I'm boiling too, anger surging through my veins at the casual way Anna is flicking through the notepad. It isn't hers. And I didn't take the phone. None of this is fair. 'For goodness' sake, Tess. Are you deaf as well as mute?'

My legs give way like maybe I've been shot. He looks at me coldly from the other side of the room. 'Can I get on now please? Is that okay with you?' He goes to the whiteboard. 'I'll see you at the end. Your behaviour today has been unacceptable.'

His voice sounds oddly far away.

There's half an hour left.

Twenty-seven minutes.

Twenty-three.

The more the clock ticks, the further away I float. The whiteboard shrinks to the size of a piece of A4 paper, the size of Isabel's little notepad, the size of a phone with a message I can no longer read from this distance. I'm vacant, drifting away from myself because there's nothing to tether me to the ground. Without Mr Richardson I have no roots, no past and no future, and no dad.

I want a dad.

More than anything, I want a dad of my own. He doesn't have to be anyone special, just someone reliable and predictable, a man who weighs up his words before he uses them. He might even say the same thing at the same time every day but it would never get boring. I'd know where I stand and I'd look forward to his catchphrases, enjoying the repetition of them, the predictable lyrics that would be music to my ears.

Mr Richardson calls me over at the end of the lesson and I obey, wanting to make amends and also leave the classroom with everyone else. I'm scared of him and I trust him and I hate him and I love him in a mix of emotion that curdles in my stomach. Isabel disappears quickly, no doubt to escape Anna, who's strolling along, reading from the notepad. Tara and Sarah hesitate, fully expecting to be asked to stay behind, but Mr Richardson lets them go.

He knits his fingers together, surveying me over the criss-crossed tips. 'What happened today was extremely serious,

Tess. You know that, don't you? From my point of view it looked as if you were either trying to break into my phone or steal it.' My lips part, but no words of protest come. 'The incident has to be reported. I can't let something like this slide. I need to tell your form tutor, really. Who is it again?' he asks, standing up and scratching his chin as if he's trying to remember. He answers his own question much too quickly. 'Miss Gilbert, isn't it?'

I make no sign that I've heard him. He moves to the door and waits.

'Come on, Tess.'

'*No,*' I say in my head, loudly and firmly. '*No.*'

My mouth doesn't move, but neither do I. Mr Richardson beckons me with one finger that curls slowly in the air.

'Come here.' His face is different. I can't see him, the Mr Richardson I thought I knew, the man whose DNA I thought I shared. 'Fine. Have it your way, Tess. But if I don't tell Miss Gilbert, I will have to tell your parents. Is that what you want? For me to phone them now? Or would you prefer to accompany me to the Art room?'

There's nothing I can do but follow, five steps behind Mr Richardson. Ten. We're not in sync anymore. He's racing ahead, desperate to see Miss Gilbert, and I'm hanging back. I think of Henry and Julie and the house they share and the man Mr Richardson seemed to be in that bedroom, joking around with his wife and his son. Clasping my hands, I pray for something to happen, like a lightning bolt or what have you, striking the Art block, blowing it up so I can go home. I want to go home, back to Jedi and the *Welcome* doormat and the pig mug and the heart water bottle that I'd fill up from the kettle and clutch to my chest all warm and comforting.

'Hello?' Mr Richardson says. 'Hello?'

Art One is empty. I can hardly believe it, rejoicing as Mr Richardson frowns. He pulls out his phone and presses the *call* button. A phone starts to ring and we look up in surprised unison to see Miss Gilbert through the door, face framed in the glass – silver moons, red hair – and then she enters the room just a little bit, staying close to the edge.

'I'm calling you,' Mr Richardson says, unnecessarily. He holds up his phone, something shining on his fourth finger beneath the skylight. The gold ring winks smugly like maybe it's making a point. He hasn't taken it off and that's a surprise, I have to admit it, to see it on his hand in front of Miss Gilbert, who doesn't seem shocked by its presence.

'So my vibrating pocket keeps telling me. Can you stop that thing?' Mr Richardson complies at once. He holds it out to show that it's done, that her wish is his command. 'Thanks, Sir. Tess isn't in trouble, is she?'

'I'm afraid so, Miss Gilbert.'

'What is it? Lack of homework again?'

'Worse than that, I'm afraid.'

'Oh dear.' They're being polite. Civil. Completely and utterly above board. I stare at them both, feeling wrong-footed. 'What have you been doing, Tess?'

'I caught her at my desk, looking at my phone.' For the first time, something real passes between them. 'There's a password.'

Miss Gilbert starts to wash some brushes, black paint swirling down the plughole. 'Were you really trying to look at it, Tess? That doesn't sound like you.'

'Well, she was holding it. Two other girls were hanging around my desk as well. Tara McCloud and Sarah Horsfall. They're not exactly innocent.'

'Tara and Sarah? About as innocent as I am.' Miss Gilbert suddenly grins. It bursts out of her, this wild smile of amusement that she sucks back in, but not before it's done its work, warming the air a couple of degrees. She scrubs the brushes with her fingers, the black paint turning grey. 'I suppose there's no major misdemeanour, is there? I mean, it's not as if she stole the phone.'

'No. Not at all.' That's not what he said after the lesson, but maybe he's doing me a favour.

'And she's never done anything like this before,' Miss Gilbert continues as I try not to think of the wallet. 'She's a good student.'

'I know that. She's excellent,' Mr Richardson replies – and there he is once more, the man I recognise, soft and kind with all this Like in his warm brown eyes. The knot

[301]

in my gut unravels and I breathe with lungs that feel as if they're floating. I'm okay. It's okay.

The water runs clear. Miss Gilbert bangs the paintbrushes on the sink and my teachers carry on chatting about nothing whatsoever suspicious.

CHAPTER 42

'Is Tess in? I'm a friend. Just thought I'd say hi.'

I'm sprawling on the sofa in my tiger-print onesie watching *Embarrassing Bodies*, hood pulled up because I'm cold. Was cold. Now I'm hot and stressed because that voice belongs to Henry. I don't want him to see me dressed like this.

'Yes, yes, I suppose she is.' Mum's taken aback. Let's face it, beautiful boys don't usually turn up on the doorstep, asking for me on a Thursday night, or any night at all for that matter. She gestures behind her back, pointing up the stairs as she keeps him talking so that I can get changed. I tiptoe past, surprised Mum is being so relaxed about it. In my bedroom, I pull on my black jeans, a black top and some odd socks. The world is okay, maybe even good, and I stare at the sky out of my bedroom window, yellow and hazy in the light of a massive moon.

Even Jack was happy when I got home from school, whistling as he printed off three copies of his script to take to the first rehearsal this evening. He was buoyant over tea, shovelling pasta into his mouth while stapling the scripts together.

'I'm going to send one to my agent as well. Make him aware. Let him see that I have a few more strings to my bow. I've loved it, Hels. And it's come so easily. I've written thirty-seven thousand three-hundred and ninety-one words almost effortlessly. Not that it's about word count, but that's a lot, eh? An outpouring. I almost didn't feel as if I was writing it at times.'

'Who was then?' Mum said, only half-listening because she was watching me devour pasta, hungry for the first time in three days. 'Do you want some more, Tess?'

'It was me, Hels, obviously. But I was channelling something else. That's what I'm saying. The spirit of Beckett, maybe.'

'There's plenty in the pan.'

'I can't wait for the guys to read it tonight,' he said, bashing the stapler. 'What could be better? A bit of a read-through over a pint.'

'Sounds good, darling.' Mum gave me another dollop of pasta, looking pleased when I started to eat it.

I walk into the lounge to see Mum and Henry chatting away as a man on the TV pulls down his trousers. It isn't exactly *Settle for Less* now, is it, so I grab the remote.

'Don't turn it up,' Mum says as I go to turn it off. She glares at me and I glare right back, my thumb hovering over the *standby* button. 'You have a visitor.' She rolls her eyes at Henry. 'She loves this programme for some strange reason. Can't get enough of it. Do you watch it?'

The man on TV is edging down his boxer shorts. 'No, I can't say I do,' Henry mutters. I cringe, but he sounds amused.

'Thank you!' Mum says. 'It's awful, isn't it? Why would anyone want to show off their weird ailments on TV?'

'The ailments aren't weird though. That's the issue I have.'

Mum points at the naked man showing something to a doctor. 'You're telling me that's not weird?' I switch it off in a fluster.

'Not really,' Henry says, grasping his foot as he leans back in the armchair. 'People don't watch this show to see something weird. They watch this show because the weirdness is familiar, and therefore not weird at all.'

I move closer to the kitchen, hoping Henry will stand up and follow, but Mum is determined to continue the conversation.

'That sounds like a paradox to me.'

'No, I don't think it is.' He's not being rude, just thoughtful, wiggling his foot up and down. 'I mean, I don't really watch it, or anything, but I reckon the appeal of the show lies in the fact we all have something secret we're trying to hide, something we're ashamed of – a rash like that poor bloke on the telly! We worry that we're abnormal and that's

[305]

why people watch it, right? Because it's reassuring. We love realising that other people are abnormal too. Flawed. Messed up. But that's the funny thing,' he says, wiggling his foot faster now. 'If we're all weird, no one's weird. In fact, if you think about it, in an imperfect world, the only truly odd thing would be perfection.'

He's mesmerising.

Mum is mesmerised.

I am practically draping myself round the door to tell him it's time to go into the kitchen.

'Wow. That's very – well, that's very interesting. An unusual perspective, certainly.' Mum seems impressed. And pleased for me. And delighted by this whole evening in general, thrilled with this smart, sensitive and, yeah, incredibly gorgeous boy turning up unexpectedly to visit her daughter. That's how I feel as she catches my eye and gives me a secret smile – like her daughter for the first time in a while. 'You should talk to my husband. He's a perfectionist.'

'It's hard not to be, isn't it?' Henry replies, climbing to his feet at last. 'But it's such bullshit . . . nonsense, I mean, sorry. If we told the truth, there wouldn't be a problem. But we don't. We're so scared of being judged, aren't we? So what do we do? Hide our flaws, airbrush our lives until they look like everyone else's, not realising they're airbrushing their lives to look like ours.'

'So what's the answer?' Mum asks, sounding awestruck.

Henry laughs as he moves towards me, Mum's eyes following him all the way. 'I have absolutely no idea. Shouting the truth louder than the lies, maybe? Or opting out completely like Tess has. Perhaps silence is the best form of protest.'

Jack returns as Henry's leaving. The two pass awkwardly in the doorway.

'Cheers,' Henry calls to Mum before disappearing down the road. I spin round to see Mum watching me with fizzy eyes.

'So that was Henry.' A smile dances on her face, trying to entice mine into a duet. I'm dangerously close to yielding so I go into the kitchen to get a drink, leaving Jack to splutter in the lounge.

'That wasn't the boy, was it? The one who drove Tess home on Monday?'

'Yes it was, actually. But it's okay. He's, well, he's extraordinary, to be honest with you.' She laughs. 'Some of the stuff he was saying, Jack. Talking with more wisdom than a seventy-year-old, never mind a seventeen-year-old. This stuff about perfectionism and the lie we're living, trying to impress each other.'

'Hmm.'

'It shouldn't take a teenager to point it out, but it's really got me thinking.'

'Has it?'

The sofa creaks – Jack flopping down, turning on the TV with a jab of the remote. I lean back against the fridge and hold a glass against my forehead. Mum picks up where she left off, babbling away as Jack hits the volume, turning it up not down so the headlines of the ten o'clock news boom around the lounge.

'I'm talking to you,' Mum says when there's a pause in the *bongs*. 'What's up?'

The volume returns to a more reasonable level. 'Nothing.'

'How was the rehearsal?'

'Good.'

I wait for him to elaborate, and Mum does too. 'Did they like it, then?'

'Yes. They got really into it. It was great. A treat for me after all the hard work on my own in the study.' He's saying the right sort of things, but in the wrong sort of tone. Mum obviously decides not to push it.

'Excellent. I'm pleased. And if it doesn't work out then it doesn't matter, darling. Nothing matters. That's what Henry seems to think. All of the stuff society's obsessed with – the effort we put in to impress other people, none of it—'

'I'm not doing this to impress other people,' Jack snaps. 'Jesus. I'm doing it for me.'

'You know what I mean,' Mum says, trying to jolly him

along. 'Worrying about what your agent might think, and Andrew next door, and Paul and Susan.'

'I don't care about them!'

'Good,' Mum says, determined not to have an argument. 'That's fine, then. Henry would say that's an excellent point of view.'

'I don't give a damn about Henry. Will you stop banging on about him as if he's some sort of prophet? Do I need life lessons from a pretentious seventeen-year-old who can't even drive?'

'He drives,' Mum says, flaring up now. 'We saw him drive.'

'You know what I mean. Tell him to come back and lecture me when he's finished puberty. *Henry would say that's an excellent point of view.* For crying out loud, Hels! Don't patronise me.'

'I'm not trying to patronise you.' I peep into the lounge. They're both on the sofa, Mum leaning towards Jack, touching his knee as he glowers at the TV. 'I'm just sharing. He said some interesting things. Some very interesting things, actually, about Tess in particular.'

Jack slams his hand against the armrest. 'Did he now? What did this total stranger have to say about our daughter, eh? No, go on,' he says as Mum crosses her legs and looks the other way. 'Spit it out. I'm interested to know what this Henry person had to say. I mean, he's known Tess for what, two minutes? Ten? I'm sure he's extremely enlightened.'

'He said it was a protest. The silence,' Mum shouts, uncrossing her legs, unable to resist the fight. 'He made it sound as though she is taking a stand.'

'Against what?'

'Us.'

They look at each other.

'Henry said that?' Jack asks, after a pause.

'Well, no. He didn't say that last bit. But that's what I think – that she's taking a stand against us. She isn't scared, Jack. She's furious. The question is, why?'

CHAPTER 43

I'm sitting on the bottom stair on Friday morning, pulling on my boots, when Jack swings round the banister and jangles the car keys in practically my face.

'I'll give you a lift, Tess.' It blurts out of him, all in a rush.

'You're giving her a lift?' Mum says, hurrying down the stairs, clutching the brown strap of her teaching bag.

'It's threatening out there.' Threatening in here, more like. Since Mum told Jack that I was furious yesterday evening, the atmosphere's been tense. Heavy. Bearing down on me and giving me a headache. I think Jack knows that I know about the blog. The secret is hanging above us, black and menacing.

Mum points at the windows, three rectangles of bright light. 'If you say so, darling.' She gives Jack a kiss then ruffles my hair. 'Have a good day.'

The words flit around the room and then they're gone, swooping out of the door as Mum leaves for work. I lace up my boots. Recheck the bows. Adjust the hem of my trousers. There is nothing else to do but stand up. I put my right foot on the lounge floor. My left. My hands sink into my thighs as I heave myself up to face the day. Maybe even The Day.

Jack's jaw sets into a determined line as we go through the motions of leaving the house. He fills Jedi's water bowl and checks the patio door is locked. I pick up my salad from the kitchen and grab my jacket off the banister. The rhythm is familiar, but there are new odd beats. A splash of water as Jack has a quick drink. A nervous cough. A creak of floorboard as he pauses by the mirror in the lounge, glaring at his reflection, psyching himself up to maybe admit the truth.

He ushers me onto the pavement as Andrew emerges from the house next to ours. Jack swears quietly before bellowing, 'Morning!'

'Morning to you too, Mr Turner! Chauffeuring again? What's the excuse this time?' Andrew shields his eyes from the sun as he looks up at a clear blue sky. 'Can't be the weather. She should be walking on a nice morning like this.'

'Should she?' Jack replies, a new bite in his tone. 'Is that so?'

'That's what I always tell my Suzie when she's being lazy. And I see you've quit the day job again.' He gestures at Jack's tracksuit bottoms. 'The acting work coming in at last?'

I expect Jack to lie, but he swallows it down then runs

his tongue over his teeth. 'Nothing much at present.' The words are slow, pushed out into the open one at a time.

'Sorry to hear that, mate. It's a tough profession.'

'It is.'

'Couldn't do it myself.'

'No, you couldn't.'

'I like this too much,' he says, rubbing his thumb against his forefinger. 'Kids aren't cheap, are they?' It even irritates me, the implication that Jack can't provide. He grimaces but doesn't rise to it. I'm impressed, and Henry would be too. 'Case in point – the school ski trip to France. That's costing an arm and a leg, isn't it?'

'I wouldn't know.'

'See if you can still get on it,' Andrew says to me. 'It's a great trip. Week in the Alps in the Christmas holidays. Brilliant.'

'We're having a family Christmas,' Jack replies. 'The three of us together.'

Andrew gives me a patronising smile. 'Bit of a home bird, are you, Tess? Our Suzie is so independent these days. We've encouraged it from the very beginning, mind you.'

'Yes, I remember you putting her in nursery full-time.'

'It's good for them, mate.'

'Good for the parents, more like, but each to their own.' Jack gives me a gentle elbow in the ribs. 'I took two years off to look after this one when Helen went back to work, and I don't regret a second of it.' My heart jolts. I must know this, but I don't really remember. Two years with Jack when I was a baby. Seven hundred and thirty days. Jack copies Andrew, rubbing his thumb against his forefinger. 'You can't put a price on that time, mate.'

We leave Andrew, flushing on the pavement, crossing the road to the car.

Jack gives him a friendly wave as we set off. 'What an idiot. Total plonker.'

Seven hundred and thirty days is seventeen thousand five hundred and twenty hours. *I don't regret a second of it.*

'I meant what I said,' Jack mutters as if he's reading my mind. He squeezes the steering wheel so the veins appear beneath his skin. I wonder if his blood feels as hot as mine. 'I don't regret it, Tess.'

It's painful, how much I want to believe him. Hope hurts. It swells in my chest, pressing against my bones.

'Two of the best years of my life, actually.'

I wait for him to elaborate, but we drive in silence. Not the comfortable kind of silence. This silence is full to bursting with all the things we want to say but can't, or all the words we don't want to speak but have to, at some point, because there's no going back. It's humming in the air above us. The cloud's beyond breaking point. A downpour is inevitable.

And yet nothing happens.

Maybe to buy himself more time, Jack drives past school and pulls into the *Texaco Garage* where I bought Mr Goldfish the night of the burned spaghetti. The sun turns into a moon and I'm back there again, the scent of charred pasta stinging my nostrils as a fire alarm beeps and my eyes struggle to take in Jack's words. I'm running out of the house. Wandering aimlessly along dark streets. Hurrying up and down the aisles of the petrol station, buying supplies to run away to London.

I need answers, but not from the HFEA.

Jack doesn't speak when he returns to the car after filling up with petrol. He pulls into the bus park amid a series of honks from irritated drivers.

'Shut up,' he murmurs, sneaking into a space. He's flustered, but I don't think it's because of the beeps. I give him five more seconds. Ten. Fifteen. Then finally step out of the car.

'Tess?'

I spin round quickly.

'Don't forget your salad.'

I don't notice at first.

At lunch, I'm still submerged in frustration, drowning in it. We were close, so close, and now the opportunity has passed. I wade through the corridor, yearning for Jack to appear at the end of it, brandishing a megaphone. He'd shout the truth louder than the Jehovah's Witness, louder than the doubts in my mind, so loudly I'd hear his words in space. *The blog was fictitious*, Jack would bellow. *Something*

I wrote for a script rather than real life. Of course I'm your dad. I chose to look after you for two years, didn't I? You don't need to search anymore. I'm here, Tessie-T. I'm right here.

I don't see the boys until I walk into them, a group of Year Nines reading something on the wall. There's another piece of paper two metres away, and another, two metres from that. I look around. The corridor is covered.

I squint to make out the words.

No. No, no, no!

Photocopies of Isabel's notepad, highlighted neatly in pink. I can see Anna doing it, oh so calmly moving the pen across the names so they don't get lost in the text. Isawynka. The Great Blade of Turner. Connoreah, a troll with a chequered past. I pull them down, swiping violently to tear them on purpose because the cool efficiency of the display angers me more than anything. This has taken time and effort and premeditation and a whole lot of Blu-tack, rolled in tight little balls by a cold, white hand.

I work faster, swipe harder, tearing down copy after copy but it isn't enough. I'm tired of sitting back and letting other people dictate.

There's something alive in my gut. I can feel it breathe, sense its steady eyes as it scours the crowd for Anna as I move towards Dining Room Three. That's where she'll be so that's where I need to go too. I've been taken over by the creature, this animal that's determined to stalk its prey – fierce and controlled, savage and rational – a thousand contradictory things working brilliantly in unison.

I shove open the double doors and march into the dining hall. People stare and snigger, but I no longer care. Henry was right. It's meaningless. Nonsense.

'Here comes Balls!' Connor shouts as if a word can hurt me, like I'm still vulnerable. I take it in, transform it, pretend he means the ones you get in a ball pool, those multi-coloured orbs that fly into the air to make a rainbow whenever a kid zooms out of a slide. I turn my whole body into them, my cells bright discs of blue, red and green so that I glow as I strut. I shine as I swagger. I glitter as I walk to the table in the middle of the hall.

I'm small and big and quiet and loud and timid and almighty as I stand in front of Anna.

'What are you doing here?'

I'm Tess, and it's very nice to meet you, I say with eyes that hold her gaze. Blaise's gaze. She takes in the paper clutched in my hands.

'Oh. You've come to confront me.' Isabel's notepad is in her lap. She holds it primly, a look of polite interest on her face. 'Go on, then.' I'm terrified and courageous, cowardly and brave. 'Is little Tessie going to stand up to the big, bad bully?' she says in a baby voice in no way appropriate. I've changed. I am changing even now. 'Go away, you stupid cow. You're not going to do anything to me and we both know it.'

I tuck my hair behind my ears in a slow, measured movement that Anna copies, but beneath the bravado I see something else, a flicker of nerves that she tries to hide in a languid yawn.

Tara and Sarah have stopped eating, their forks hovering above their plates. The other girls are wary too. They're scared of me and I almost laugh. I don't need to do anything else. I snatch the notepad then turn to leave.

There's no applause. No standing ovation. Most people in the dining hall have no idea that something incredible has just happened, but one girl did witness the miracle. One girl saw it, and she's standing at the edge of the room, always on the periphery, holding a ham and cheese baguette high in the air, sort of like a sword – The Great Blade of Turner.

'Stop!' Anna cries. 'I mean it, Tess. Stop right now.'

I smash through the doors and race down the corridor in the direction of the Art block.

'Give me the notepad!' Anna's thirty metres away, but gaining. 'Give that back, or I swear I'll make your life a misery.'

I look back to see her charging towards me, her cheeks

unusually red. This isn't about the notepad. It's about saving face because I embarrassed her in front of her friends and she can't stand it. She isn't big enough to take it. Henry was right about that too. We're all scared, deep down. We're all vulnerable, even Anna, and she can't bear to have it exposed.

I turn around and face her.

She almost runs into me, just about managing to skid to a stop. Lurching forward, she makes a swipe for the notepad but I shove it down the front of my trousers. It's utterly bizarre and maybe even a little bit brilliant as well. She looks horrified anyway, and I enjoy that, the expression of disgust as I push the notepad deeper into my trousers then hold out my hands, palms skyward like I'm channelling the energy of the universe. I am part of it, or it is part of me, and I am no longer afraid.

She glances at my crotch – the part of me she's scorned for weeks and attempted to expose in the bar. I point at it, daring her to go there, calling her bluff. She has no idea what to do. She's smaller than I realised and there's a spot I didn't notice before, red with a yellowish tinge on her temple. She's tried to cover it with foundation and I see a different girl now, one scrutinising herself in the mirror, twisting her head this way and that, frowning at the spot still visible beneath the make-up.

She becomes real to me and I don't want that now, do I, so I fight to hold onto the image of the villain with the smooth black hair and flawless skin, cold and hard as marble. I don't want to see her vulnerability, but it's right here in front of me, in that heavy blob of foundation and that faint smudge of mascara beneath her left eye and that random tomato seed, a spot of orange on her bright white shirt.

'Do you think I care what you think?' she says, following my gaze, but her voice is quieter now, her eyes filling with tears as she slaps at the seed. 'I liked him, you know. Henry. I really liked him,' she whispers, and then she's gone.

CHAPTER 44

I pull out the notepad, shaky and triumphant. The front is torn but easily fixable. I'm near the Art block, so I head into my form room to look for some sticky tape. Isabel's going to be so happy to have it back. I can't wait to give it to her, patched up and pristine, to see the look of delight on her face as the warm feeling blossoms in her chest and also my chest because we are symbiotic creatures, reunited for all eternity.

I search the store cupboard. We're allowed in here so absolutely there will no problem if Miss Gilbert walks in to find my hands in this drawer. Or this drawer. Or this one, full of glue sticks and paperclips and one small roll of Sellotape. I get to work on the notepad as someone enters the room, probably Miss Gilbert. I can't shout out to alert her to my presence, so I move forward to pop my head around the door, retreating quickly when I realise she's not alone.

'This is better than eating in the staffroom,' Mr

Richardson says, and there's a rustle like he's getting out sandwiches. 'Chicken. What've you got?'

'Tuna mayo for me. A bit stinky.'

'Good job I won't be getting too close.'

'Why do you think I chose it?'

They laugh because it's a joke – just a joke I tell myself firmly, but my pulse is galloping. I check the storeroom, but there's no way out except through the classroom. I'm trapped in a prison of stationery.

'We should have invited our chaperone too. To be on the safe side.'

'Shall I go and find her?'

'No,' Mr Richardson says. 'I think Tess realised yesterday that three's a crowd.'

'She's lovely though.'

'Yes, she is. Very lovely and very, very useful.'

My hand flies over my mouth.

'Stop it! That's mean,' Miss Gilbert replies, but she giggles as I whimper into my fingers.

'You're right. We have a lot to thank her for. We wouldn't even be talking if it weren't for Tess, I don't suppose. When I saw her with my phone – well, I was pleased, to be honest with you. I had to hide how happy I was. Might have laid it on a bit thick.'

I remember his words, his cruel words, uttered quite clearly on purpose. *Are you deaf as well as mute?* I wish I was deaf right now, like I wish I could turn off my ears and not hear these things, spewing out of his mouth. He's my Jack, and I'm supposed to be under his wing. I shiver, feeling suddenly, horribly cold in my black jumper and odd socks that maybe don't suit me after all.

'I made it seem as though I had no choice but to march down here and see you,' Mr Richardson goes on.

'You're very cunning.'

'What choice did I have when you sent me that message? *I never want to see you again. Don't come to my room. Don't call because I won't answer.*'

'It's how I felt at the time.' I can hear a shrug in Miss Gilbert's voice. 'I make no apology for it.'

I shove Isabel's notepad in my bag then press my eye to a gap in the door to see a thin sliver of room, both my teachers crammed inside it. Mr Richardson has his back against a desk and Miss Gilbert is directly opposite, her bum pressed against a cupboard. Their legs are jutting out, their toes almost touching. The sandwiches lie forgotten at their side.

They're not friends.

Not at all.

Their body language is screaming out in big bold letters that they want each other. Right now. Probably on that table. Henry deserves more than this, and Julie too – Julie with her chocolate cake and warm caramel eyes. I turn away, unwilling to see anymore, but I can't block out their words.

'The text was a bit over the top,' Mr Richardson says, his tone gently mocking.

'It was entirely appropriate, actually. I was hurt. You lied to me.'

'I never said I was single.'

'You never said you were married! You took off your wedding ring every time you spoke to me.'

'So you were right,' I tell Mr Goldfish, going for my pocket, my fingers closing around nothing. 'You were right all along.'

'I'm sorry,' Mr Richardson says. 'But it wasn't a direct lie, was it?'

'It's lying by omission, which is lying in my book!'

'Woah. Do I need to go and get Tess to stop you laying into me?'

'Yeah, that was sly. Coming down here with a student so I couldn't have a go at you.'

'Like I say, Tess has her uses, even if she is a bit creepy. The silence. All that black hair.' I stifle a sob. 'Talk about spooky.'

'We can't keep doing it. It isn't fair. I'm no good at lying.'

Mr Richardson chuckles like I'm the punch line of a bad joke. 'A room swap, was it?' I force myself to look. They're smiling, basking in each other as I experience something of a solar eclipse. There's no warmth in this store cupboard. No light. No hope. The sun's rising between them, this hot ball of passion, setting their faces on fire. 'That was inspired.'

Miss Gilbert groans, but she's enjoying the agony. 'Why did I say it?'

'It was ridiculous!'

'Maths and Art! Oh God! As if that would ever happen in a million years. No offence, but what could someone dull as a Maths teacher possibly want with a room like this.'

'Maybe it's not the room he wants.'

'Don't,' she warns, but she moves closer, stopping herself at the very last second. 'Don't say that if you don't mean it.'

'I can't stop thinking about you, Laura. I've tried, and I can't stop.'

'But you said you wanted to be friends. You said you'd made a mistake.' She's quivering on the precipice, body pulsating with the effort to stay put, keep rational, resist the urge to jump.

'All last night. In the shower. In bed.'

'What about your wife?'

'Don't talk about my wife.'

'And your son?'

'I don't know.'

'They're your family, Jack.'

But he doesn't hear, because he's pulling her towards him, their bodies colliding with a BOOM that shatters my world.

Stop!

The word bounces off the bones of my skull, boomeranging back on itself, stuck in the cage that is my head as Mr Richardson drags Miss Gilbert round a corner, out of sight of the window, but in full view of me. The sliver of room becomes a slice as I slowly open the storeroom door.

'Stop!'

It isn't me who says it. This word is free. Untrapped. It bursts out into the classroom as Miss Gilbert half-heartedly pushes Mr Richardson away.

'Stop!' she says again, but then she moans because he's kissing her neck and jaw and ears, his lips on the crescent-shaped moons. 'Stop. No. This isn't right! This isn't—'

She looks up, sees me, and gasps in dismay. She shoves Mr Richardson away, properly this time. He stumbles then stops, facing the opposite direction, his body tense because he knows.

'It's Tess, isn't it?'

Miss Gilbert's silence says it all.

'If you mention this to anyone,' he whispers, without turning around, 'I'll ring your parents and tell them I caught you trying to steal my phone. Do you hear me? Do you hear me, Tess?'

The only reply is the door slamming closed. I stagger into the corridor, weaving through a crowd of people inexplicably having an ordinary day. I hurtle out of a fire exit next to a girl wrapped up in a thick red coat, biting into a browning apple. It makes me think of Henry and the rotten core he sees at the heart of the world. It's more true than he could ever have imagined. There is something rotten at the heart of his world – and it's his dad.

But not my dad I suddenly know with absolute certainty, and there's a glimmer of relief, even as I stumble out of the school gates, grieving for yet another Jack.

CHAPTER 45

I plunge my hand into the bin. Mr Goldfish is at the bottom, buried beneath I don't know what, tucked inside a polystyrene cup, no doubt in an effort to keep warm. My heart bleeds for him, weeping scarlet tears in my chest that's getting bigger or smaller, or wider or thinner, or maybe all these things at once because definitely my body feels peculiar. My head too, wobbling about on my neck a thousand miles long as I gaze down at myself, watching my hand grab Mr Goldfish and flick his switch.

Nothing.

I flick it again.

No light. No voice. No magical bursting into life.

'I'm sorry. I'm so sorry.' I strain my ears for a reply that doesn't come. He's lifeless, lying on my palm, eyes open but seeing nothing because – 'No. Definitely not. No way.'

I give Mr Goldfish a shake, just a gentle one, stroking his beautiful golden head. He's alive. He has to be alive. Hoping for a miracle, praying for it, I click the button to resurrect him from the dead. No words emerge from his lips. No reassuring ray of hope shines out of his mouth. There is nothing but darkness, and I am alone – a Pluto, lost at the very edge of the solar system where I thought I wanted to be.

I walk in the opposite direction to school, even though afternoon lessons are about to start. I guess I'm skiving, and isn't it strange how easy it is, how completely and utterly simple to break the rules when you no longer care. I trudge with Mr Goldfish, cradling him in my palm as if he's asleep, not dead.

People are possibly staring. I don't know and I don't care because I only have eyes for my fish. My friend. I hold him tight as I process down the road, carrying him to his final resting place, which will be somewhere warm and protected with—

'—Some hot lady-torches for me to lie with for the rest of eternity?' Mr Goldfish says weakly. I spin him round in disbelief and, wow, there's an abundance of light, but it's from my face, not his. It's my eyes that are radiant, my joy that is golden, my happiness that is dazzling my friend.

'You're alive! I thought you were dead!'

'Nope. Not dead. No thanks to you, mind. You left me.'

'I know.'

'In a bin.'

'I know that too.'

'Do you also know what people put in a bin, Tess?' He

sounds frail but irritated. I'm so thrilled to see his grumpy face, I laugh out loud. It's a whoop, a holler, a huge great big shout of delight. Definitely people are staring now, and definitely I don't care because Mr Goldfish is here. 'Get off me!' he says, as I cover his puckered brow in kisses. 'Tissues, Tess. That's what goes in a bin. Used tissues. *Poo bags from dogs.*' I giggle at his look of revulsion. 'It isn't funny.'

'I know it isn't. I'm sorry. I wasn't thinking straight.'

'You admit it now, do you?'

It comes back to me in an excruciating rush – the lies and the betrayal and the kiss, burned on my retinas so I can see Mr Richardson's writhing body when I close my eyes. He'll know I'm skiving by now. Probably an email will have gone round, alerting all staff that Tess Turner didn't turn up for French five minutes ago.

'You were right about Mr Richardson.' Mr Goldfish doesn't say *I told you* so or gloat in anyway whatsoever, just nods sadly. 'He isn't my dad, is he?'

'No, I don't think so. I'm sorry.'

'Don't be. It's a good thing. I'm glad. Honestly. He's an idiot.'

'It's okay to be upset,' Mr Goldfish whispers because my bottom lip is trembling. I bite it hard as I can, drawing blood.

'No, it isn't. Not for him.'

'You're bound to be disappointed.'

Tears fill my eyes, but I blink them back. 'I thought

we had a bond. A connection. He said he felt it too, but it was a lie, wasn't it? To get closer to Miss Gilbert?' The gap between how I viewed Mr Richardson and how he really viewed me opens up and I stare into the void in disbelief. 'None of it was true.'

I've been walking without paying attention to my surroundings. I blink again, trying to work out where I am – a quiet street, a petrol station in the distance – the road where I flagged down the cab to go to the HFEA the first time I ran away. A black taxi with an orange light glowering on its forehead chugs into view. It would be so easy to stick out my hand and race to London on the pretence of needing answers I'm too scared to ask the only man who can give me the information I seek. Whizzing to Manchester Piccadilly station, I could catch a train to anywhere in the country, vanish in Scotland, disappear in Wales and never have to see either Jack again.

I could forget the words of the blog. The words spoken in the Art room.

The words Jack said this morning to Andrew.

The words Mum uttered in my bedroom when she handed me the hot water bottle.

I could live without words. Without a name. Without a past.

'Tess?' Mr Goldfish says. The taxi is approaching, the exact colour of night, of space. It would take me far, far away. My hand quivers as I hold it out and step closer to the kerb. The car slows . . . slows . . . slows . . . but does not stop because I jerk back my arm and shake my head.

No.

It roars past, the light flashing like a shooting star as I stand on the ground – as I stand *my* ground.

I'm not going to hide from the truth anymore.

CHAPTER 46

I wander about until the end of school then buy some milk and Eccles cakes for Gran, the fattest ones I can find. I run to her house, relieved to have chores that need completing. I'll dust. Pick up the bits off the floor. I'll even do the skirting boards, scrubbing them until they shine. I'll clean Gran's street then move on to Mr Richardson's, getting rid of the filth until it's pure. Untainted. Fit for Henry and his mum.

The doorbell chimes and for once Gran hears it.

'Tess! Everyone's worried sick about you. Where have you been?' Gran is white as her hair. I hold out the Eccles cakes, wanting to make amends, but she doesn't take them. 'Your dad's been on the telephone. Your school called to say you'd disappeared. You've caused a lot of upset.' I hold out the milk too. 'Come on in. I'll let your dad know you're here.'

Gran goes into the kitchen to make the call. I enter the lounge. The fire is overpowering, a wall of heat, but I move closer to it, determined to dust the ornaments on the mantelpiece, to do something nice for Gran to make up for the stress I've caused. With my sleeve, I polish as many animals as possible before she returns – a horse, three birds, two pigs and the lion – then drop onto the sofa as she shuffles through the door.

'He's on his way,' she says, lowering herself into a rocking chair. 'He's relieved you're safe, but truancy, Tess? He isn't happy about that, and I can't say I blame him.' Gran's never been angry with me before. I can't stand the disapproval in her eyes. 'What is going on with you?'

'Where do I begin?' Mr Goldfish asks, heaving himself out of my pocket, his voice weak but determined. 'She convinced herself that a teacher was her dad and then she kissed a boy even though he could have been her brother.' I push him back down as Gran points at a photo on the windowsill. A tiny blonde toddler peers out of a silver frame with big bright eyes that can't wait to see what the world has to offer.

'I assume that little tot is still inside you somewhere. We don't lose the people we once were, Tess.' She glances at another picture. 'Believe it or not, I'm still that girl on her wedding day.' I can just about make out two black and white figures in front of a village hall. Gran and Grandpa look like ghosts. Happy ghosts, but ghosts all the same. 'We had a buffet. Chicken legs. Meat pie. All the lot. The guests brought along a dish to cut back on costs. No point frittering your money away for one day. Just look at Aunt Susan and that ridiculous Mark she married, spending thousands on a fairytale wedding, only to get divorced two years later.'

Gran crosses her ankles and rocks herself quickly. She seems agitated, not like herself at all. 'How much did Susan say the cake was? Eight hundred pounds? Far too much. It was too expensive to enjoy! Susan went green when that Archie, the Wilsons' boy, dropped half a slice and his brother mashed it to a pulp with his toy car. I know what Susan was thinking. *Ten pounds. That piece cost me ten pounds.*'

Her glasses catch the light of the fire as she shakes her head. 'I don't know, Tess. It used to be keeping up with the Joneses. Now it's keeping up with those Beckhams. I mean, honestly – Aunt Susan and Mark sitting at the reception on a pair of thrones? He's an accountant, for Heaven's sake. What was he playing at? The world's gone bonkers.' The chair squeaks as she rocks herself even faster. 'I feel sorry for you all. You think you've got it better nowadays? I'm telling you – you don't. Yes, there were fewer choices when I was young, but people knew where they stood, at least. They had a role. A purpose. Time to commit to things – jobs and family and community. Now there's too much choice. People try to have it all, and they end up with less. Funny that.'

She goes quiet for a few seconds, the chair creaking more gently. 'Like your dad, Tess, having that nervous breakdown in his twenties.' I sit up sharply because no one's ever said anything about this before. 'Working all the time, audition after audition after audition. *I'll be happy when I've made it*, he always used to say. *Made it where?* That's what I asked him once. He couldn't answer, but he's still doing it, isn't he? Still running round trying to prove himself. Well, I blame his parents for that. He can never do anything to impress them, his dad in particular. That's all your dad wants, really. A bit of praise from his own father. Tragic.'

It is tragic. I think it before I'm aware of it, this wave of sympathy washing over me for the man with the half-empty wall and the Sellotaped skull and the need to exaggerate about everything he's ever done. Another wave crashes over me as I remember something else, a conversation in the car park outside the Methodist church in Didsbury. *Can you imagine if he had been in the audience? Or my dad, for that matter, if he'd said yes to those tickets? It would have been even more humiliating than it already was.* Jack invited his dad to the play, and his dad said no.

Jack is many things, but he isn't neglectful.

'The opposite, you could say,' Mr Goldfish mutters. 'Supportive in an overly-pushy, annoyingly in-your-face kind of way.'

'He does love you, Tess,' Gran says, watching me closely. 'Whatever you might think, his heart is in the right place.'

I want to believe it, but it's hard when I know what I know, when I've read what I've read.

'He is irritating sometimes, always trying so hard to be

more than he is.' I nod, glad Gran understands. 'But you're irritating too,' she goes on as my head freezes, 'trying so hard to be less. This isn't you, dear. These clothes. This silence. It's the denial of you. And it's getting a little bit silly.'

Someone knocks loudly on the front door. Gran climbs to her feet and hobbles stiffly across the lounge, past the porcelain ornaments shining on the mantelpiece.

'You might not be a lion, Tess. That's fine. Neither am I. But we're still cats, aren't we? Just because we don't roar, doesn't mean we have to hide ourselves away.'

I throw my bag onto the back seat then climb into the front, waiting for the explosion that absolutely is coming. I skived school today, and definitely Jack will have a lot to say about that. I'm ready for the showdown. Craving it, almost. I want Jack to shout, to prove me right, or wrong, or whatever it is. I want him to scream the words from the blog, over and over again. More than that though, I want him to say that he's sorry, that he takes them all back, every single one of those six hundred and seventeen words because he never meant them in the first place.

But Jack just drives.

When we pull up outside our house, Jedi appears in the window – ears pricked, tongue hanging out – delighted to see both of us. We smile at him and almost, but not quite, at each other, sharing yet another okay moment that makes no sense in the grand scheme of things.

'Tess.'

Jack's voice is gruff, urgent, totally at odds with his fading grin. He turns to look at me, his seatbelt pulling tight across his chest like he needs to be strapped in for the turbulence that's about to hit. I harden myself, getting ready for his criticism and his outrage and his lecture about school that no doubt will go on for hours.

'I'm here, okay. Ready to hear, if you ever want to talk.'

That's all he says for thirty seconds or so, pretty much the quietest and most remarkable half a minute in the history of the universe.

'I know I'm not always the best at listening, but I'll try. I really will. What your mum said, Tess, about your silence being a protest. It doesn't have to be like this. You can talk about whatever it is that's making you angry,' he says, not quite daring to meet my eyes – but then he does, fully. 'Your old man is big enough to take it. Okay?'

He pats my leg then shoots out of the car, busying himself in the boot. I grab my school bag off the back seat, my phone slipping out under the passenger seat. I lean down to get it, and there, hidden in the shadows, are three copies of Jack's script, not given to Mr Darling or Nana the dog at all.

'These are for you, by the way,' Jack says, opening my door. I sit up quickly, pretending I haven't seen the scripts. He hands me a plastic bag. 'Socks. Matching socks. I thought you could do with some new ones.'

CHAPTER 47

I barely sleep all weekend, unable to relax as I pace up and down my room, trying to work out how to act in front of Miss Gilbert and Mr Richardson on Monday. When it finally arrives, my eyes are puffy, my shoulders tight.

'I'm going to blow it,' I tell Mr Goldfish when Mum drops me off in the car park. 'My face feels weird. They're going to take one look at it and think I've blabbed.'

'You still could.'

'You heard what Mr Richardson said. He'll tell Mum about the phone.'

'That's blackmail, Tess.'

'Yeah, and it's working.'

'See you in a bit, then,' Mum sighs. She's taken the morning off work to attend a meeting with Mrs Austin to *discuss the consequences of my truancy*. That's the phrase Mrs Austin used on the phone, and the one Mum has been repeating for two days solid.

'Be prepared for the fact that the consequences of your

truancy might be fairly severe, Tess,' she said over breakfast on Sunday morning, picking up a slice of toast. 'We just have to hope that Mrs Austin's in a lenient mood, though I don't suppose that's very likely. The poor woman has to be seen to be doing something. She can't let students get away with walking out of school in the middle of the day. What sort of precedent would that set?' She points the toast at me. 'Truancy, Tess? Skiving? What's the matter with you?'

'Leave it, Hels,' Jack said, carrying two bowls of porridge to the table. He put one in front of me and I huddled round it, breathing in the creamy warmth. 'We don't know the details.'

Mum put the toast back down again. 'What?'

'Maybe Tess had her reasons.'

'Oh, don't give me all that.' Mum made a beak out of her hand that she opened and closed at the side of her head. 'That's what I've been trying to tell you.'

'Yes. And I've listened.' He grabbed the bird and held it tight so it couldn't peck his fingers. 'Obviously she shouldn't have done it, but I don't think Tess would have run out of school without good reason, that's all I'm saying.' Mum's expression was an odd mixture of irritation and surprise at this man who didn't sound like Jack, or look like him either. He was smaller, somehow, his manner more serious, less brash. For some reason I thought of a peacock with a closed-up tail. 'She'll tell us when she's ready.'

I was ready then, actually, and I'm ready now. I look back into the car.

'What is it?' Mum asks. *If you mention this to anyone, I'll ring your parents and tell them I caught you trying to steal my phone. Do you hear me? Do you hear me, Tess?* 'Go on, now. I'll see you at nine thirty.'

I make my way to the Art block – via the toilet I don't really need, stopping at a vending machine even though I'm not hungry and pausing at my locker to drop off a French textbook that actually I'm more than capable of carrying around. It kills five minutes, and I get to practise my innocent expression so it's ready for Miss Gilbert and Mr Richardson. I stick my head in my locker.

'How about this face? Or this one? No, this one.'

'All good.' Mr Goldfish sounds sleepy, lying on the textbook, fins tucked behind his head.

'You're not even looking.'

He scrabbles around. 'I am. I am, I am,' he lies and then he laughs, which turns into a violent cough, his pale light flickering as he gasps for breath.

'No!' I grab him and give him a shake, tapping his back with my fingers. 'No! Please!' His light is fading and his breath is rasping and his eyes are clouding over. I whack his back. His light returns, but it's faint, barely shining in the darkness. 'Are you okay?'

'Just do the face again.' Neither of us wants to consider the answer to that particular question. No doubt about it, he's getting weaker. I do as he asks, exaggerating it to make him smile, even though nothing whatsoever about the situation is funny.

'Tess, I owe you a thank you.' I pull my head out of my locker to see Isabel, grinning broadly. 'Seriously, Tess. Thank you.' She hurries over to me, cello bouncing at her side. I am so happy to see it, I almost yank it out of her hand and play a song myself. Instead, I pull her into a hug.

'I'm sorry. I'm so sorry,' I say with my arms, squeezing her tightly.

'Oh, Tess. Will you forgive me?'

'Of course you're forgiven,' Mr Goldfish cries. 'Don't worry about—' but I turn him off gently because actually this moment belongs to Isabel and me. We step back and look at each other.

'You, in the dining hall! Blimey, Tess.' She starts to laugh. 'Total respect. I mean, it was insane, but in the best possible way, like in *The Return of the King* – film not book – when Merry and Pippin break rank in the Battle of the Black Gate, charging at the orcs before Aragorn has even moved.' She acts it out, roaring with a sword held high above her head. I drink in the sight of her off-kilter ponytail swinging madly as she swipes at an orc.

She's a mentalist, all right.

'You're a mentalist, Tess,' she says and that makes me smile because we are symbiotic creatures, let's be clear about that. 'But it worked, didn't it? I haven't seen any copies around school this morning, and I came in early to check. There's nothing in the toilets, or the corridors, or anything. You totally saved the day.'

I take the notepad out of my bag. She clutches it to her chest then holds it out, admiring the job I did to patch up the front cover with the sticky tape in the storeroom. Where I heard that conversation. And saw that kiss.

'What's wrong?' Isabel whispers. 'What's going on?' I can't tell her – I can't tell anyone – but it helps to have my friend by my side as I walk to Art One to face Miss Gilbert.

A supply teacher is sitting behind her desk, a woman with grey hair and a dull brown suit and absolutely no lunar sparkle. Weak with relief I sink onto my stool. Miss Gilbert isn't here, so maybe Mr Richardson has decided to skive as well. Maybe they're together, checked in to a hotel, a *Do Not Disturb* sign swinging from the handle.

When registration is over, I head outside to get to the Geography block. There's a clearing in the fog, as if the day is slipping off its black cloak. Definitely the outlook seems more positive, a hint of sun in the sky. Mr Richardson might have done a runner. Or he might have realised the error of his ways, resigning from his post, deciding to recommit to his wife and son, vowing to stay away from Miss Gilbert and all women, actually, until the end of time.

I take my seat in Geography. There's only half an hour until the meeting with Mrs Austin. I'll accept my punishment, whatever it is, and I'll try hard, refocusing on school. Mr Holdsworth will be back after Christmas, so even if Mr Richardson hasn't done the honourable thing and left of his own accord, things will soon return to normal. I feel good, safe, so I don't jump when there's a cough in the corner of the room.

'Sorry to disturb you, Sir, but I need a quick word with Tess.'

'Right you are. No problem at all. Go on, Tess,' Mr Hughes says, pointing a pen at Mr Richardson, who's smiling benignly, hands in his pockets, waiting for me to stand. 'You don't need her for long do you, Sir?'

'Five minutes,' he replies. 'That's all it should take.'

CHAPTER 48

He's a member of staff so I have no choice but to follow. It takes forever to move across the room, like it seems about three miles long with hundreds of tables and chairs to manoeuvre around, not that I'm complaining. I would take this endless trudging if it meant I didn't have to speak to Mr Richardson.

'Thanks, Mr Hughes,' he calls, leading me into a corridor that's eerily deserted. He makes quite sure the door is closed behind us, that there is no one around before he starts to speak.

'Tess.' He has no right to say my name and I bristle. 'It's good to see you back in school. I was worried when you ran off like that.' I can hear it now, how manipulative he is. 'You were upset, weren't you? I'm not sure why.' He nods – up and down, up and down – in a slow, hypnotic rhythm. 'We understand each other, don't we? We're still on that same wavelength?' He touches my arm and my skin buzzes like an electric fence. 'I just wanted to make quite sure of it this morning.'

I snatch my arm away and his head jolts back in surprise.

'Don't be like that, Tess. I'm simply double-checking that you didn't see anything untoward on Friday. That's all I need to know, really. Clarify that, and you're free to go.' He waits for some sort of response. 'Your silence, Tess,' he sighs, still treading carefully, like definitely he thinks he can work his way around me with a bit of clever footwork. 'It's problematic in these sorts of situations, is it not? Or then again, I suppose it has its uses. If you can't speak, well, let's just say that the problem is solved.'

My lips open but no sound comes out.

'Precisely.' He smiles at my frustration. 'Clearly there's nothing to be concerned about here. We can forget about Friday. Go back to how things were before. Put it behind us.' He nods on my behalf. 'Yes, definitely. You're a good student, Tess. That's what everyone seems to think and we want to keep it that way, don't we? I would hate for certain things to get out. Certain things such as the fact that I caught you with my phone. Hiding in Miss Gilbert's store room. Rifling through my bag,' he says as my stomach drops. 'I know you looked inside my wallet, Tess. I don't know why you did it, but that hardly matters. All it would take is me complaining to Mrs Austin that some money of mine has gone missing, and you would probably be expelled. We don't want it to come to that, do we?'

It's a rhetorical question because he doesn't expect me to

answer. He doesn't expect anything of me at all, nodding again as if the problem is solved.

Mrs Austin appears at the end of the corridor, marching towards us, skirt tight around a pair of squat calves as she comes to collect me for the meeting.

'Good morning,' Mr Richardson calls brightly. 'Just having a word with Tess about some homework she was supposed to hand in this morning.'

'And failed to hand in, I'm guessing?'

'Unfortunately so.'

I fold in on myself, my fury bending double as I glower privately, quietly, words fluttering in my throat, noiseless and frantic as moths. My vocal chords are disintegrating, decaying to nothing, turning to powder like the dust on Gran's mantelpiece, covering her ornaments. The animals. That porcelain lion.

You might not be a lion, Tess. That's fine. Neither am I. But we're still cats, aren't we? Just because we don't roar, doesn't mean we have to hide ourselves away.

'He's lying, Mrs Austin. He's a liar.'

My words are quiet but clear. Henry is wise and brilliant, but he was wrong about one thing.

This is a better form of protest.

The Head's office is smaller than I remember, and redder. The rug is red and Mrs Austin's cheeks are red and Mum is crimson and Jack is ruddy, pulling at the tie around his neck. He plays with it, holding it out then letting it flop back down on his shirt. It looks like a tongue. It looks like my tongue, free to move for the first time in weeks. I thrash it about behind my teeth, checking the muscles still work.

Only Mr Richardson is a normal colour, a cool, calm beige. He smiles patiently at Mrs Austin as if he can't wait to clear up this little misunderstanding just as soon as the secretary has arrived with another chair for me.

She appears at last, pushing an old, creaky one into the office, the stiff wheels getting tangled in the rug.

'Sorry. Would you mind, Mr Richardson?'

He gets up to help. 'There you go, Tess.' He pats the back of the chair, daring me to sit down and take him on. 'Make yourself comfortable.'

I move it half a metre to the right, closer to Mum. Mr Richardson sits back down next to Jack. It's strange seeing them together, just inches apart – blond versus ginger, tall versus small – no idea they share the same name, totally unaware of the duel they have fought in my mind.

'We'll make a start, shall we?' Mrs Austin says, shuffling some paper on her desk. 'We need to discuss the truancy on Friday, but I'm afraid there is another matter we should address first.' Mum and Jack exchange a worried glance. 'This morning, Tess accused Mr Richardson of being a liar.'

'Because of an issue with homework,' he says at once. 'A silly thing, really.'

'Accused how?' Mum asks. 'Did she write it down?'

Mrs Austin purses her lips. 'She said it to his face.'

'Really!' Jack's delight jars with Mrs Austin's disapproval. 'She spoke?'

'Out loud?' Mum says, clutching the Mulberry bag. I don't mind it being here. I've done something worthy of it for once. 'Are you sure she spoke?'

'Of course.'

Jack laughs. 'Fantastic! Not the words, obviously. I don't mean that. But this is, well . . . *Helen.*'

'*I know.* It's a big step, Mrs Austin. We're not condoning what she said but you have to understand this is wonderful news for us.'

'She accused a member of staff of lying, Mrs Turner. That's serious.'

'Because of an issue with homework,' Mr Richardson says again, no doubt banking on the fact that what just happened in the corridor was a one-off, an anomaly, never to be repeated. He wants me to shut up, to be mute forevermore. Jack is the opposite, nodding encouragingly, keen to hear my voice, big enough to hear my truth, whatever it is.

'It has nothing to do with homework.' I don't need to shout. The words are powerful enough.

'Don't say something you'll regret now, Tess.' Mr Richardson looks insistently at Jack. 'She was supposed to hand in a worksheet this morning, but for some reason she's denying all knowledge of it.'

[349]

Jack stares him down, blue eyes overpowering brown. 'I think we'll let my daughter speak for herself, thank you.'

'But she can't be trusted! She's going to tell you a pack of lies!'

Mrs Austin is startled by the outburst. 'Perhaps it's better if you step outside, Mr Richardson.'

'That's hardly fair!' His composure is falling apart in spectacular fashion. He's on his feet, waving his arms. 'Do I even get the chance to defend myself against her fibs?'

'You'll have the opportunity to put forward your case but for now I must ask you to leave the room.' Mrs Austin marches round her desk on adamant legs that stop at the door. She turns the handle with a firm twist of her wrist. 'Step outside, Mr Richardson.' He flares up, eyes bulging, nostrils wide. 'The waiting area, if you please.'

The door *clicks* behind him and the office is quiet.

'Right,' Mrs Austin says, and she's back shuffling paper on her desk, but it's different now. She's uncertain, searching for a blank sheet and a pen. 'In your own time, Tess. There's no rush.'

A computer screen. Running away. The HFEA. A Methodist church in Didsbury. Mr Richardson's brown eyes. A driving licence. The kitchen window. Henry. Miss Gilbert. A wedding ring. And a kiss in a classroom.

Slipping my hand in my pocket, my fingers close around Mr Goldfish, squeezing him tightly as I turn him on.

'You can do it, Tess.'

I'm not so sure. Mum and Jack are waiting. Mrs Austin's fountain pen is poised.

'Say it, Tess,' Jack urges. 'It's okay. You can explain. Nothing's off-limits here.' He rubs his face. I know what's coming, but it takes him a while to ask the question. 'You saw it, didn't you?' I nod, just once. His whole body seems to sag. 'I'm so sorry, sweetheart.'

'Saw what?' Mum asks. 'Saw what, Jack?'

'It's okay. Tell her.'

And so I do. I talk. I explain everything, my words captured on paper by Mrs Austin's glistening ink. She traps the truth. Makes it real. Undeniable. Impossible to ignore.

It takes ages and it's exhausting, but somehow I get to the end, finally repeating the words Mr Richardson used when he blackmailed me in the corridor.

When it's over, no one speaks. Mrs Austin glances back over her notes. Mum cries quietly into the yellow handkerchief. Jack puts his arm around my shoulder. He pulls me to him, and I resist, and I resist, and then I don't.

'Can I take my daughter home?' he asks.

'Absolutely,' Mrs Austin replies. 'And rest assured that Mr Richardson will be suspended with immediate effect, pending investigation.'

'If he comes near Tess again, I swear to God I'll knock his block off.'

'That won't happen, Mr Turner. I know tensions are running extremely high, but please trust me to handle this.'

Jack goes to argue, but Mum stops him by fetching his coat. 'Take this. Come on. Let's go home. Have a cup of tea.'

'That's an excellent idea,' Mrs Austin says, and I agree.

CHAPTER 49

A scurry of paws announces Jedi's arrival as he tears down the stairs to greet all three of us, not quite a trio but more than a bunch of individuals. I kick off my boots on the doormat. *Welcome* it says. *Welcome back.* Falling to my knees, I bury my face in Jedi's fur.

'Hello, boy.' He wags madly at the sound of my voice, jumping up to lick my mouth before collapsing on his back, paws stuck out in all directions. A giggle bubbles out of me. It feels good, sort of tickly. 'You are a silly dog.'

'I've always thought that,' Mr Goldfish mutters, moving ever so slightly in my pocket. 'Silly and smelly.'

Mum pauses midway through removing her shoes. 'Your laugh, Tess. I never thought I'd hear it again. It's a nice noise.'

'A great noise,' Jack says.

I'm embarrassed by the compliment so I give Jedi a stroke. Mum stumbles towards me, pulling off her other shoe and tossing it to one side. Jedi darts after it.

'No, boy! No! Damn it,' she says as he shoots into the kitchen with his trophy. 'Listen to me, Tess. You have to understand that your dad and I wanted you, whatever it said in that blog.' She glares at Jack. 'We fought for you for years and that's why we used a, well, a thingy.' She takes a deep breath. 'A sperm donor.'

Jack's reaction is identical to mine. We both flinch and look for an escape route, but decide to stay put.

'It's because we were so desperate to have a child of our own that we ended up in this situation. We'd tried everything, hadn't we, Jack? Herbal remedies. Pills. IVF.'

He clears his throat. 'Yes.'

'Is that all you've got to say?'

He clears his throat again because there's a blockage, something stopping him from saying these words. He's kept them hidden far longer than I have. 'It isn't easy, Hels.'

Mum softens at once, pulling him onto the armchair. He sinks into it, exhausted. Mum perches on his knee and rubs the base of his neck. 'That time in our lives was really hard, Tess. Getting our hopes up every month only to have them dashed. Trying week after week. It was tiring.'

'That's maybe too much information,' Mr Goldfish whispers.

'It was a struggle, devastating at times.'

'And it was my fault,' Jack says in a low voice, 'as you've probably guessed. I was the one with the problem.'

'That's definitely too much information,' Mr Goldfish hisses.

'I couldn't give your mum the thing she wanted more than anything. We didn't tell anyone, not a soul, because I was too proud. Your mum had no one to talk to. No one to confide in.'

'Neither did you.'

They hold hands. 'It was stupid to try and keep it to ourselves, but there you go.'

Jack shifts on the armchair, rubbing his nose, adjusting his trousers, uncomfortable with the conversation we've had so far, or maybe where it's heading. He's upset, shaken like a snow globe, all these dormant words agitated and restless for the first time in years. He pulls on his tie, freeing his throat.

'Even when it came to using a donor, I wanted it to be a secret so no one would ever dispute that you were mine. I was determined to be a good dad because I'd failed as a husband.'

'You didn't fail, Jack. Don't be daft.'

'That's how it felt.'

'So, Gran and Aunt Susan and Uncle Paul?' I ask slowly.

'They don't know. Nobody knows.' Something eases in my chest as I nod. 'The day we found out we were expecting you, I made a vow, cheesy as it sounds. Looked in the mirror and said it out loud. I would love you like my own. I'd be there for you in the way my own dad wasn't for me. Support you. Encourage you to do well at school and outside it. But then you were born and—'

'What?' Mum says. 'This is what I don't understand. We were over the moon, weren't we?'

'I wasn't. I'm sorry, Hels, but if we're being honest then I have to say it as it is.'

'You didn't love her?'

'Not straight away. I couldn't.'

I wait for the hurt and the terror and the anguish, but I'm strangely calm, almost at peace, which makes no sense at all. I've dreaded this for weeks, built it up in my mind, run from it at every opportunity, but now it's actually happening, I'm relieved. For a glorious instant, Mr Goldfish appears before me, resplendent, puffing out his orange chest. *The only way to conquer your fears is to face them. True courage—'*

'Is what?' I ask.

'I don't know,' he admits, sheepishly. 'I had no idea where that was going first time round, either.'

'She didn't feel like mine,' Jack says. 'You and Tess, you were a twosome, right from the start. You were brilliant, Hels. Got the hang of it straightaway. A total natural. Breastfeeding. Winding. Nappies, all that stuff. You were the one who could soothe her if she was crying. Send her off to sleep. She'd settle on your skin because it was her skin, wasn't it? That's how it seemed. You smelled the same. You were made of the same stuff. And I was on the outside.' It's a flurry of words. I can almost see the blizzard. 'I felt useless, to be honest.'

'You should have told me, Jack.'

'How could I? This is what we'd wanted for years. What we'd tried so hard to get. I was ashamed, wasn't I? I couldn't be a proper dad, and when it came to manning up and taking on Tess as my own, I couldn't do that either.'

Tears shine in Mum's eyes. 'I had no idea. No idea!'

'That's why I wrote the blog. Partly to get it off my chest and partly to help other men who might feel the same. There was something on TV a few weeks ago about dads who struggled to bond with their babies and it brought it all back. I wanted to reassure people that, just because things start off badly, doesn't mean they always end up that way, but I didn't end up posting it in the end. It seemed wrong when Tess didn't know the truth. Can I show it to you? To both of you?'

'I'd like that,' I reply, surprising myself again.

We follow him into the study, the curtains closed and the radiator switched off so the room is dark and cold, almost as if it's no longer in use. The skull is nowhere to be seen and the frame that contained the Robert Frost poem is empty. It makes me sad to see it, but hopeful too.

'I'll just get the computer going,' Jack says, and there's a bizarre five minutes of practicality where a wire is untangled and a plug is inserted in a socket and an *on* button is pressed.

We huddle in the gloom, waiting for the laptop to wake up. When it finally does, the screen is bright as sunrise.

Jack finds the file and opens it up for us to read. Six hundred and seventeen words – only there are more of them now, three thousand and seventy-one in fact. The start of the blog hasn't changed, and it isn't easy to be faced with Jack's experience of me as a newborn, his struggle to bond with another man's daughter, his disappointment – in himself most of all, for not being able to give his wife a child, and for being incapable of loving the one she had when it arrived.

Mum backs away from the computer. 'I can't believe you felt like that.'

'Read on,' he urges. 'Just read.'

And so we do, and the blog transforms the instant he writes about the first time he saw me smile, just this ordinary Saturday morning. Mum had a lie-in and he sat in the kitchen and ate a bowl of porridge, cradling me in one arm, looking down to see me grin. It was faint, maybe even wind, but that was the second he felt like my dad.

'That was the point I was trying to make, Tess. When you read it, it wasn't finished. I'm so sorry you saw it, love, that you found out like this and that I didn't ask you sooner if you'd seen it. I wasn't absolutely sure that you had. You already seemed so upset. I was scared of telling you something you didn't know and making everything worse. What if you hadn't read the blog? What then? I'm sorry. We should have been honest with you from the start.'

'It was difficult. I get that,' I say. I didn't at first, but now I do.

'There was never a good time,' he goes on, reassured by my response. 'You were too young. And then you were too old. You'd been my daughter for years. I didn't want to tell you otherwise. Put ideas in your head so you'd run off, trying to find some other bloke who didn't know you like I do. Love you.'

An image of Mr Richardson floats into my mind, and just as quickly, disappears again.

'I'm not the best dad, Tess. I know that. But I am your dad.'

The words are quiet and simple – my sort of words, drifting out of his mouth to settle on my skin like snowflakes in first dawn, melting into me as I accept them as truth.

We drink tea, a lot of tea, my hands snug around the pig mug. I tell my parents about Isabel, who agrees to come over this evening when I give her a ring after school.

'You can talk,' she says.

'I can talk.'

'Tell me you love me.'

'I love you, Isabel.'

'More than Mr Holdsworth?'

I snort. 'Don't push your luck.'

Henry calls round later, upset and ashen-faced, insisting he doesn't blame me.

'Well, that's generous of him,' Mr Goldfish says, his voice quieter now, not even a whisper, more of a breath with words swirling around in it. 'You have sort of destroyed his parents' marriage.'

I'm pleased Henry doesn't agree. 'This is his fault, Tess. Do you hear me? Totally his fault. He came home and admitted everything. Didn't have a choice, did he? There's going to be an investigation. The union is involved. Everyone's going to know about it. I've already had messages from Anna and Tara, taking the Mick. *What a total bastard,*' Henry snarls, pacing up and down the kitchen, his lethargy gone, his air of world-weariness replaced by genuine anger.

There's a flash of ginger as Jack peeps around the door. I catch him and he grins guiltily then bows out, excusing himself with a wave of his hand. It's nothing like my hand, but that's okay. Some things are more important than biology.

'He promised it would never happen again. Oh yeah,' Henry goes on, as I look at him in shock, 'he did it at his last school too. Mum forgave him, and the time before that. She's had enough now though. Thrown him out. He's staying at a Holiday Inn in Moss Side.'

Mr Goldfish laughs, or tries to, because it turns into a cough. 'Couldn't have happened to a nicer guy.'

'Let me find a battery,' I say, as Henry leaves, promising to be in touch when things have quietened down. I can't wait to introduce him to Isabel, maybe even Patrick. We could be a four – a strange four but a great four, pretty much the world's most fabulous bunch of misfits. I dash into my bedroom to take the battery out of my clock. The ticks are loud and fast, like time really is running out. 'Here. This will do.'

'That's major surgery, Tess. An organ transplant,' Mr Goldfish jokes as he lies on my bed, his tail twitching every now and again. 'No offence, but I don't think you're qualified.'

'It will only take two seconds.'

'You'll put it in the wrong way and my head will explode.'

'Please let me try.'

His light turns off, then on, then off again so I give him a shake, not wanting him to go. 'Back,' he says with lips of flickering white. 'But not for long.'

I shove on my silver boots, putting the battery and Mr Goldfish in my pocket one last time before racing downstairs.

'Where are you going?' Jack asks at once. He's curled up on the sofa with Mum, their legs entwined in a knot. I am lucky to have them, still together, still happy after all they've been through.

'Out. There's something I need to do.'

'What kind of something? How long will it take? If

Isabel's coming round later, don't you think you should do a bit of work on the subjects you missed at school today?'

'Jack.' Mum nudges him with her big toe. 'This is precisely what we've just been talking about.'

'Right.' He waves cheerily. 'Okay then, Tess. Off you go. Be back whenever. Next week, if you like. There's no rush. No need to do your homework this evening. I'm totally relaxed. It's your life.'

'Ha ha,' Mum says, but they're laughing for real by the time I close the door.

It's dark now, inky, like Mrs Austin's fountain pen has leaked over the sky, releasing the words. I'm free of them at last. I take my time, enjoying the walk with Mr Goldfish. Sometimes he wafts in front of me, the faintest smudge of orange; mostly he sits in my pocket, too weak to move. Stars begin to appear, one by one. Pluto's out there somewhere, but I'm glad to be here. In Manchester. My home city.

The man with the hen-like face is behind the till in the *Texaco Garage*, staring at his phone. The aisles are quiet, the squeak of my silver boots the only sound as I pass the bottles of de-icer and stop at a shelf of plastic goldfish.

'Some hot lady-torches for me to lie with for the rest of eternity,' Mr Goldfish grins. 'I approve, Tess. I approve wholeheartedly.'

I stroke his fins, his tail, his golden face that seems paler now, waning before my eyes.

'I'm going to miss you. Who else is going to give me

advice? Get on my back? Tell me I'm deluded and naive and generally pig-headed?'

Mr Goldfish chuckles. 'You are. Because it was you all along.' His light shines brighter for a second then disappears to almost nothing. 'I don't exist, remember?' he whispers, and then he fades to black.

I swap his battery quickly then flick his switch. A dazzling ray of light beams out of his mouth.

'Goodbye,' I say – out loud this time.

There's no reply.

Acknowledgements

The book in your hands is the culmination of the hard work and expertise of many people. Thanks to all at Orion and the Hachette Children's Group who have played their part. I know how lucky I am to work with such a stellar team. In particular, I am indebted to Fiona Kennedy (my wise and wonderful editor and publisher), Nina Douglas (publicist extraordinaire), Catherine Clarke (uber agent) and the rest of the crew at Felicity Bryan Associates.

I have the utmost gratitude for the bloggers, tweeters, reviewers, librarians, teachers and booksellers who continue to support my career. Without you, no one would read my books. Thank you.

A big shout-out to Jane Handley, who took the time to explain the ins and outs of speech therapy and mutism in young people. Thank you! Any errors in the novel are mine, not hers.

A woof of thanks to my dog, Inca, for greeting me happily when I got up in the middle of the night to write. Her wagging tail almost made the early starts worth it. Thanks for keeping my toes warm while I typed.

A million thanks to my incredible mum, Shelagh Leech, for helping me out with my son. I decided to scrap thousands of words and restart this book a few months in to maternity leave, and it was only possible because of the support of the world's best grandma. Thanks, too, to my family and friends, for listening patiently, cheering me on and generally just being the loveliest group of people to hang out with. Sorry for the times I had to say, 'No, I can't. I need to work,' over the past couple of years.

Above all, I would like to thank Steve Pitcher – super-husband, super-dad, and my best friend in all the world. Managing two busy careers, a beautiful baby and a crazy dog in the past eighteen months has been a spectacular juggling act for both of us. You've never once dropped a ball. Thank you for being the very best person that I know. I love you and our son so much, and I can't wait for our new arrival.

Annabel Pitcher
West Yorkshire
April 2015

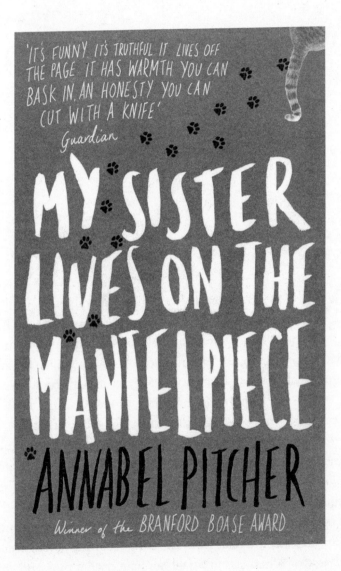

MY SISTER LIVES ON THE MANTELPIECE

ANNABEL PITCHER

1

MY SISTER ROSE lives on the mantelpiece. Well, some of her does. Three of her fingers, her right elbow and her kneecap are buried in a graveyard in London. Mum and Dad had a big argument when the police found ten bits of her body. Mum wanted a grave that she could visit. Dad wanted a cremation and to sprinkle the ashes in the sea. That's what Jasmine told me anyway. She remembers more than I do. I was only five when it happened. Jasmine was ten. She was Rose's twin. Still is, according to Mum and Dad. They dressed Jas the same for years after the funeral – flowery dresses, cardigans, those flat shoes with buckles that Rose used to love. I reckon that's why Mum ran off with the man from the support group seventy one days ago. When Jas cut off all her hair, dyed it pink and got her nose pierced on her fifteenth birthday, she didn't look like Rose any more and my parents couldn't hack it.

They each got five bits. Mum put hers in a fancy white coffin beneath a fancy white headstone that says *My Angel* on it. Dad burned a collarbone, two ribs, a bit of skull and a little toe and put the ashes in a golden urn. So they both got their own way, but surprise surprise it didn't make them happy. Mum says the graveyard's too depressing to visit. And every anniversary Dad tries to sprinkle the ashes but changes his mind at the last minute. Something seems to happen right when Rose is about to be tipped into the sea. One year in Devon there were loads of these swarming silver fish that looked like they couldn't wait to eat my sister. And another year in Cornwall a seagull poohed on the urn just as Dad was about to open it. I started to laugh but Jas looked sad so I stopped.

We moved out of London to get away from it all. Dad knew someone who knew someone who rung him up about a job on a building site in the Lake District. He hadn't worked in London for ages. There's a recession, which means the country has no money, so hardly anything's getting built. When he got the job in Ambleside, we sold our flat and rented a cottage and left Mum in London. I bet Jas five whole pounds that Mum would come to wave us off. She didn't make me pay when I lost. In the car Jas said *Let's play I Spy*, but she couldn't guess *Something beginning with R*, even though Roger was sitting right on my lap, purring as if he was giving her a clue.

It's so different here. There are massive mountains that are tall enough to poke God up the bum, hundreds of trees, and it's quiet. *No people* I said, as we found the cottage down a twisty lane and I looked out of the window for somebody to play with. *No Muslims* Dad corrected me, smiling for the first time that day. Me and Jas didn't smile back as we got out of the car.

Our cottage is the complete opposite of our flat in Finsbury Park. It's white not brown, big not small, old not new. Art's my favourite subject at school and, if I painted the buildings as people, I would turn the cottage into a crazy old granny, smiling with no teeth. The flat would be a serious soldier all smart and squashed up in a row of identical men. Mum would love that. She's a teacher at an art college and I reckon she'd show every single one of her students if I sent her my pictures.

Even though Mum's in London, I was happy to leave the flat behind. My room was tiny but I wasn't allowed to swap with Rose 'cos she's dead and her stuff's sacred. That was the answer I always got whenever I asked if I could move. *Rose's room is sacred, James. Don't go in there, James. It's sacred.* I don't see what's sacred about a bunch of old dolls, a smelly pink duvet and a bald teddy. Didn't feel that sacred when I jumped up and down on Rose's bed one day when I got home from school. Jas made me stop but she promised not to tell.

When we'd got out of the car, we stood and looked at

our new home. The sun was setting, the mountains glowed orange and I could see our reflection in one of the cottage windows – Dad, Jas, me holding Roger. For a millisecond I felt hopeful, like this really was the beginning of a brand new life and everything was going to be okay from now on. Dad grabbed a suitcase and the key out of his pocket and walked down the garden path. Jas grinned at me, stroked Roger, then followed. I put the cat down. He crawled straight into a bush, tail sticking out as he scrambled through the leaves. *Come on* Jas called, turning around at the porch door. She held out a hand as I ran to join her. We walked into the cottage together.

I'VE DONE SOMETHING WRONG.
AND DO YOU KNOW THE
WORST THING?
I GOT AWAY WITH IT.

KETCHUP CLOUDS

ANNABEL PITCHER

By the Author of MY SISTER LIVES ON THE MANTELPIECE

1 Fiction Road
Bath

August 1st

Dear Mr S Harris,

Ignore the blob of red in the top left corner. It's jam
not blood, though I don't think I need to tell you the
difference. It wasn't your wife's jam the police found on
your shoe.

The jam in the corner's from my sandwich. Homemade
raspberry. Gran made it. She's been dead seven years and
making that jam was the last thing she did. Sort of. If you
ignore the weeks she spent in hospital attached to one
of those heart things that goes *beep beep* if you're lucky
or *beeeeeeeeeeeeeeeeeeeeeeeeeeeep* if you're not. That was the
sound echoing round the hospital room seven years ago.
Beeeeeeeeeeeeeeeeeeeeeeeeeeeep. My little sister was born six
months later and Dad named her after Gran. Dorothy
Constance. When Dad stopped grieving, he decided to
shorten it. My sister is small and round so we ended up
calling her Dot.

My other sister, Soph, is ten. They've both got long blonde hair and green eyes and pointy noses, but Soph is tall and thin and darker skinned, like Dot's been rolled out and crisped in the oven for ten minutes. I'm different. Brown hair. Brown eyes. Medium height. Medium weight. Ordinary, I suppose. To look at me, you'd never guess my secret.

I struggled to eat the sandwich in the end. The jam wasn't off or anything because it lasts for years in sterilised jars. At least that's what Dad says when Mum turns up her nose. It's pointy too. Her hair's the same colour as my sisters' but shorter and a bit wavy. Dad's is more like mine except with grey bits above his ears, and he's got this thing called heterochromia, which means one eye's brown but the other's lighter. Blue if it's bright outside, grey if it's overcast. The sky in a socket, I once said, and Dad got these dimples right in the middle of his cheeks, and I don't know if any of this really matters but I suppose it's good to give you a picture of my family before I tell you what I came in here to say.

Because I am going to say it. I'm not sitting in this shed for the fun of it. It's bloody freezing and Mum would kill me if she knew I was out of bed but it's a good place to write this letter, hidden away behind some trees. Don't ask me what type but they've got big leaves that are rustling in the breeze. *Shhhhwiiishhh*. Actually that sounds nothing like them.

There's jam on my fingers so the pen's sticky. I bet the cats' whiskers are too. Lloyd and Webber meowed as if they couldn't quite believe their luck that the sky was raining sandwiches when I chucked it over the hedge. I wasn't hungry any more. In actual fact I never was, and if I'm being honest I only made the sandwich in the first place to put off starting this letter. No offence or anything, Mr Harris. It's just difficult. And I'm tired. I haven't really slept since May 1st.

There's no danger of me dropping off in here. The box of tiles is digging into my thighs and a draught is blowing through a gap underneath the shed door. I need to get a move on because just my luck the torch is running out of battery. I tried holding it between my teeth but my jaw started to ache so now it's balancing near a spider web on the windowsill. I don't normally sit in the shed, especially not at 2am, but tonight the voice in my head is louder than ever before. The images are more real and my pulse is racing racing racing, and I bet if my heart was attached to one of those hospital things, all the fast thumping would break it.

When I got out of bed, my pyjama top was sticking to my back and my mouth was drier than probably a desert. That's when I put your name and address in my dressing-gown pocket and tiptoed outside, and now I'm here face to face with all this blank paper, determined to tell you my secret but not sure how to say it.

Tongue tied doesn't exist in writing, but if it did, like if my hand was a great big tongue, honest truth it would be all tangled up in one of those complicated knots that only Scouts know. Scouts and also that man off BBC2, you know the one with wild hair who does survival programmes and ends up in the middle of the jungle, sleeping up a tree and eating snakes for dinner? Now I come to think of it, you probably have no idea what I'm talking about. Do you have TV on Death Row and if so do you watch British shows or just American ones?

I guess questions are pointless. Even if you wanted to write back, the address at the top of this letter is false. There's no Fiction Road in England, so Mr Harris don't go thinking you can break out of prison and turn up out of the blue on my doorstep because you hitched a ride from Texas and you're looking for a girl called – well, let's pretend my name is Zoe.